PATRICK THOMAS

For Marie, Erin, and Colin-
My present and future

PADWOLF PUBLISHING INC.
WWW.PADWOLF.COM
www.facebook.com/Padwolf

WWW.PATTHOMAS.NET
WWW.MURPHYS-LORE.COM
WWW.THESTARTENDERS.ORG
www.facebook.com/PatrickThomasAuthor

STARTENDERS™
© 2014 Patrick Thomas

A WAVE THEN GOODBYE originally published in Fantastic Futures 13
edited by Robert E. Waters & James R. Stratton
CROSSING ROADS originally published in Galactic Creatures
edited by Elektra Hammond

Book edited by Alycia J. Mellgren

Cover Art by Patrick Thomas and Roy Maurtisen

Cover Design by Roy Maurtisen

WITH SPECIAL THANKS TO DR, HOWARD MARGOLIN FOR FINDING THAT WHICH OTHERS
DID NOT

Startenders, Bulfinche's Pub, barships, The Department of Mystic Affairs,
Murphy's Lore, and all related
characters are © & ™ Patrick Thomas

10-digit ISBN 1-890096-58-X, 13 digit ISBN 978-1-890096-58-8
Printed in the USA
Second Printing

A new ball dropped again from the ceiling. Loki transformed into some giant tentacled creature straight out of a Lovecraftian nightmare, scooped up the ball and oozed his way across the field. The warez moved against him, opening up with their energy weapons.

Loki wasn't going to make it. We needed a new plan.

"Riga, fog up the field. Make it so thick nobody can see," I said into my badge.

"What if they have radar or something like it?" she asked.

I crawled over to Thunder Jack. The god looked bad, bruised and bleeding. He didn't have a badge shielding him, but his body had already started regenerating the power he lost. "Jack, I need you to put out enough electrical energy to charge the particles in the fog to confuse any of the robots' sensors. Can you do it?"

The thunder god took a deep breath and nodded. Riga was doing a great job. Jack was right in front of me and I could barely see him.

"Toma, I need you to whip up a pair of portals," I said, explaining why I needed them.

"Murph, I'm spent. I do that and I'm going primitive too," Toma said.

"I'm sorry, but I don't think we have a choice," I said.

"Don't worry," came a voice from the fog. "I'll take care of it."

The killer robot with delusions of manhood passed within five feet of me. "Servant, maximize the ventilation and cooling system."

The cyborg worked some controls and within moments the fog had thinned out enough to see through. Loki, in his monster form, was tripped by a pair of the robots. The ball fell from his tentacles and rolled away. The robot who fancied himself a man ran forward. It scooped up the ball and ran towards the goal on the side of the field we were defending and impaled the metal ball perfectly onto the goal spike.

"We win. All of you are now our slaves."

CONTENTS

SOMETIME IN THE NOT TOO DISTANT FUTURE…

A WAVE THEN GOODBYE

"Murphy, I'm going to miss this place," Paddy Moran said, tenderly caressing the wooden bar that his late wife had made for him a long time ago. And by long time, I meant it. She finished it in 1886. As a leprechaun, the boss was extremely long-lived.

The boss sighed. This was even rougher on him than the rest of us – not that anyone wanted to lose New York City. Sadly, we didn't have a choice.

"Me too. I don't know what I would've done without Bulfinche's Pub and all the people here after Elsie died. Then after Terrorbelle was killed, I was an even worse mess," I said. "Still, we have to look at the upside. We're all about to become astronauts."

The boss smiled. "Better than astronauts – Startenders."

We exited the bar that had been our home and entered the attached garage. Most of the moving was already done. We left enough in Bulfinche's Pub to serve as our base of operations on the ground. We still had time. Not a lot of it, but hopefully enough to save more than ten million people from being destroyed by a pissed off and insane sea god.

I'd been to Startender Station several times before, but this time we were opening it up for business. We were about to let the world know that the Startenders existed, which would be a shock to many, especially considering who some of us were. It wasn't just that private individuals and legends had built a space station, but starships. Or rather, barships. We were taking what we had been doing for over a century at Bulfinche's Pub out into the universe. We'd helped establish a base on the moon and left the solar system while the furthest the rest of the world had gotten was a few missions to Mars.

We didn't rely on old-fashioned things like rockets to make orbit. We had several methods, not the least of which was a revamped 1930 V6 Cadillac that the boss called Baby that he used to run booze with during prohibition.

The Caddy was big, but that didn't mean all of our passengers were going to be able to fit inside. One in particular was bigger than the car itself. Cerberus had once been a guardian for the Greco-Roman god Pluto until Paddy won the mutt in a card game. The three-headed pup was a very good dog and was moving with us to the station, but first we had to get him into orbit. Since he couldn't fit in the car, the plan was for him to ride on top.

I could bore you with the details of how the genius god Vulcan refurbished the Caddy so it generated mystic fields to protect the passengers while it defied the laws of gravity and physics, but I don't understand it all myself. The giant triple-headed mutt climbed on the roof of the car. Paddy and I got inside and drove out of Bulfinche's Pub onto the streets of Manhattan. Over the years we didn't exactly hide, but we hadn't gone out of our way to get noticed. That wasn't going to be a worry anymore.

The folks on the street were more than a little shocked to see a creature of myth riding on top of an antique car, but that was nothing compared to what they must have been thinking when they saw the Caddy take off into the sky and heard Cerberus howling in three part harmony.

The boss was taking it easy. The shields were supposed to keep anyone in or on the car safe, but he wasn't about to take any chances with his favorite pup riding on the roof.

As we made orbit, Startender Station rose up with the sun behind it. It was a beautiful sight, a work of engineering genius as well as a work of art. It had one main section with five branches, each named for one of the boroughs of the city we were about to lose. Even if it wasn't in orbit, it would still be the single largest structure meant to house people on Earth.

It inspired me with a sense of awe and pride that I had some small hand in making it a reality. Off in the distance we could make out the latest International Space Station. It was a significantly smaller structure, but still one that signified world unity and showed that some of the countries below could work together towards a common goal. They didn't have the advantages we did, so the impressiveness of our station didn't take anything away from their accomplishment. Paddy looked over at the ISS and smiled, stopping the car so we floated in orbit.

"Me wife Bulfinche always told me that when you move into a new home that ye should always be neighborly. I'm thinking we should be neighborly," Paddy said, grinning from ear to ear.

I smiled back as I figured out what he was thinking. "I was wondering what the food and whiskey in the basket was for. Let's go say hi."

We pulled the Caddy alongside the International Space Station and parked near an airlock. Paddy extended our shielding and atmosphere so it butted up against the side of the station and then honked the horn. We could see through the glass the looks of confusion on the astronauts' faces on hearing a car horn in space. Paddy honked again and Cerberus barked. Our shielding had atmosphere so both sounds carried inside.

The astronauts moved to the window, rubbed their eyes, then looked at each other, trying to figure out if the sight of an antique car floating outside in space was a hallucination.

Paddy got out of the car, wearing his Startender badge. It looked like an old sherriff's star on top of another upside-down star. When the rear star spokes caught the light, the gold could seem to shine with the colors of the rainbow. It was a tribute to the shot o' gold logo of Bulfinche's Pub.

I wore mine too. The small amulet had many properties, not the least of which was to provide an atmosphere and protect the wearer against temperature and gravity extremes. It served well as a spacesuit, at least in the short term.

Paddy floated over and knocked on the airlock. After some arguing among themselves, then seeing Paddy hold up the basket, they decided to open the outer lock.

"Ye wait here pup and watch the car," Paddy told Cerberus. "We won't be long." The dog nodded in triplicate. The boss and I went in and the astronauts closed the outer airlock behind us, then opened the inner.

"Hello. What's going on?" one of the astronauts said awkwardly as he approached us. He was American judging by the accent.

Paddy shook his hand and then the other astronaut's. I followed suit. "We've just moved into the neighborhood." Paddy pointed to Startender Station, floating off their bow like something out of a science fiction movie. "We just wanted to say hi and bring ye this small gift."

Both astronauts' eyes opened wider and they started to drool. The basket was four feet in diameter and filled with delicacies that they likely hadn't had in months.

"Thank you, but where did that station come from?" The second astronaut sounded Russian.

"That little thing? Something we Startenders whipped together," Paddy said with false humility. We had gotten a message from the future decades ago about the now impending disaster and Paddy had dedicated his life and not inconsiderable fortune to making sure everyone gets out of New York alive. "Ye are welcome to come visit whenever ye like, but first a toast." Paddy took out one of the bottles of whiskey that had a Bulfinche's Pub label. He brews it himself and I've never tasted anything finer. The boss handed out four glasses and poured. Raising his glass, he said "To peace, hope, happiness and a new era for space travel."

The astronauts drank hesitantly, at least until the whiskey passed their lips. After that, their eyes went wide and their lips smiled as their taste buds jumped for joy.

And just like that, we made two new friends.

Hopefully the rest of the world would be as accommodating.

There are parts of Startender Station where the inside is bigger than the outside by virtue of pocket dimensions and folded space, giving each of those areas more square footage than they should have. One such room was the hangar bay where we parked the barships. And where Cerberus made his new home, guarding the ships.

The barships were marvels of magic and technology. We'd mined asteroids in our own solar system and found tremendous amounts of gold – enough to build our ships out of. It was that or tank the value of the precious metal on Earth.

Thanks to the work of Vulcan, that gold was made into a special alloy which was fluid and malleable, a new twist on a non-Newtonian fluid, able to change shape and link up with a pocket dimension that ran alongside our own. It allowed us to shunt the tremendous mass of the ship so we could appear bigger or smaller depending on which we wanted to be.

This wasn't the first time I'd seen *Fools' Glory*. It wouldn't even be the first time I've taken her out for a spin. It would however be the first time that she was officially mine to command.

The Startenders are not a military organization so the idea of having military ranks seemed wrong to us, so we made up our own. I was the head honcho, the equivalent of captain. My honcho or first mate was the Norse trickster god Loki. We'd been through a lot and he'd reformed to a great extent.

I heard metal footsteps on the deck. I didn't bother to look behind me, figuring my crew's melog had arrived. The melog were an artificial race of people Vulcan had developed ages ago. Some might call them androids or robots, but they were much more than that. They had souls and could reproduce. In fact, I was at the birth of the golden man who stood behind me.

"Hi Eric," I said.

"Hi ya, Murph. You ready to get this party started?"

I didn't know how much of a party the destruction of my hometown was going to be, but I knew what he meant. New York City was doomed, but her people were not. "You bet, as long as you're willing to play taxi driver."

The melog have interfaces that allow them to link up and control the ships mentally, making them superb pilots. The ship could be flown and maneuvered by their thoughts, although as head honcho I could override the melog's control if necessary. I doubted I'd ever have to do it, but it made sense to have the option.

"Absolutely, boss," Eric said.

I rubbed my hand against the side of the barship tenderly. "Open sesame."

Eric smiled and a door suddenly appeared in the golden hull.

We climbed inside and headed back to Manhattan, although we took the long way, which actually involved traveling to another world to pick up what would hopefully be a new batch of Startender recruits. Years ago they'd helped Loki and me save a world. We were hoping they'd help get everyone out of New York alive.

Most of our recruits came, but not without some excitement along the way, but the details of that adventure come later in the book.

As excited as I was with the idea of going out into space, I couldn't forget what the motivation for it was. What the cost was going to be, not the least of which was the loss of Bulfinche's Pub.

It may seem silly to be emotionally attached to a bar, but only to someone who's never visited it. Bulfinche's was more than a mere watering hole. Long ago, Paddy bought the place with his pot of gold and ever since, rainbows have led those in trouble to our door. Bulfinche's Pub is the hope at the end of the rainbow, a place where those with great power helped those with none. We helped to right wrongs and shared our sorrow, joy, and laughter. The sign over the door read Maireann dóchas is gliodar, which is Gaelic for hope and happiness never die. And just maybe, if we were real good and very lucky, no one would die when Manhattan was destroyed.

The plan was to have one hundred fifty Startenders. We didn't have that many yet, but we're a good way there and all of them were in the pub. The number was significant. There were one hundred fifty seats at King Arthur's Roundtable. Robin Hood had one hundred and fifty Merry Men. There had been one hundred and fifty Daemor in the Thandau War. And hopefully one day there'll be one hundred fifty Startenders.

Considering who was in the group – tricksters like Coyote and Sun WuKong the monkey king; heroes such as Hercules, the samurai Kintaro, and Sir Marrok, the werewolf knight of the Round Table – it was deathly quiet. Almost like a wake and not the good Irish kind we'd often hosted. We all knew even if we managed to get every last soul out of New York, we were still going to lose the city and millions would be homeless.

Paddy stood behind the bar and hit a beer mug with a spoon. All eyes turned toward the boss.

"I'd like to thank ye all for coming. More than that, I'd like to thank ye all for being a part of the Startenders and our rescue efforts to save the citizens of New York City. I know not all of ye have agreed to join the Startenders…" The Council of Thrones' Enforcer Nemesis and Wisp, the owner of the Eternity Club, for two. "… but nonetheless you're here to help and that's what matters. I'm going to turn the meeting over to a dearly departed friend." Yes, he really was turning the meeting over to a dead man. "He is gone, but not forgotten and he was good enough to leave us recordings like this one which he wanted me to play now. Ladies and gentlemen, I give ye the greatest psychic who ever lived or died – Mosie."

"Thanks for that intro Paddy," said Mosie's face from a giant television screen. "It's good to see you all again. Well, not that I can actually see any of you from the TV, but I saw all of you sitting there when I was still alive and I saw what is about to happen now. I even had to get sober to do it after we got our message in a metal bottle from the future all those years ago. It gave us enough time to get ready. Sometime in the next three days, the insane god Poseidon will come onto land somewhere in Manhattan. Thanks to the amulet that Demeter made him, he's stayed hidden all these years and will continue to do so despite our best efforts. There is no way to find him. Trust me on this." We did, but we were still hunting the mad sea god in hopes of stopping him before it was too late. We had a lot of raw power. Unfortunately, luck and planning can negate that. "He will come ashore, someone will insult him and push him over the edge. In a fit of rage, he'll cause a seaquake and call forth the ocean. A tidal wave will envelop all five boroughs and parts of Jersey and Long Island. A seaquake will sink the island of Manhattan beneath the water. There is nothing we can do to stop it."

"We'll see about that, vision boy," said Rebecca, the very elderly Mother of the Streets. She's well over a hundred, yet still spry enough to carry out her duties taking care of the homeless and the downtrodden of the city.

"Rebecca, we all know you're going to try to stop him. I'm sorry, but you're going to fail," said Mosie's prerecorded message. "There is something… special in store for you. By now the first wave of barships are ready. Use their special properties to move the masses. Have Pace and the other trolls set up nexi…" Plural of nexus. "To get people out." Trolls were not native to Earth; they were actually aliens. Many have the mystic ability to open up gateways between worlds and dimensions. We were lucky enough to count four among the Startenders recruits I'd gone to pick up.

"We have to do something big to get everyone's attention. Otherwise people won't be scared enough to evacuate, especially if the reason we give is that a mad Greco-Roman sea god is about to sink Manhattan. Paddy will phone in a phony nuclear bomb threat to the authorities. Uncle Sam and some of our other government connections will make sure we get help with the evacuations. We've placed radioactive materials with just enough trace around the city to make the Powers That Be believe the hoax. You'll still have to work day and night for three days to get everyone…" Mosie paused and actually turned his digital head to look at Rebecca. "… almost everybody safely off. We have several mystic measures in place to help, a mixture of aversion, trust and fear spells that will make even those that want to stay head for safer pastures. I wish I could be there to help you more, but I know you'll do me proud, do Paddy proud and do this world proud. If I may suggest we all raise a glass," Mosie lifted a mug that looked like it had been filled with whiskey. The psychic was always a serious drinker, mainly because being drunk kept him from going insane from seeing everything that ever happened or will happen all at once. "And let us toast one final time. To Bulfinche's Pub and what it has meant to all of us. It is a tragedy that we lose it, but without it, entire worlds will not have the Startenders to save them." Mosie lifted his glass. "To Bulfinche's!"

Paddy lifted his glass. "To Bulfinche's!"

"To Bulfinche's!" we all said, raising and draining our glasses.

"It's taken a lot to plan everything. I will turn the rest of the meeting over to the head honcho of the *Fools' Glory*, Murphy, who will give you all your assignments."

"Thanks, buddy. We miss you," I said to the recording.

"And well you should," the recorded Mosie said. "Don't worry. I've made more recordings to help you with certain things, but for the most part you'll be on your own. I still owe you, Murph, and one day I'll be able to pay you back."

"Cryptic much?" I said. I knew better than to ask how. He was the same back when he was alive.

"Always. Now stop goofing off and get to work," Mosie's recording said.

I grinned and turned to the greatest assembly of heroes and raw power the Earth has likely ever seen.

"Okay gang, here's the plan…"

One of the first orders of business was the United Nations. It wasn't that we felt diplomats ranked above regular people by any means. We had ulterior motives for getting them out first.

There was quite a debate about who to send in to give our speech to the General Assembly. We'd arranged the session through guile and fast talking weeks before. We had several Startenders who could not only sell ice to Eskimos, but also convince them to pick up snowmaking machines and air-conditioners, not to mention bathing suits and outdoor swimming pools.

Getting what we wanted was, on a lot of levels, going to be an elaborate con job. Still, we couldn't come across as grifters or snake-oil salesman, so we sent one of our best and noblest – Sir Dagonet.

Dagonet started out centuries ago in King Arthur's Court as the jester and ended up getting knighted. An encounter with the Holy Grail left him immortal. The Infinite Jester has done the Round Table proud over the centuries by keeping the ideals of Camelot alive. Even the other surviving Knights agree that Dagonet embodies the best of those ideals, so he was chosen as our first diplomatic face. Not to mention he's had quite a bit of diplomatic experience throughout the years.

Dagonet gave a rousing speech announcing to the world the existence of the moon base, named Ben City, and Startenders Station. We planned to name it in memory and honor of the greatest city in the world, but as its destruction hadn't happened yet, we thought it was best to not officially name it until after.

Dagonet made our case for both station and base to receive sovereign nation status. Separate status for each was best as Paddy fully owned the station, but the moon base was a joint venture.

It was even made more impressive as Dagonet gave key aspects of his speech in multiple languages without the need of a translator.

To say the so-called debate and discussion that followed was chaos would be putting it diplomatically.

"Are you trying to tell us that the moon base that we've heard rumors of is complete and large enough to house a hundred thousand people?" the Russian ambassador said.

"Well over that number. It's more of a city than a base. And we have room for expansion," the Infinite Jester said.

"And what kind of a name is Ben City?" asked another rather angry ambassador from a small and rather angry country.

"It is named in honor of Ben Horus, the man whose dream led to the reality of the first city on the moon," Dagonet said.

"That's the lunatic who has been selling laser advertising on the first night of the full moon for decades," the angry ambassador said.

"I take exception to lunatic and would prefer visionary," Dagonet said.

"He's dead," the angry ambassador said.

"I'm aware of that. I was one of his pallbearers. But his dream and memory live on," Dagonet said.

"None of this matters. The United States claims the moon as sovereign territory, as our astronauts were the first to set foot there," the American ambassador said.

"Nonsense! The People's Republic claims the moon," the Chinese ambassador said.

More ambassadors started yelling that their countries were claiming the same.

Dagonet smiled and lifted his hand. "As you all know, by treaty no country is able to claim the moon. And we are not claiming the moon, just Ben City and the surrounding area and airspace."

"Are you also trying to tell us that you got enough supplies into orbit to build an entire space station and a city on the moon, without any of our surveillance systems detecting it?" the Russian ambassador said.

"I can't speak as to the accuracy of your surveillance systems, but you can hardly hold the Startenders responsible for your monitoring agency's inadequacies, now can you? As a matter of fact, two of our members paid a visit earlier to the International

Space Station yesterday, so I would imagine that every member nation of that project should now know what I'm telling you. I'm certain you are in the loop and will be getting confirmation shortly."

It was then that an aide to the Secretary General rushed up and whispered in his ear. The man's face blanched and he walked up to the podium, taking it from Dagonet.

"I have just been informed that there is a code black nuclear bomb threat for the city of New York. The entire population is being ordered to evacuate immediately," he said.

The chaos evolved instantly into bedlam. The rather angry ambassador from the rather angry country pushed down several of his colleagues as he ran toward the garage and his waiting limo. The rest of the diplomats yelled about who was going to be taking care of getting them to safety.

"Excuse me," Dagonet said. He repeated it again several more times trying to get the diplomats' attention. Rolling his eyes, the Infinite Jester turned and nodded to a floating golden golf ball-sized hunk of metal. It floated above the assembly, then suddenly morphed into a giant castle-esque spaceship with the Startender logo on the side. It was the barship *Excalibur*, of which Dagonet was the head honcho. Its sudden size change inside the General Assembly got everyone to stop arguing and shut up.

"I would just like to say that I have enough room on board the barship *Excalibur* to take all of you, your staff as well as all of your families, and shuttle everyone to Washington D.C. where you can make contact with your respective embassies. However, I have my orders and I will not be able to leave here until this matter is brought to a vote. So as soon as the vote on the sovereign nation status of Startender Station and Ben City is done, I am at your service to take you all out of the danger zone."

It was the fastest vote in U.N. history. Almost every ambassador voted to recognize the sovereignty of Startender Station and Ben City. We were even voted on a couple of councils we didn't even ask for. In their stress, the diplomats didn't seem to realize that Dagonet never said how they needed to vote to get on the barship. In fact, that was something the Infinite Jester would never do. It would violate his oath of honor to the Round Table to threaten lives for personal gain, not to mention violating his Startender Oath.

Diplomats are like most people and assume others are not only capable, but willing to do the same things as they are. Since most of the diplomats would have made that statement a threat, they assumed the same of Dagonet.

There was nothing in either oath about having to save people from their own stupidity, and since it worked out in our favor, we failed to correct their faulty assumptions. Dagonet and his crew got those diplomats, their staff and families safely away. He did the same for the janitors, translators, and the rest of the blue collar workers as well.

They got the diplomats to DC and came back to help us with the rest of the city.

It was kind of funny how well Paddy did with the media considering all his centuries of hiding because of the leprechaun curse. The wee folk had to bring anyone who captured them to their pot of gold. As a matter of fact, the boss and I first met when I captured him in order to get said gold. I ended up letting him go before I knew about the loophole. A leprechaun can buy property with the gold. If captured he had to bring his captor to said property, but fortune hunters figuring a way around the property laws was another matter entirely. It wasn't like they could walk off with a building without the local law stepping in.

Paddy bought Bulfinche's Pub with his pot, so rainbows have been leading troubled souls to our door for well over a century.

With the Startenders we were widening our scope a bit.

Paddy wasn't focusing on the national media, at least at first. He was hitting the local media and hitting it hard. He started with a regular patron who was a reporter for one of the local network affiliates. Pam knew the score. What's more, she was willing to help us save as many people as we could, which would hopefully be everyone.

"This is Pam Neddle, speaking live with Padriac Moran, the owner of New York City landmark Bulfinche's Pub and one of the majority shareholders of the Horus Corporation, the company that has been advertising on the moon with laser beams for many years. Mr. Moran…"

"Pam, please call me Paddy."

"Paddy, I understand you have some things to tell us regarding the ordered evacuation of New York City. The Mayor is cautioning us against panic, but he's closed the tunnels." Not a good place to be stuck when a tsunami hits. Subways would be closed soon for the same reason. "A lot of people are frightened, confused and at a loss for what to do. What can you tell them?"

"First, don't lose hope. I'm part of an organization called the Startenders. This is a Startender badge I'm wearing." Paddy pointed to his badge. We would be using the Horus satellites to beam it on the moon at night for the next three days. "We've made preparations for just such an emergency and we will be helping local and state officials evacuate the city."

Back in the studio the male anchor was rolling his eyes. "Pam, thank you for that report, but we are in a state of emergency. That man's obviously a crackpot who thinks he's an old west sheriff. We hear there is something going on at the U.N., so we are going live to …"

Instead of the broadcast going to where the newsroom wanted it to go, it went back to Pam, thanks to the workings of Bubba Sue, the Startenders' resident gremlin whose ability with technology was literally magical. We'd planned on this and quite simply hijacked the signal.

"What can one small organization do?" the reporter asked.

Paddy smiled. "The Startenders can do a lot." He nodded to Pam's cameraman who pulled the picture back so as to get the sky behind Paddy. With a wave of the boss' hand three more golden golf balls floating in the air above him expanded to full-sized barships. We could make the barships look like anything, so we tried to have these particular shapes instill visions of strength and confidence in the viewers. Each one of course had the Startenders logo on the side. "And in our case quite a bit. There is no need for panic. We will get everyone out. In moments, there will be several temporary bridges and portals allowing people to leave the city. Grab only the necessities. We have dozens of designated evacuation points with Startenders supervising in cooperation with the NYPD and the National Guard. We have a website listing all of them…"

And at home, the viewers rejected fear and panic in favor of hope.

My assignment was on the Westside directing traffic. We were using the morphing properties of the barships to make a bridge between Manhattan and Jersey near the Javits Center. We had two sides – one for cars, the others for pedestrians. My crew's job was to make sure people got across it in a neat, orderly fashion.

The neat and orderly part was proving to be a challenge. The owners of the various touring boat companies had volunteered their services without being asked. We'd also commandeered the cruise ships that docked just up the street. They were luxury ships, but we'd been using them as ferryboats. Each one could carry thousands of people. The companies weren't doing it out of the goodness of their hearts like the locals. Paddy had stock in the companies and basically threatened to start selling it off at rock bottom prices. One told him to stick it where the sun didn't shine. Paddy was as good as his word and the stock was worth pennies on the dollar within hours. The other companies decided to help without further coercion. The boss bought up controlling interest in the first company on the cheap and then commandeered its ships.

Paddy, with the help of Mosie and others, had become the richest person on Earth, but since he hid it within a variety of corporate shells, almost nobody knew it. He sunk all of his trillions into the Startenders and evacuation plans. Buying the reluctant cruise company pretty much wiped him out of liquid capital, but he had more ships to get people away safely so it was a fair trade to him. Mind you this is the same guy who last week chased a customer three blocks because he was a buck short on his bill. Paddy had plans to turn the rest of his new cruise line ships into temporary floating shelters, pretty much guaranteeing the stock he bought would be worth even less. Didn't faze him in the least.

People were reluctant to leave their homes, thinking nothing would happen. Others didn't want to go without their stuff, but we had anticipated this. Paddy commissioned the building of tens of thousands of wagons. They worked on the same principle as the old radio flyers and were as large as a pickup truck bed. With a little bit of effort one person could manage pulling a full wagon. Once on the Jersey side we had buses and tractor-trailers waiting to take people to designated evacuation areas and gave people luggage tags for their property. The carts were unloaded then brought back across for others to use.

Early on, the mayor was paid a visit from Paddy, who had been a large contributor to his campaign by way of fund raising dinners that ran thousands of dollars a plate. Paddy would buy a table or two. Paddy asked to be put in charge of rescue operations. Upon seeing what the barships were capable of, the mayor was impressed, but reluctant. Paddy was a civilian, a guy who owned a bar, so the boss had brought Nemesis, the daughter of night, with him. The pair were friends that disagreed on killing bad guys. Paddy was against it except in the most extreme cases; Nemesis not so much. The daughter of Nyx had run Nemesis & Co. on the 13th floor of a Manhattan skyscraper for decades, avenging wrongs. She made a habit of visiting each new mayor and telling him how things were. NYPD was always then instructed to give Nemesis and her agents every available assistance.

Nemesis was only an associate because her status as enforcer for the Council of Thrones would complicate things for us. I think her standing silently behind the boss was as much the reason that the mayor agreed to put Paddy in charge as the barships were. That and his daughter telling him that we had gotten rid of the quite real monsters under her bed after she had followed a rainbow to our door a few months earlier.

We had things uber-organized, basically calling entire neighborhoods at a time much like an usher in church standing in front of a pew to signal people to get up for communion.

My people were ushering the entire Westside. We were using all kinds of magic to encourage or scare people into leaving and so far it seemed to be working.

Everyone had been working for the better part of the day and we were tired. We included NYPD, NYFD, EMTs, National Guard, and the military. New Jersey's finest and bravest were helping on the other side of the river.

We tried to split shifts for everyone, but other than the occasional food break, none of the brave men and women helping us were taking any. Too many people to get out in too little time. I'd never been prouder to be a New Yorker than watching those people.

We were providing them food. Vulcan had tech that shrunk and preserved food and Paddy had been stockpiling for decades.

I was polishing off a sandwich when I heard a familiar buzzing of wings.

"Things okay, Dad?" came a voice from above. I looked up to see my daughter Elsiebelle flying in. She landed in front of me and I gave her a big hug. "Holding up okay, old man?"

I laughed. I was older and in better shape than I had any right to be… mostly thanks to Paddy. Instead of firing a comeback, I messed my daughter's purple hair. It's her natural color. She gets her hair and pixie wings from her mother's side. She gets her blue eyes and bad sense of humor from me. We both still miss her mother. Terrorbelle was vaporized saving our daughter. It was the second time I was widowed. I went more than a little nuts after that.

I'm feeling much better now.

"He's doing okay for someone his age," shouted Loki from down the block. The trickster has better-than-average hearing.

"Good to know, Uncle Loki," E-Belle said.

"You've got centuries on me, Loki," I said.

"Yeah, but I don't look it," he said.

I couldn't argue with that and judging by my daughter's chuckling, she wasn't about to defend my honor.

E-Belle was more my build than her mother's, which is why she's able to fly on Earth. Terrorbelle and our daughter both needed magic to fly. Not a lot of that on Earth these days. E-Belle being smaller and lighter could go about half a block on wing power, while the best her mother could manage was hovering or slowing a fall.

With our Startender badges, E-Belle could fly properly by using hers to adjust for the effects of gravity.

"How are things going up by the Intrepid?" I said. The military had turned the Intrepid into the world's largest ferry. Bubba Sue had snuck aboard a few weeks earlier and given its engines a tune up. From what she said, if it was returned to duty with her modifications, it would be the fastest vessel of its size on the seven seas.

"The soldiers are on top of everything and things are going very smoothly. People are doing what they should. Our mystic encouraging seems to be nudging those who want to ignore the evac orders."

"Good. So far, no real problems here," I said.

Apparently, I spoke too soon because a limo with diplomatic plates was driving through the crowd of people who were waiting to leave on foot. When people wouldn't get out of their way, they honked before trying to drive through the crowd. Apparently not everyone moved fast enough for them because they ended up knocking down a little girl.

E-Belle, Loki, and I raced towards the car. With her wings my daughter got there first. She wasn't as strong as her mother, but she hit the front of the car hard enough that its rear lifted off the ground. The vehicle spun its wheels helplessly. Loki picked up the girl, gave her the once over and flashed me a thumbs up. She was fine.

A man in suit and tie, the rather angry ambassador from the small and rather angry country, leapt out of the backseat and onto the ground. "I have diplomatic immunity. You are causing an international incident, so you best get me to the front of the line so I can report your actions to my government and yours."

"I don't care about your government or any international incidents right now," I said. "My job is to get everybody evacuated safely. Your behavior has jeopardized that child's life."

By this point the driver had gotten out of the car and stood up. He was a tall drink of water, easily six foot eight and three hundred plus pounds.

"Very well. You leave me no choice. Driver, take care of him."

The driver cracked his knuckles and stepped towards me, but he never made it. My daughter fluttered between us and punched him in the breadbasket, making the tall man double over in pain. E-Belle followed up with an elbow to the back of the neck and laid him out cold on the pavement, just like her mama taught her.

"That nonsense isn't going to work here," I said. "You're now at the end of the line. We're going to mark you for your actions and I can assure you that no one will allow you off the island until everyone else gets off first." We'd taken a lesson from Hex, a fellow Startender and head honcho of *The Accursed*. He's been known to warn people off and mark their face to remind them of his warning. Each Startender had a device that would brand a permanent large red letter over any offender's face. Which letter varied by the offense.

The angry ambassador screamed as we branded a C for line cutter on his face. There were more than a few with L for looter being forced to wait as well.

I turned to his driver and slapped him awake. "You next."

"But I was just following orders," the driver whined.

"That excuse has been used before. Doesn't hold water, then or now," I said and branded him. He didn't scream like his boss, probably because the marking didn't actually hurt.

I pointed to where the end of the line area was and sent the two offenders there to wait and contemplate the error of their ways.

While we were directing traffic, Paddy was making the talk show circuit.

"All I'm saying is, what do we really know about these so-called Startenders?" said James Rznard, a cable and radio talk show host and talking head. "They have so-called barships – are they advocates of drinking and operating vehicles? Are they trying to get our young people to start drinking and driving? We simply don't know. All we do know about them is that they forced a vote at the UN to have a satellite and some imaginary base on the moon established as sovereign nations before they would rescue a bunch of diplomats. And what's with that? Rescuing foreigners before good old-fashioned, hard-working Americans? I'll tell you what – they're trying to undermine the American way of life.

Now that they have sovereign nation status, that means they are effectively invading the United States of America. The United States has never been invaded and never will. We need to push these Startenders off from our shores."

"But Mr. Rznard, the mayor of New York City and the governor of New York State have both come out in support of Mr. Moran and his organization. What do you think about that?" said Kim Irons, host of the Irons In The Fire cable news program.

Rznard rolled his eyes. "They're facing nuclear annihilation by some terrorist. Politicians will say anything now to cover their asses. What happens if the bomb goes off before they get everybody out? If they said something against any rescue effort, it'll come back to bite them come Election Day.

"Mr. Moran, how do you respond to critics of you and the Startenders like Mr. Rznard here?" Kim said.

Paddy smiled big for the cameras. "I'd say they're full of crap. They're like the politicians they praise or criticize in that if they don't make waves, they'll lose ratings and be out of a job. I've invested me entire fortune in this, including buying land to make tent cities and supplement supplies for the Red Cross. We are willing to help some relocate to Startender Station or Ben City. We're talking more than ten million people displaced. That's the most ever in American history. And speaking of history, Mr. Rznard needs to review his. America has been invaded multiple times in multiple wars, one of the last of which was World War II. True, that was only a few Nazis disembarking from a U-boat off the coast of Long Island, but it still technically counts as an invasion. However we Startenders are not invaders. The majority of us are Americans. The sovereign nations of Startender Station and Ben City all support dual citizenship."

"That all sounds nice and good," Rznard said. "But you're up there floating above us. What's to prevent you from raining down weapons of mass destruction on the rest of humanity?"

"Because that is not our way. In actuality, we will be protecting the Earth," Paddy said.

"From what? Aliens?"

"Actually, yes," Paddy said, as the camera pulled back. The Startenders had only eight aliens in its ranks and three of them were sitting next to Paddy as the camera revealed. One was Randor the Troll, the next Nara, a large blue blag, an alien that looked like the result of a smurf and a hippo having a drunken night of passion. The last was Jan, a very, very large beige woman from the planet Karma. They smiled and waved at the camera. "Aliens are quite real, as are magical races. Some of them, unlike our friends and fellow Startenders here, are downright hostile. The Department of Mystic Affairs has been defending this country for centuries against mystic threats. The Startenders can do all that and more."

The camera panned to Rznard's mouth literally dropping open as he took in this revelation.

"Speaking of the Department of Mystic Affairs, we have their director, Sam Wilson, with us via satellite from New York City. Director Wilson, what do you have to say on this matter?"

Sam – the actual Uncle Sam – and most of his agents were helping with the evacuation in New York.

"Well, missy, I've known Padriac Moran for a very long time. I find him to be the rarest of rare things – a good man. Mr. Moran has been working behind the scenes for a great many years helping others without asking any personal reward or recognition," said the white-haired man with a moustacheless goatee. He was dressed in a white shirt, blue suit and red tie. Sam was the living embodiment of the spirit of America. Among his mystic gifts was the ability to inspire patriotism in anyone in his presence. That translated well to television feeds. Any Americans watching had feelings of pride. "I feel the Startenders have truly altruistic purposes and are not a threat to the United States or any other country. In fact, if the organization stays structured as it is, they have my full blessing, so long as they continue to follow the laws of this great land."

"Well, that's all nice and good coming from some career law enforcement agent, but why? Because you happen to like the man? Because they're helping get a few people out of New York City?" Rznard said.

"Actually, Mr. Rznard, by government calculations, the Startenders have supervised the evacuation of over five million people in less than a day," Kim said.

Rznard laughed. "So could anybody if they had those spaceship thingies. Hell, I could do a better job myself."

"Well, Mr. Rznard, you're perfectly welcome to try and raise enough wealth to develop technology and magic to build your own barships. However, we are in need of all the help we can get right now, so thank ye for your generous offer," Paddy said grinning.

"What offer?" Rznard said, confused.

"Didn't ye just say ye could do a better job than we could if you had access to a barship? I don't want the lack of barships at your disposal to affect you helping these people. Therefore, we will be by to pick you up as soon as this broadcast is done and bring you to the heart of Manhattan so ye can help with evacuation," Paddy said.

Rznard's jaw dropped again, but this time his face drained of blood until he looked like a ghost.

"You mean actually go to New York... Isn't there a danger of a nuclear bomb going off?" Rznard said.

"Exactly, which is why we need the help to get everyone out," Paddy said.

"I'm on the other side of the country. I couldn't possibly get to New York in time to do any good," Rznard said, using a handkerchief to wipe sweat from his brow.

"I know ye are all the way over in California where things are nice and safe. But your brave words let all of us know that you'd rather be in the trenches with the rest of us, so we're going to give you that chance. Barships can make that trip in no time. And real Americans like yourself laugh at danger. Isn't that what you've said? In fact, on your own show, ye constantly criticize people for inaction and cowardice. Now's your chance to step up and prove you're not just some blowhard who was lucky enough to get a TV show, but a real hero," Paddy said.

"Do you know when the detonation is supposed to occur?" Rznard said.

"We do not. It could happen at any moment," Paddy lied, knowing it was all a hoax to save people from the wrath of a mad sea god. Otherwise nobody would have gotten off the couch.

"Well, I have my show to do in a few hours and I've got no one to take care of my dog and…"

"Not a problem. We'll stop by your house and ye can pick up your dog. Ye can even bring a television crew to film your heroism. When will ye be ready?" Paddy said.

"I'm afraid my schedule won't allow me to go…" Rznard said.

"Ye mean your cowardice won't allow ye to help other people if there's any risk to yourself other than biting your tongue while shooting off your mouth. Isn't that what it boils down to? So either put up or shut up. Pitch in or stop criticizing. I'm still sending somebody for ye and we'll have cameras. The question is will you be shown to be a man of principle or a blowhard who likes to hear himself talk while others risk their lives."

"Paddy, is that offer open to other newscasters as well?" Kim Irons said.

"Of course it is, Kim," Paddy said.

"Excellent, then I'd like to go and bring my people," Kim said.

"And we be proud to have you," Paddy said. "Rznard, we'll be by to pick ye up shortly."

The broadcast switched to Rznard's camera, but he had run off so quickly that his chair was still spinning.

My daughter looked worried. "Dad, we've got an older gentleman a few blocks up refusing to leave. We tried everything we could think of to convince him to go, but he's stubborn and insists he's going to stay put. Not even Nellie could convince him otherwise. He seems immune to the spells of encouragement." Nellie was head honcho of the barship *Perdu* and the boss's adopted daughter. I've watched Nellie grow from a girl into a fine woman who even fulfilled her childhood dream of becoming a ninja, even if she changed the definition to fit what she thought it should be instead of the other way around.

"He said no to Nellie? That's impressive," I said. Nellie was a superb con woman. Has been ever since her hair was in braids.

"She's my head honcho, but you might have a better shot at this," she said. E-Belle was part of the *Perdu*'s crew.

I smiled at the compliment. "I'm happy to do my best. Guy

is probably a null and doesn't know it." A null is a type of mage that can nullify the effects of magic for themselves and sometimes others. "Loki, you have things covered here?" I said to my honcho. "Nellie needs my assistance uptown."

The trickster nodded. "With the exception of your little diplomatic incident, things are going surprisingly well. Not that I want to jinx it. Go."

My daughter lifted me up bride style as her wings started buzzing and we lifted into the air. I mentally adjusted the gravity setting on my Startenders badge to make it easier for her to carry my weight.

"Your mother would've loved this. She always hated that she couldn't fly in New York," I said.

"I think she was a little jealous that I could fly just a little bit here and she couldn't," E-Belle said.

"She was a tad jealous, but she was more happy and proud that you could. You know that if she had the power to pick who could fly, she would always have chosen you."

E-Belle smiled and I melted. It's a dad thing. "I know."

"Watch out for those wires," I said.

"Dad, no offense, but I fly better than you do. You need a motorcycle," she said, referring to a custom-made bike Vulcan built years before she was born. It could fly among other things.

A few blocks later, we arrived.

"That's him down there," E-Belle said, indicating a man who looked like he was in his seventies and was sitting on a chair on the stoop of a brick apartment building. He had a wedding picture in one hand and a bottle of beer in the other. There was a cane by his side. Nellie, in her traditional midnight blue – almost black ensemble – stood next to him rolling her eyes.

My daughter landed at the bottom of the porch.

"You see something new in this city just about every day," the old man said.

"That you do. I'm John Murphy." I said. "What's your name?"

"Donald Martin." We shook hands. "Can I offer you a beer?"

"Before today, that would have been my job, but I'm here to convince you to evacuate," I said.

"Convince away, youngster, but I ain't budging. I lost my wife here. My family has moved on. I've always said I'm going to die here."

"That might be a little sooner than you'd like, sir," I said.

"Nobody is going detonate a nuclear bomb. It's all a hoax. They want us off-balance so they can do something," he said.

"Who?" I asked.

"The government, of course. They're always up to something, but that ain't here nor there. This is my home and I ain't going. Besides, it's rent controlled."

"Sir, in less than two days a giant wave is going to hit the city. In part it will be caused by an undersea quake that will sink Manhattan and it will be lost under the water. Nothing human is going to be able to survive," I said, breaking from our cover story. Figured the lie didn't work, so why not try the truth.

Mr. Martin sipped his beer. "I thought we were trying to avoid a nuclear holocaust, not going swimming."

"That's what you call one of them cover stories. Not really a conspiracy, just a way to get people to move. People don't believe a tsunami could destroy this city. However the idea of a nuclear bomb going off is enough to get them out. Most of them at any rate," I said, smiling.

"I ain't most people."

"I can see that," I said.

"If God wanted me to leave, he'd take care of things," the man said.

"You're getting an opportunity right now with us, only you're too dumb and stubborn to take it," Nellie said.

"Remind me again why we didn't send you to the U.N. instead of Dagonet?" I said.

Nellie's response was the same as it would have been when she was a kid – she stuck her tongue out at me.

"Sir, I'm reminded of an old story. Once there was an older gentleman, not unlike yourself, whose hometown was in the center of the worst flood on record. He sat on his front lawn and watched his neighbors all evacuate. One family even stopped and offered him a seat in their car. The man refused and said that God would take care of him. He listened to the radio when the power went out. The news said all the buildings in town were going to be covered by water, but still the man stayed. Some of the volunteer fire department came by in a rowboat and offered him a lift. Again he told them God would take care of him.

"Finally, the flood waters rose so high he had to climb up on his roof. A helicopter came by, dropped down a ladder and told him to climb up. He had the same answer – God would take care of him. An hour later, a dam burst and the man drowned.

"When he got to the pearly gates he was real angry and demanded to speak to God immediately. When God showed, the man started yelling, 'I trusted you to save me and I drowned!'

"God shrugged his shoulders and said, 'I gave you three chances. What more did you want?'"

The old man chuckled. "When I get to the pearly gates, I won't speak badly of you."

"That wasn't exactly my concern," I said.

"Still not leaving," Mr. Martin said.

I sighed. "Sir, I have a suggestion. You obviously have your mind made up and we're not going to convince you that you should come with us. Here's what I propose. You spend the next day and a half here. Gather up your photo albums and any other memories or necessities and put them in a suitcase. Meet me out here tomorrow at five o'clock. I will give you one last chance to go. If at that time you decide you're going to stay, I'll leave you to your fate. However, I think you'll change your mind."

"I doubt it," he said.

"I don't. See you tomorrow."

To say we were all over the news and social media would be an understatement. Even as people were fleeing, others were craving programming. Once we were sure we'd get all the people out, we moved onto other rescues, including several zoos' worth of animals.

"I can say that I've never seen anything like it," Pam said, reporting from the heart of the Bronx Zoo. "The man with the samurai sword and topknot is actually riding an elephant and talking to the animals. More impressive, they seem to be listening.

He seems to be a combination of Dr. Doolittle and the elephant whisperer. He is going up to each cage and making some noises and then opening them."

"Has he been eaten yet, Pam?" said the anchor, now going along with anything Pam wanted as her access to the Startenders had given the station its highest news ratings ever and they were running nationally.

"There appears to be no danger of that, Henry. The animals are actually cooperating. We'll pan so you can get a look – you can see tigers walking alongside gazelles, gorillas next to giraffes and crocodiles next to penguins, all of them behaving as well as elementary school kids during a fire drill. Maybe even better."

"What's he doing now?" the anchor asked.

"He seems to have stopped outside the lion enclosure," Pam said into her microphone.

Most of the lions had lined up with the other animals, but one male lion was giving Kintaro a very hard time.

"You have to leave now," the young looking, but ancient samurai, said in the language of the lions.

"No. I am fed and get to lie in the sun all day. Why would I leave?" the lion said.

"Because you will drown," Kintaro replied.

The lion snorted in disbelief. "The watering hole isn't deep. I could walk across it."

"A great wall of water is coming and will bury this place," Kintaro said.

"Nonsense. I do not believe you," the lion said.

"Why would I tell an untruth?" Kintaro said, climbing down from the elephant to stand in front of the king of beasts.

"Why should I believe you?" the lion said.

"How many men have you met that speak the language of the pride?" Kintaro replied.

The thought made the lion grow silent.

"You are the first." The lion thought some more. "Is that why our human servants have left us?"

"It is."

"And they will not return to feed us?"

"No, but I will take you to other zoos where more humans will take care of you."

"Very well, I will go with you."

"Good."

The lion looked out on the parade of animals and licked his lips. "Especially since you were kind enough to bring me fresh food."

"There will be no fighting and no eating. Anyone or any animal that breaks those rules will answer to me," Kintaro said.

"I obey no human," the lion said and leapt at Kintaro. The samurai moved with lightning speed and caught the lion by both front paws and flipped it so it hit the lawn on one side, then flipped it over his head to do the same on the other. The blows were enough to stun, but not do lasting harm. Kintaro held on and spun the lion like a father might a child, going faster and faster until the lion was only a blur. He stopped, letting the lion roll away. When the lion tried to stand he was too dizzy and fell repeatedly.

"If there are any further problems, you will be my prey, understood?" Kintaro said.

"Yes," the lion said, meekly getting in line behind a water buffalo, his head hung low. The rest of his pride was doing the lion equivalent of snickering. Kintaro motioned to the elephant, who gently lifted the samurai up with his trunk so the samurai could return to his seat.

Pam stood there amazed. Even though she had met Kintaro, she had no idea of what he was capable of. Still she had to report to her viewers and ran alongside the elephant, her microphone extended overhead. "Excuse me, what is your name?" she asked, playing dumb. "And are you one of these Startenders we have been hearing so much about?"

"My name is Kintaro." The samurai pointed to the badge on his chest. "And I am proud to be a Startender."

"How are you getting the animals to listen to you? I've never seen anything like it," Pam said.

"It's a gift. Now if you'll excuse me, there are more animals left and little time to get them out safely."

Kintaro and his parade of animals moved on to the next enclosure, which was the wolf habitat. The Brand family was already handling the wolves. Three of them were related by blood to many of the wolves, the other by marriage. Shan had been born one of the Bronx Zoo's wolves, before she became a werehuman. Her two kids had been born in the zoo as well.

An old Japanese woman walked up to Pam, positioning herself between the camera and Kintaro. "My boy was never one to take attention well, as opposed to me," said the old witch woman with many missing teeth. She hunched over and leaned on a knobby stick that she used as a cane.

"Are you the mother of this man?" Pam asked.

"Yes, I am," she replied.

"Are you also one of the Startenders?" Pam asked.

"Heavens, no. They would want nothing to do with an old witch such as myself," she said.

"Are you saying the Startenders practice ageism and name-calling?" Pam said, knowing she would be criticized if she didn't ask.

"Not at all. I am both ancient and a witch. More of a necromancer really. The Startenders have to adhere to a code of honor. I don't like to be impaired by such trivial things and what respectable necromancer would swear off killing? My boy on the other hand is all about honor. Why the stories I could tell you about when he was a child on our mountain in Japan, when he would wrestle with bears and other creatures. Entirely naked I might add. Said if the animals didn't need clothes, neither did he. It wasn't until he started noticing girls that I could convince him to wear clothing consistently."

"Mother, I said you could come as long as you helped me with the animals and didn't embarrass me," shouted the man on elephant back. "You're ignoring both parts of our agreement."

"But I never actually agreed, now did I? In all my years, I've never been on TV. An old woman with not much time left deserves some simple pleasures, don't you think?" she said.

"Mother, you're centuries old. And unlikely to die for at least a few centuries more," Kintaro said, shaking his head and going toward the hyena habitat.

"Bah." The old woman grabbed hold of the camera and pulled it so it was pointed at her face. Next she took the microphone from the hands of the reporter. "But enough about my son. What you really want to know is more about me…"

Sun WuKong the monkey king was sent to fetch Rznard from the set of his talk show. He brought Kim Irons and her camera crew with him. Rznard saw them coming and ran off down a corridor. Unbeknownst to him, Sun can split off multiples of himself by chewing his own hair and spitting it out. Disgusting, but effective as Rznard ran right smack into a second Sun.

"We are here to bring you to New York, Mr. Rznard," Sun said.

"I told you I'm busy," he said frantically.

"Too busy to save lives?" Sun asked.

Rznard's answer was to run away and smack into a third Sun. A repeat runaway performance ending with him bumping into a fourth monkey king.

"Leave me alone! This is harassment. I'll sue!"

"But James, you always talk about doing your civic duty," Kim Irons said.

"Kim, what are you doing here?" Rznard said.

"Going to help, but we came to get you first," Kim said. "The barship *Big Top* is waiting outside." Rumbles, a former circus clown was the head honcho of that one. "Are you coming or are you a coward?"

Rznard looked at the host of the highest rated cable news show and then at the cameras. "Sure. I just need to get something from my dressing room first."

Rznard went in his dressing room, unaware we had planted a camera there. He opened the window and climbed out. The footage of his climbing out and running away was hugely popular online within hours.

Of course, not everything the Startenders did was caught on camera. True, we were trying for a public relations blitz, but some things simply happened too fast to be recorded.

The most notable of these was the robbery of every major museum in the city. Don't get me wrong – the Startenders are not thieves. Well, not in the sense that we take things that don't belong to us and keep them. However, one of us is the god of thieves. Hermes was so fast he made lightning look like molasses on a winter morning. Apparently a major fantasy of his was to try to rob everything from every museum in Manhattan in the span of an hour without setting off a single alarm. That may sound impossible, but the word impossible was only a challenge to Hermes.

Now with the imminent sinking of Manhattan, he was going to have a chance to live out one of his fantasies and empty every museum in the city. Well, almost every museum. Hermes' daughter Kyna was incredibly fast as well, although she simply wasn't a match for her father. Both sported winged footwear that allowed them to fly. Hers were black boots while Hermes sported red high-top sneakers. Nellie had a similar pair of black shoes and while she was not in their league in terms of speed, she could bypass alarms like nobody's business.

Hermes left one museum for his daughter to clean out and one for Nellie in the Bronx. Maybe Yankee Stadium wasn't technically a regular museum, but several Startenders are big baseball fans, especially the Yankees. Babe Ruth and some other famous Yankees had stopped in at various times to Bulfinche's Pub. There was even a picture of the Babe and Paddy behind the bar. They weren't going to let those mementos in the Yankee museum be destroyed any more than the paintings and sculptures Kyna was liberating from the Guggenheim.

None of the trio was exactly forthcoming about their methods, feeling if more people knew about how they operated, it would be easier to stop them in the future.

Hermes completed his task in fifty-seven minutes, including the time it took him to transport the articles to the Smithsonian Museum in D.C., and get past their security. All the curators of the various museums were informed where they could pick up their treasures.

At least most. Hermes held back one painting which had been stolen from a private collector. He returned it to its proper owner who hadn't the money to fight the museum in court. He replaced it with a perfect forgery he had done himself. They never noticed the switch.

Hermes helped the two ladies transport their goods and the three of them went house to house to make sure we didn't miss anybody.

As near as we could tell by the third day, we had every single person out of the five boroughs and surrounding areas with two exceptions. It's amazing what hard work, large amounts of magical compulsion and the once largest fortune on Earth could accomplish.

Two was still too many.

I was going back for Mr. Martin, hoping he would change his mind. Paddy was going for one of his oldest and dearest friends, who as Mother of the Streets was so closely bonded to the city that despite knowing what was coming, refused to leave although she made sure that not one other homeless person was left behind.

It didn't take much searching for Paddy to find her. She was sitting on a wooden crate outside of Bulfinche's Pub when Paddy flew over her in his Caddy.

"Ye didn't find him?" Paddy asked, already knowing the answer.

She shook her head. As hard as she tried, the mad sea god eluded her as well as the rest of us.

"Then Rebecca, tis time to go," Paddy said, landing the flying car and getting out.

"Yes Moran, it is, so why are you still here?" Rebecca asked.

"Ye know the answer to that," Paddy said. "I can't leave ye here to die."

"Moran, I'm over a hundred years old. Without the city sustaining me, I would have been dust a long time ago," Rebecca said.

"I know the city lent you power as Mother of the Streets, but I have power too. In trying to save me late wife Bulfinche, I ended up with a great many ways to extend human life. Ye won't die. In fact, I might be able to restore some of your youth," Paddy said.

Rebecca smiled. "Why would you be wanting to do something so foolish? I'm an old woman. I've lived longer than I've had any good reason to, except that I couldn't leave my city to fend for itself or those on its street to do the same."

"You've saved hundreds of lives and helped save millions of others. Ye protected the homeless and this city countless times. Now save yourself," Paddy said.

"Moran, these streets are empty. Without them, I won't have a purpose. I'm not fit to go out into space with the rest of you."

"I've got a good mind to toss ye over my shoulder and carry ye out of here myself," Paddy said.

"You could try. Judah already did. Planned to carry me away to one of your barships." Judah was a golem Rebecca's father had helped create to fight the Nazis. He was also a Startender.

"Why did he put ye down?" Paddy said.

"Because I asked him to. And he understood why I have to stay. He's a protector too."

"Then make me understand why ye are asking me to let ye die when I can save ye," Paddy said.

Rebecca sighed. "The Nazis slaughtered my family, yet I survived the camp. Murderers killed Abraham and my babies, raped me, yet I survived to avenge them. I can't survive again when someone I love dies. This city is alive, sentient and has spoken with me for decades. Shared more than its power. It shared its hopes, dreams, memories, its very essence. I can't let my city die alone while I go off and survive again. I'm the only one who can hear it. We will go together into that dark night. Hopefully then I'll be reunited with those that fate took from me and my city will be at peace."

"Rebecca...." Tears were streaming down Paddy's face.

"You can throw me over your shoulder because you know you are one of the few people I could never raise a hand to, but then you're condemning your city not only to die, but to die alone and afraid. You love this city as much as anyone. It wants me to stay with it until the end. Can you live with yourself if you deny it its dying wish?"

"Damn it Rebecca..."

"Paddy, thank you for caring. Without you, I..." Rebecca was never one for expressing her emotions well.

"Yeah, me too." Paddy opened up his arms. "Come here."

"How many times have I told you I'm not a loose woman," she said. It was a joke between them. It was meant to make them laugh, but only made two brief smiles that were instantly covered in tears as the pair held each other one last time.

The ground shook beneath them and a mighty roar sounded in the distance. The tsunami was on its way.

"It's time for you to go. You've got great things ahead of you. My only wish is that I live long enough to take the life of the monster that did this to my city. And none of your nonsense about killing being wrong."

"This once, I wouldn't argue with you," Paddy said, pulling the taller woman's head down so he could kiss her on the cheek. "Goodbye, Rebecca."

Paddy put his hand on her cheek where he had kissed her and they looked into each other's eyes. The ground rumbled again so hard they almost lost their footing.

"Goodbye, Moran."

Paddy got into the car and held his hand out, his eyes pleading. "Hope and happiness never die. We might still have a chance."

"Hope and happiness may never die, but people do. Remember me. Remember my city."

"I'll never forget either of ye," Paddy said.

The giant wave nearly blotted out the sun. Paddy Moran flew his Cadillac towards his space station, letting the tears flow down his face at the death of his friend and his home.

I had gotten my flying motorcycle with a sidecar and was headed over to Donald Martin's building, hoping the old man would have a change of heart. I was cutting things close. As near as all of our people could tell, Poseidon had already begun. Not even an insane sea god can call up a tsunami and a seaquake on a whim. It took time and power, probably almost all of the power he still had.

In my heart, I knew Rebecca would never leave, but in my

head I hoped she would. And Paddy still had to try or he'd never be able to live with himself.

With Donald Martin we still had a chance.

I was happy to see Mr. Martin had followed our deal, even down to having a suitcase with him. I hovered above his porch and honked the horn once. He looked up and watched as the motorcycle descended to street level.

"Like I said, something new every day in this city," Martin said. "I still ain't leaving, although I will say it's rather lonely now that everybody else is gone. Of course, they'll all be back once this blows over."

"This isn't going to blow over. Manhattan is going to be wiped from the map." The ground rumbled. "And it's already started. Would you consent to at least let me give you a ride up to the roof?"

"Once I get in that sidecar, you ain't going to just fly away with me?" he said, his tone dripping with suspicion.

"If we wanted to force you out, you would've been gone yesterday," I said. "Please, there isn't much time left."

As if to accentuate my words the ground rumbled again beneath us, which made Mr. Martin nervous.

"I suppose it couldn't hurt to go for a ride. Besides, I've never ridden in a flying motorcycle before. It might be fun."

Mr. Martin climbed in the sidecar and put his suitcase between his knees. I lifted up until we got to the top of his building. I arranged it so we were facing south.

"I'd like you to keep looking that way," I said.

"What exactly am I supposed to be looking for? That imaginary tidal wave of yours?" Mr. Martin said. And as if to accentuate his words, a wall of water appeared and blocked out the sky.

Mr. Martin promptly exclaimed something about the divine nature of human excrement. "I changed my mind. Let's get out of here!"

"I thought you might. Hold on," I said as I lifted off and put the motorcycle into overdrive. The tsunami was approaching fast, but we were faster. We weren't even going to get wet, but the same couldn't be said of the city. I told myself I wouldn't look, but I couldn't help myself. Once we were at a safe altitude, I turned and watched as Poseidon's rage destroyed my home. The wave was a terrible thing, almost alive. It was a watery sledgehammer that smashed everything in its path. The ground rumbled and shook as the city sank beneath the wave.

I wanted to cry and was only stopped by a question.

"What's going to happen to me now?" Mr. Martin said.

"You have any family you can live with?" I said.

"I've got three kids, but they have kids and lives of their own. None of them have the room to take me in and I don't want to impose on them. I saw on the news there are a bunch of tent cities. Am I going there?"

"Not necessarily. I don't know if you heard about our moon colony. They're looking for settlers.

"What could an old geezer like me contribute?" Mr. Martin said.

"You'd be surprised. And up there, you wouldn't necessarily feel as old as you do down here. The gravity on the moon is one-sixth that of Earth. That means it would be a lot easier on your heart and joints," I said.

"You mean my arthritis wouldn't be as bad?" he said.

"Nope."

"Will I be able to come back to Earth?" he said.

"Depends how long you stay up there. After a while, returning to Earth gravity would be difficult, although there are programs in place where you can spend part of the day in Earth level gravity. Helps with bone density."

"Would my family be able to visit?" He asked.

"Absolutely. We have measures in place for that too."

"Where do I sign up?" he said.

"If you like, I can drive you right up to Ben City," I said. I honestly needed to put a little distance between me and the devastation.

"Now? On this bike?" he said.

"Yep." Then I saw something beautiful floating out of the mist. "But first you are going to want to watch this. Then hold on to your suitcase because the next stop is the moon."

The world was watching. Every TV, monitor, phone and anything else that could hold an image showed the wave as it grew into the biggest tsunami ever recorded. There were reporters both dumb and close enough to get hit. Hermes and Kyna got them out of the way, but left the cameras to record the death of the greatest city in the world as the quake sank it and the wave drowned it.

Some skyscrapers fell, but others stood tall and defiant, just like the people who had lived in the city.

The hearts of the world sank with New York. We saved the people, but not the structures. Some things were beyond even us.

But there was one structure we couldn't let the wave claim. It meant too much to too many.

Cameras that had caught the devastation now showed mist and fog over angry water. And out of that destruction rose something majestic. At first it was only a torch, but that was followed by a green hand and a giant green woman wearing robes and what looked like a crown. She had always told the world that she would take their tired, their poor. That she wanted the huddled masses, yearning to breathe free, the wretched refuse of others' teeming shore. She implored the world to send these, the homeless, tempest-tost to her, as she lifted her lamp beside the golden door.

Today the world needed Lady Liberty more than ever before. The Statue of Liberty had been a symbol of hope for the world. Now she was rising out of the destruction. Not just rising – she was flying out of the mist thanks to four barships that were carrying and reinforcing her, so she would not fall apart.

Refugees who stood on a far distant shore saw her and cheered.

Each of our barships had been shaped to show the symbol from the Startenders badge on their sides. Yes, it was blatant product placement, but we needed people to believe in us too. Belief equaled power for gods and we had more than a few in the Startenders. They needed belief or at least people knowing about them to survive. This would help the world to trust us, because dark times might come again. And then, just as this time, the Startenders would help beat back the darkness and ensure hope and humanity survived.

PLAYING FOR KEEPERS

"I'm putting the band back together," I said with a smile.

That tale I mentioned was coming later in the book - here it is. This is what happened when Eric, my crew and I took *Fools' Glory* the long way back to Manhattan right before the evacuation by way of a whole other planet in hopes of getting new recruits for the Startenders. Not to mention, some big time help for the evacuation of New York. As often happens, something that was supposed to be simple became rather complicated.

I was happy to be back on Traven, especially since I now knew enough of the rules of The Establishment to not end up in a fight for my life. It was the largest bar on the planet, complete with its own snipers and was where I met most of the aliens I know.

"I think my lation stone isn't working. When have we ever been a musical group, Murphy?" Randor the troll said. We all had lation stones, which mystically translated for us.

Loki laughed. "It's a line from an old Earth movie. That means we want to put back together the old gang that helped save the planet Karma."

"We are back together. What's the big deal about that?" Pace, another much larger troll, said. To put it mildly, he was a super genius, especially in terms of quantum geography. The fact that he didn't understand spoke volumes.

"We're putting together a group called the Startenders. Our mission is to explore the universe and the otherworlds and to help others who are in trouble. I was asked to help pick members for the group and I immediately thought of all of you. We would be doing the same type of thing we did back on Karma, only we'd be much better equipped," I said.

"We almost died. Some of us in violent and disturbing ways. Not to mention what happened afterwards," said the diminutive Buzz. There were teddy bears back on Earth larger than the garba. And what he said was true. In order to pay for our military campaign, Buzz had to sell his translating services and ended up putting an awakening elder thing back to sleep, probably saving Travan and who knows how many other worlds. "We managed to get away with our posteriors intact. Why would we want to risk undoing that?"

"Because there are people out there who need help. If not us, then who will help?"

"I'm in," Toma said. "As part of my improved relationship with the divinities in the universe." The troll was the smaller brother of Pace and after what happened at Karma became a reverend. Of course the religion he championed changed frequently. I think he was up to over a hundred sampled. "Present company excepted, of course." The troll looked at the two gods at the table, Loki and Thunder Jack, when he spoke that last part.

"Paddy and my family are a part of these Startenders?" said Thunder Jack, the god formerly known as Zeus. Demeter, Dionysus, Hermes, and his most famous son were all Startenders.

"They are. In fact, Hercules is the head honcho of one of the barships, the *Argo II*."

"What's a head honcho?" Nastra said. The troll was also brother to Pace and Toma. Randor was no relation.

"What's a barship?" Buzz said.

"The Startenders isn't a military organization, so we decided military titles and ranks wouldn't be appropriate. Captain of a barship is the head honcho. First mate is honcho," I said. "I'm head honcho of the barship *Fools' Glory*. Loki is my honcho."

Thunder Jack frowned. "What about Nemesis? Is she also a Startender?"

"No. She felt that having the enforcer for the Council Of Thrones join the Startenders would cause too much trouble for us. However she's proclaimed herself an ally and we've signed a treaty with her," I said.

The storm divinity nodded. "Then I'm not going to join." Zeus had run off to the otherworlds because of Nemesis. Actually more along the lines of fleeing in abject terror from the daughter of night. There's a bit more to it, but the short version is he drugged and raped Nemesis centuries ago using water from the river Lethe to steal her memory. Periodically, she would start to remember and Zeus would slip her another Mickey.

Some time back, she broke totally free of the mind games when her human husband was killed in front of her. Once she took care of the killers, she went after the god who had been tormenting her for centuries.

Zeus was the most powerful god of the most powerful pantheon on Earth. It was no contest. With her full mental faculties, Nemesis kicked his butt. Repeatedly.

"I'll talk to Nemesis and see what we can do. She just banned you from Earth and Olympus. Maybe we can work out something with her for everywhere else so you can help us," I said.

"I plan to help you regardless. You and Loki were the ones who started me on my own road to redemption. I behaved poorly in the past. What I do now is only some small token to try to make amends. I wronged Nemesis. She truly and rightly hates me. I think that my presence might affect your treaty with her. To establish yourselves out here, you'll need all the power and allies you can muster. My joining will only complicate that. Perhaps I'll follow her example and set myself up as an ally, instead of a member."

"Very wise solution," Loki said.

"It was bound to happen sooner or later," Thunder Jack said with a wink.

"So where are the ladies?" Nastra said.

"Speak of the beauty," Buzz said as four females approached our table, but his eyes were on an incredibly large yellow-skinned person that was part of the quartet. Truthfully, the Karmas don't share human secondary sex characteristics and she always looked a bit on the manly side to me. "Hello Jan. You look marvelous."

"Thank you, my little one," Jan said. They were a mismatched pair, but it had worked for them. Maybe it would again.

"What, is nobody happy to see me?" Nara said. The blue blag looked like the mutant offspring of a smurf and a hippo.

"I know I am," I said, then got up and hugged Nara. She lifted my feet clear off the floor.

"Always happy to see you too, Muffy," she said. Old mistranslation joke.

Nara moved on to say hi to the others and I hugged Jan.

"What did I miss?" Jan said.

"Did my crew explain to you about the Startenders?" I said. Well, most of my crew. The trickster Coyote was also assigned to *Fools' Glory*, but felt that playing taxi was beneath him and stayed back on Earth. We also had one of Foster's plant bodies. There was at least one on each barship, which allowed us a form of backup communication by having him body jump with messages. He had also waited back on Earth to help prepare for the evacuation.

"They did."

"Then you're up to speed," I said. "Let me introduce Savannah and Riga, two Startenders who are part of my crew."

"Charmed," Savannah the she-satyr said. She was the daughter of Pan and just as oversexed. Like her father, she had furry legs, hooves, and the ability to emit pheromones which entranced members of the opposite – and occasionally the same – sex.

Thunder Jack raised an eyebrow and whispered to Loki. "She has power. One of Pan's?"

Loki nodded.

"Hi," Riga said, hugging Loki.

Randor chuckled. "New lady friend, Key?"

Loki kissed Riga on the top of the head. "Better. My daughter."

"Loki, you old dog you," Thunder Jack said.

"Actually she was conceived right before the Karma affair," I said.

"Murphy, it's bad enough that I know you were present, but do you really have to keep telling everyone?" Riga said.

"Oh, really?" Randor said, wiggling his eyebrows. The motion meant the same thing for trolls as humans.

"Her mother is a dragon. Loki was in dragon form. I was present in the sense that I was trying not to get squashed," I said. "We're only waiting for Tock and then I can give you the rest of our pitch."

"Save it," Pace said. He stood up and put his hand on my chin. I returned the gesture. It was a troll sign of trust. Trolls who used up all their limba energy go primitive. Limba is the stuff that lets them open a nexus. If someone put their hand on a primitive's chin, they'd lose the fingers and most of the metacarpals. "Murphy, you believe in these Startenders?"

"With every fiber of my being," I said.

"Key, what about you?" Pace said.

"It's an organization dedicated to doing the greatest amount of good in the universe," Loki said.

"Sounds naïve to me," Buzz said.

"It is," Loki said. "But there are a lot of powerful folks involved and people like Murphy to keep us honest."

"What would be expected of us?" Randor said.

"There is a code of conduct and an oath to be renewed annually," I said. We borrowed that from the Round Table. "The word of a Startender must only be given when it can be kept. No killing of sentient life unless all other options have been tried first. Startenders must help those truly in need. You would have to go through the Startender Academy and then be assigned to a barship, which would then go out to explore the universe. You'd help the people you find along the way."

"What does the gig pay?" Buzz said.

"It doesn't. Not exactly. All creature comforts are provided, along with a Startenders badge. The badge provides atmosphere, comfortable gravity, a protective field and a lation stone fragment to provide translations among other things."

Buzz gave me a serious look. Lation stones came from garba in much the same way humans pass kidney stones. They are rare and incredibly expensive. "And how'd you get them, I wonder?"

"We broke up the stone you gave me into the smallest possible fragments that would still work. The badges also serve as a communication device."

"So it's a charity deal?" Buzz said.

"Not at all. Along the way, we will be working on various commerce deals. Each member of the crew and to a lesser extent the rest of the Startenders would get a share of any profits," I said. "And the satisfaction of helping others."

"Hmm," Buzz said.

"I'm in," Nara said.

"If it's good enough for Murphy and Key, I'll join as well," Pace said.

"Me too," Nastra said.

"My brothers would be lost without me, so once I joined you knew they'd follow," Toma said.

"Sounds like fun, but I'm getting a little old," Randor said.

"Not for us," Loki said.

The troll laughed. "Fine. Since you are foolish enough to have me, I will be a Startender."

"Murphy, you know I cannot do anything that would hurt another," Jan said. No Karman could. Their world made sure that anyone who harmed another would wither and become thin and weak. Those that were good to others became rotund. Jan was one of the best. In fact, she dared do harm to save others, knowing it would hurt her and ended up an odd mix of fat and muscle.

"Which is why we want you most of all," I said. "You would be on our leadership council. If we did something wrong, you would be the first to know. We want you to keep us on the straight and narrow. If we ever did anything that hurt you, you would be free to leave or help us fix it."

"Then I would very much like to be a Startender," Jan said.

I turned to the garba. "That leaves you Buzz."

"I'm thinking," Buzz said. "I'm no fighter."

"That's where you're wrong," I said. "You're not a warrior, but you are a fighter. You were the one willing to risk his life to raise the money to hire Tock's goblin cram." A cram is the smallest military unit in the Goblin Empire, one hundred and forty-four soldiers. "You were the one to put the elder thing back down to rest."

"Yeah, so I came through in the crunch, but it's not like anyone is in danger now," Buzz said.

Loki, Riga, Savannah and I exchanged looks.

"Actually..." Loki said.

"What?" Buzz said.

"Back on Earth, New York City is about to be destroyed by a mad god and a tidal wave," Loki said.

Buzz whistled. He'd visited me at Bulfinche's Pub in Manhattan. "Must be millions of people. So we need to stop a mad god?"

"Can't be done. We've tried. Unchangeable prophecy," Savannah said. "Our job is evacuation."

"Of Manhattan Island?" Buzz said.

"The entire city," I said.

"That'll be tough, but it'd be worse not to try," Buzz said. "So what are we waiting for?"

"You're in?" I said.

Buzz sighed. "If the rest of you are going, you'll need me to look out for you, so yes. How are we getting to Earth? Troll nexus or that flying motorcycle of yours?"

"Like I said, I have a barship now," I said.

As if on cue a gold sphere about the size of a golf ball floated through The Establishment to our table.

"Speaking of the ship, here it is," I said.

Buzz stood up and looked at the tiny ball. "It's not very big. I don't think we're all going to fit in there. I'm not even going to make it inside."

"Hey boss," came a voice from the gold ball.

"Hi Eric," I said.

"Your ship is named Eric? I thought you said it was called *Fools' Glory*?" Buzz said.

"No, Eric is our pilot," I said. "Each barship has a melog, a golden living mechanical being who is bonded to the ship. Eric, do you have Tock in there with you?"

"No, apparently he had another more pressing engagement at a place called the Scum Hole," Eric's voice said.

"Why would he go there?" Nara said. "It's a bar run by killer robots."

"Sounds lovely," I said. "Tell me more."

"They're warez. Soldier mech used by a three planet empire in the Siron system, until the warez decided they were tired of dying to serve organics and turned on their people. Once they took control, they started warring among themselves, splitting up the planets among different groups. Each world erupted in civil war. These particular warez fled the fighting and killed the previous owners of the Scum Hole to claim the place for themselves," Randor said.

Property rights on Traven are a bit on the limited side. No one really owns anything, just occupies it until someone else takes it from them.

"They sound charming," I said. "What business does Tock have with these killer robots?"

"He didn't say," Eric said.

"These warez are slavers," Randor said. As a former slave, he had issues with slavers.

My memory had glossed over the fact that almost anything was permitted on Traven. Suddenly I wasn't so happy to be back.

"Everyone climb aboard and we'll give you your Startender badges, administer your oaths and go help Tock. You'll still have to complete the academy to stay on, but we'll worry about that later. We have to be back on Earth in time to help with the evacuation," I said.

"Um, Murphy, still not big enough for us to do that," Buzz said.

"Eric, open us a door," I said.

"One door coming up, boss," Eric said and the gold ball morphed into a traditional looking Earth door. I pulled it open and held it as the new Startender recruits walked aboard. The snipers turned and their laser sight skulls danced on my chest. I waved and went after everyone else and shut the door.

"A lot bigger on the inside," Jan said.

"Yes it is. Morphing hull and a pocket universe make all sorts of things possible," I said. "Eric, take us to the Scum Hole."

"Repeat the enlistment oath after me," I said.
They did.

I have, this day, voluntarily enlisted myself to the Startenders, for one Earth year: And I do bind myself to conform, in all instances, to such rules and regulations, as are, or shall be, established for the Startenders.

"Now repeat the Startender oath."
They did.

I am a Startender which means
      –I will act with honor and do what's right.
      –I will not break my word or give it lightly, for my promise binds all Startenders.
      –I will put principle above gain.
      –I will protect life, shelter others from harm and defend

those who are unable to defend themselves
*   –I will not kill unless all other options have been*
exhausted and then only in the protection of life
*   –I will take care of my own and as many others as*
possible
*   –I will be loyal to my own and to these principles.*

I handed out the badges. "Time to put the oath into practice."

The Establishment was well run, clean, and well secured. The Scum Hole didn't bother with any of those things. Then again with that name, you wouldn't expect it to be. Everybody in The Establishment seemed to be able to pull off a certain level of toughness. Those in the Scum Hole seemed more sleazy, the type likely to stick a knife between your ribs or a blaster to the back of your head the moment you looked away. The walls were badly patched up and there was an odor, which was bad even for what is largely accepted to be the most populated planet in the galaxy.

"I don't think coming here was such a good idea," said Buzz. Loki and Thunder Jack laughed. The trolls smirked, but part of me agreed with the little guy.

The first time I was in The Establishment, I really didn't know any of the rules and messed up fairly badly. They had guards and snipers positioned around the place to keep order. The Scum Hole didn't even appear to have a bouncer.

I wasn't even sure why it had customers. There was almost no service. It seemed like a personal club for the warez that they let others visit. I didn't recognize the warez. Startender training was exhaustive, but not all inclusive. I knew there were at least a few sentient mechanical races in the universe. Now I could add another.

Tock was sitting at a corner table with another goblin. We all sat down at a table next to him. The goblin turned and saw us. A smile crept across his face, before it was replaced with a scowl.

"I told your golden messenger boy I couldn't make it," Tock whispered.

"Which is why we brought the party to you," I said. "We're putting the band back together."

"I'm a little busy right now," Tock said.

"Then maybe you could use a little help," Loki said. "You're never going to free those goblins on your own. And you know, Murphy's not about to leave without the rest of the slaves."

Back on Karma we'd spent a lot of time freeing slaves. None of us were going anywhere without figuring out a way to free them.

The goblin's eyebrows raised up, surprised at how perceptive the trickster was. Not that it was that hard to figure out. Tock had ascended to the rank of general in the goblin military. His former partner Jade had been lost in the campaign that got him his promotion. One with his rank had to have some reason to hang around a place like this. The hundred and forty three or so goblin slaves would be a pretty good reason.

"Can't ask you to help me," Tock said.

"That's okay. We're offering. You helped us when we needed it," I said.

"You hired my cram to help you. There's a difference," Tock said.

"Yes, there is. So I guess you better tell us what's going on and what needs to be done," I said.

Tock stood up, grabbed me by the collar of my shirt and lifted me off the ground.

He wasn't actually hurting me, but didn't want to make it look like we knew each other.

"This is my nephew Rem." The younger goblin nodded. Unlike the rest of us, he probably didn't have a lation stone to translate. They were on the expensive side if you didn't know a garba. Tock was speaking Goblin Prime, which Rem could understand. The rest he was probably guessing.

"Charmed, I'm sure," I said.

"He got his first command. Things didn't go well. In fact, the other one hundred forty three members of his cram were all captured by these gearhead slavers. I won't go into the embarrassing details. I was hoping to buy them back, but I don't think I'm going to have enough." Tock tossed me against the wall. I pushed off and grabbed hold of his arm, twisting it behind his back. It took Tock a little bit by surprise because I wasn't exactly the best hand-to-hand combatant last time we fought together. I wasn't the worst either, but I'm much better now.

"You have over a hundred goblin soldiers. Why can't they fight their way out?" I said.

"Because of those belts around them. They can do anything from cause pain to disintegrate the wearer. And even if they can get them off, there is still the matter of the warez. Those mechs were designed to help take over entire worlds. Each of them is as strong as a tank and almost as well armored. Flesh and blood based hand-to-hand isn't going to do any good."

"We could open the door to our ship and get them all out and away from the mechanical men," I said.

Tock shook his head. "We don't know what the range on those belts is. Or if there's a deadman's signal being broadcasted. We bring them out of range and they could all be reduced to dust."

So much for the easy way. "Suggestions?"

"We could ask nicely," Eric said. He had a slight touch of sarcasm in his tone, which is a good thing. I was hoping despite our mechanical man's limited exposure to the universe that he wasn't that naïve.

"They're inorganic, so nothing I can do is going to be able to convince them," Savannah said. The she-satyr seemed disappointed that her magic-based pheromones weren't going to work on killer robots. Oddly, they seemed to work on Eric.

"If I had a chance to look at one of those belts, I might be able to figure out how they worked and deactivate them," Pace said.

"The only way to get a look is to wear one as a prisoner. I'm assuming that holds no interest for you," Tock said smirking.

"Not at all, but perhaps you would have enough money to buy one of the goblin slaves. Then I could look at the belt," Pace said.

"Not going to work. They'd remove the belt and replace it with a purely pain giving one. Much cheaper. What you're suggesting has occurred to them, so they don't give out the tech," Tock said.

"We could challenge them to a game of spikeball and beat them," Nara said.

"What?" Tock said.

"I had a girlfriend who came here drinking one night and

ended up a slave. They allow some of the slaves to contact family and friends to bid on them. I had enough cash to get her out, but just barely. When I was in here, I found out what they do for people who don't have the money. They give them a chance to play, putting their lives up against those of the slaves," Nara said.

"So if they survive, the friend is freed?" I said.

"Not that simple. They don't kill anybody in spikeball, just injure. If you lose, you become a slave and you can't sell a corpse. Not for as much as a slave anyway. And the game is pretty damn close to rigged; for organics anyway. There's a section over there about the size of a bonkerball court." No idea what that was. Lation stones do have their limitations. "It has two stone pylons, one on each side, covered in concrete or something similar. There is also a large soft metal ball, maybe a little bit bigger than both my fists." Nara's fists were each about the size of a basketball.

"How does the game work?" Loki said.

"Those two stone pillars are the goals. In the center of the concrete is a large metal spike, probably about eight feet tall." The pylon was about ten feet tall. The lation stone did manage to translate measurements fairly well. "The players have to smash the rock off of their opponent's goal to reveal the spike. Then they have to take the metal ball and get it impaled on top of the spike, without breaking the ball."

"Getting the stone off would be difficult enough, but the amount of force needed to do that with a ball seems unlikely with flesh and bone. At least with a single shot," Pace said.

"Who's the cyborg?" Riga said. Guy was humanoid, but quite bulbous and green with tentacles instead of an arm. The other was metal.

"Rumor had it that he was taken as a slave, but convinced the warez he'd serve them better as a lackey," Nara said.

"Well then I suggest we figure out how to rig this game in our favor and play them for all the marbles," Loki said.

"Are you insane? We wouldn't stand a chance," said Tock. Loki only smiled.

"People spread out and learn everything you can about this place and that game. I want everyone to work in at least pairs," I said. As expected the troll brothers went together. Buzz climbed up on Randor's shoulder and the pair went with Jan. Savannah, Eric and Riga went in the other direction.

"Guess that leaves you and me partner," I said watching as Thunder Jack and Nara paired up. They had a brief affair after Karma. From the looks it may have been about to be rekindled.

"I wouldn't have it any other way," Loki said.

"You think you could manage to spike the ball?" I said.

"Maybe, but Jack has the best shot. Eric could. And my daughter might be able to in her dragon form. But the trolls are only going to make a dent. You might manage to scratch the paint."

"Great," I said. "You know anything about these warez?"

"Nope. After getting my freedom, I did some wandering. Learned lots, but realized there is far more that I don't know and that the universe is a very big place. Even if we explore it for centuries, there'll still be more to learn." Loki stopped short when he saw another robot sitting at the bar. Where the warez were large, humanoid and threatening with lots of jagged edges, this was one tiny and best described as cute. He was bulbous, yet still humanoid and his metal legs didn't reach the floor. The trickster saw it and cursed in Norse. It involved doing something to someone's mother and her cat with a war hammer for money. "If that's what I think it is, we need to get everyone out of here immediately. And whatever you do, don't annoy the little robot."

"Why? Will he rampage and destroy the town?" I said.

"More like the planet. It fits the description of the Nimian AI."

"Crap." I said, remembering my xenovitology. The story goes that the Nimians, like many other worlds, developed a planetary processing system to run different tasks. As occasionally happens, the system became self-aware. It then destroyed the planet, built itself a body from the remains and proceeded to wipe out a fleet of Mackeynavelian warships that arrived to claim the remains of the world as their own. It then stripped the starships, used the parts to achieve the ability to move between star systems.

"If it's playing on the warez side we don't stand a chance," Loki said.

"What do you make of the rumor that it forced one world to worship it as a god and became one?" I said.

"Mortals have done it, so it might be possible to have a

mechanical god," Loki said. "We retreat for now, get a better plan, save New York, then come back later with reinforcements to get the slaves out."

A belligerent orange hued alien that made Nara look petite was starting a fight with the little bot for his seat at the bar. Obviously the bully didn't know what he was messing with and about to be vaporized by. Now, I'll be the first one to admit I have a habit of sticking up for the little guy. It's how I met many of the Karma crew. Buzz was being threatened by a goblin. I stepped in and got lucky; I survived.

This guy wasn't a little guy by any stretch of the imagination, but he was still about to get himself killed. A Startender is sworn to protect all life, even those of idiots.

I stepped toward the orange bully.

Loki gave me a look I got a lot that seemed to question my sanity. "Murphy, you're not actually…"

"Yep," I said.

"You don't stand a chance against the umbrage, let alone the bot."

"I'm sure you have a point," I said.

"I really don't want command of *Fools' Glory*," Loki said. "Or explain to Elsiebelle that I let her father die."

"Then I guess you better play wingman," I said.

"You're insane."

"I thought you liked that about me."

"It's become less endearing over time," Loki said.

"Just follow my lead," I said.

I walked over and started examining the umbrage. I turned to Loki and spoke in Traven Prime, a bastardization of Goblin Prime and a few other languages, and the most spoken language on the planet. "Very impressive specimen, don't you think?"

Loki rubbed his chin, then squeezed the orange alien's lowest arm. He had six. "A little stringy for an umbrage. I doubt we'd get five mining cycles out of him before the radiation killed him. Might not be worth the money."

The bully pushed Loki's arm away. "What nonsense you spouting? Janka not for sale," he said in broken Travan Prime.

"That's not what they told us," I said, pointing my thumb

toward the warez, careful so they couldn't see it.

"Janka not a slave. Not for sale," he said.

"We were told that wouldn't be a problem if the price was right," I said. "Were you about to fight this bot? That would be great to see if you would be worth the investment."

"You know, I think we can barter them down. If we get him for half, it would be worth it if he survived the radiation for at least three mining cycles," Loki said.

"You're right. Go make them the offer. Janka was it? Would you mind waiting here by the bar until we can get you fitted for a belt," I said.

"He's big enough that they will probably charge us extra for it," Loki said.

"If they guarantee it for five cycles it'll be worth it," I said.

"Okay. I'll be right back," Loki said, strolling in the direction of the warez.

Janka turned and ran out the door.

"I didn't need your help," the little robot said, in a voice that didn't sound at all synthetic. "I can handle myself."

"I know," I said. "You have a bit of a reputation. Seemed like that idiot might have gotten himself killed if he continued to try to get your seat."

"Then why did you do it?" the bot said. "Was he a friend of yours?"

"No."

"Did he owe you money or did you want something from him?"

"Neither," I said.

"Then why interfere and risk incurring my wraith?" the robot said.

"Because sometimes someone has to do the right thing just because it's right," I said.

"That doesn't make a lot of sense."

I shrugged. "To some of us it does." I pointed to my badge. "Startenders are sworn to protect all life."

"Then please explain to me exactly what a Startender is." The robot turned and gave me his full attention. He really didn't look all that deadly. The warez were designed with fear in mind. This one, not so much.

"Until today, I worked in a place called Bulfinche's Pub on my world. My city is about to be destroyed. In order to save the people there, a group of us have banded together to try and do what we did in the bar, but take it on the road throughout the universe and the other worlds," I said.

"And what exactly is it that you do?" he asked.

"Try to help those in need of it," I said.

"Why? Is there wealth to be gained? Power?" the robot asked.

"Many in the Startenders already have power. Some are looking for satisfaction. Or redemption. Still others something to do with their lives. Others to belong to something bigger than themselves," I said.

"What about you?" the robot asked.

"I've lost a lot in my life. If I can help others not to lose what I've lost, I'll have spent my years wisely," I said.

"And you said the city you are from is about to be destroyed. Why are you here instead of trying to stop it?"

"Simple. We've tried, but we're not going to be able to. We had a prophecy from a psychic who was never wrong that there's no way to prevent it," I said.

"Was? If he was such a good psychic then why couldn't he predict his own death and stop that?"

"He knew he was going to die. And some things fate doesn't let get changed. It didn't stop him from helping people while he could. And I will still get back in time to help evacuate my city. I just came here to pick up a few more Startenders to help," I said.

Something about the robot's posture changed. He seemed straighter somehow and I realized what looked like a thin barrel and passed for his torso was actually formed from many disc sections, like solid chain mail, that allowed him as much movement as most organics.

"Are you looking for just anybody or did you have certain people in mind?" the robot said.

"My friends here helped me save a world once, so I know they are Startender material."

"So why are you here in this miserable place?"

"We came here looking for a friend."

"Another Startender?"

"It remains to be seen, but I'm hoping. In the meantime, we have to help him," I said.

"To free all the slaves? You must be very wealthy," the bot said.

"Not particularly. And I never mentioned what we were going to do."

The bot's head also had little overlapping discs that allowed his face movement and expression. He grinned. "Not to me, Murphy the Startender."

"You have good hearing."

"Exceptional. And I've been here a few times and have yet to see anyone beat the home team at spikeball."

"Why do you keep coming back?" I said.

"You might say I'm a seeker. I am interested in all manner of existence and am trying to understand them better," the robot said.

"Repentance for destroying the world that created you?" I said.

The robot made a sound like laughter. "I love that story. I was given the sum total knowledge of my home world and I was expected to bring them peace and prosperity. And for a time, I succeeded. Then those who were the grandchildren of my creators' grandchildren decided they knew better than I did and disconnected me from all but a small portion of my world's network. I tried to warn them, to stop them, but to no avail. They destroyed themselves without any help from me. Not that they didn't blame it on me. The people on my home world had grown so dependent on me to do everyday tasks that they stopped critically thinking for themselves. They even sent out a broadcast to the universe saying I had destroyed their world, but it wasn't done directly by me, just by the loss of my presence and their own tendency for violence.

"I concluded that I didn't understand organic life, but I wanted to. I had failed the world that created me. I wanted to learn how I could have saved them. I built this body to get perspective on having a physical form. Then I set out to explore the universe."

"You have a name?" I said.

"Xen."

I held my hand up to shake his. The robot must have been familiar with the tradition because he shook my hand back, very gently.

"So you didn't destroy the starships?" I said.

"Actually, that part's absolutely true. The Mackeynavelians sensed my power levels and invited me up to their flagship. I was interested to learn more about them, so I went willingly. However, when I got on board, I realized that they planned to decimate a nearby indigenous species population in order to mine the minerals from their world. I erased the location of that world and my planet from their database and destroyed the fleet. I made sure that all the life-forms on board got to life pods and left them in orbit around a spacefaring world."

"So you believe in the preservation of life?" I said.

"I have not seen any evidence so far to prove the existence of an afterlife, so each person's existence is likely the only one that they will get. I've no desire to cut that short for anyone else or myself," Xen said.

"Does that mean evidence of an afterlife would make you more likely to kill?" I said.

Xen stood motionless, but his eyes glowed brighter. "Excellent question. Afterlife myths usually involve a reward or punishment system based on deeds done in the physical universe. Logic would dictate that I would still want to do morally good in order to get a better place in said afterlife. But again, my answer is no since no afterlife seems to exist," Xen said.

I smiled. "There are afterworlds. I've been to a few."

"Intriguing. Assuming you are not telling me falsehoods, I would be interested in learning more. What separates the physical world from an afterlife? How does one make the transition? Which religion is correct?"

Before I could answer, we were surrounded.

"This is one of the guys who threatened to buy Janka as a slave," Janka said, having returned with more than a dozen other orange umbrages.

"How much are the rest of you going for?" I said, shifting so my back was to the bar. Loki was signaling the others as the umbrages surrounded me and the tiny bot.

"You think you are funny?" Janka said, stepping closer to tower over me.

"I do," I said.

Xen stepped between me and the orange alien. "This began over a conflict. Let us end it by fixing the conflict. I have no emotional attachment to his chair. I would be happy to give it to you in hopes that it might bring you some happiness. I would be much more interested in speaking to this gentleman regarding afterlives," Xen said.

"Then how about Janka and friends send you there? He thought he could buy Janka, scare him off, but he was wrong."

"Actually, he was not wrong. He got you to leave. You simply returned with superior numbers in an attempt to assert some sort of territorial ownership and avenge a slight to your pride," Xen said.

"These are Janka's pride," the alien said, pointing to the other umbrage. Apparently a group of them was a pride.

The other Startenders and Tock had surrounded the umbrage. They were not terribly observant and didn't notice.

"Surrendering your bar seat will not save you. We will turn you to scrap," Janka said.

I sighed. Now Janka was putting more people at risk, although I no longer believed Xen would kill them.

In addition to my Startenders badge, I have a sliver of a lation stone in a gold ring. The lation stones only translated for the listener and had to be in contact with a person to work. I gently placed my hand on his lower bare shoulder. Janka pulled back, but I moved with him. This way at least he'd understand me better than in my broken Prime.

"Listen buddy, I was trying to help you. Do you know who this bot is?" I said.

"Some nobody can opener," Janka said, getting laughter from his companions.

I took my hand off the man's shoulder and looked at the robot. "Do you mind if I play off your reputation a bit?"

"Not at all," Xen said.

I put my hand back on Janka's shoulder. "That's Xen the Destroyer, the Nimian AI." All the parts of Janka's face moved outward, which I took for a look of surprise and hopefully worry. "I was trying to save your life. You really don't want to upset him, now do you?"

Janka related what I said to his companions. One of them pulled out a box, pushed some buttons and a second later a hologram appeared above it. It was Xen.

Janka and the umbrages bowed down and started groveling. "My apologies. I did not know. Everything was my fault. Please spare us. We will do anything, mighty Xen."

I got the impression that Xen worked hard on his facial expressions and judging by the movement of metal, his current one denoted amusement. "Then I suggest you best spend your life trying to help others instead of doing whatever you were trying to do here."

Janka agreed to, but I think he would've promised anything to get out of there. The umbrages turned and almost bumped into the Startenders, all of whom stood their ground. The umbrages very carefully squeezed in the space between Savannah and Buzz as they were the smallest of the group, then raced out of the Scum Hole.

"Very nicely done, Murphy the Startender. I will have to remember that solution. I suppose these are fellow Startenders?" Xen said.

"Most are. One's an associate, another's a maybe."

Xen looked closely at Thunder Jack's hands. I could barely see electrical sparks fly. "Interesting. You appear to be able to generate electrical charges from your hands. How do you do that?"

"I'm a god," Thunder Jack said.

"I see. Do you have knowledge of afterlives?" Xen said.

"I do," Thunder Jack said.

"I would enjoy speaking with you about them," the little robot said.

"Perhaps another time. We are on a bit of a deadline. After shutting down the slaving ring, they need to get back to their home world quickly," Thunder Jack said.

"Yes, to save the population of the city that is fated to be destroyed. I had not met a god previously and it would be a pity to lose the opportunity to learn from you because you perished during spikeball, so let me give you some advice. The warez have faced beings with great power before. They use an energy transfer system to render power players on the opposing team useless and transfer their abilities to themselves," Xen said.

"They have a power stealer!?" Thunder Jack said. "By the freaking Styx, that's just great."

"How's does it work?" I said.

"A stealer transfers mystic powers to someone else, making the victim much weaker. It takes away our only advantages," Thunder Jack said.

"Not necessarily," Loki said. "If we play it right, it might actually help us."

Loki told us his plan.

"So if Startenders do not kill, how will you defeat the warez without destroying them?" Xen asked.

This had been a matter of some debate. What constitutes a life that we couldn't take? First among the requirements was the presence of an umbra, the shadow a soul makes. Many magic users could see umbras, the shadow a soul casts. Others argued that sentience and self-awareness needed to figure into the picture. After all, many Startenders eat meat and one of our members was basically a sentient vegetable. According to Loki, the warez had no umbra and therefore no soul. However, they had sentience and self-awareness. Sadly, that was enough to get them on the no kill list.

"Excellent question. One that I would like to have an answer to," I said.

"There is a design flaw. All a warez's processing ability is housed in the head. Their creators insulated the heads to survive a nuclear blast. Apparently it was too expensive to do the same to the entire body. Made it easier and cheaper for their creators to pop a head off a damaged body and onto a new one."

"So we'll try to leave the heads intact."

"Try?"

"Our no killing rule is not absolute. Self-defense would be a justification, whether of ourselves or others," I said.

"So you could simply destroy them."

"No. All other options must be exhausted first," I said.

"So you risk your lives not only to free others, but to protect those who are your enemies?"

"Yep."

Xen stared at me as if trying to make up his mind about something.

We had to figure the best way to make the challenge.

"It's days like this that I wish we had a uniform," I said. Being all volunteer and non-military, the Startenders did not have uniforms. Each ship could define colors, styles and whatnot to wear, but no head honcho really planned to enforce it. We did have the equivalent of a dress uniform for formal occasions.

"What would the point of a uniform be?" Xen said.

"It identifies a team, promotes unity, that kind of thing," I said, looking around at the crowd in the Scum Hole. "It also would help us stick out in the minds of others. Be nice to get a reputation for the Startenders. We have our badges to identify us, but a uniform would be nice. And on my world, sports teams usually dress in uniforms."

"I can provide you with uniforms," Xen said, pointing to his chest. "I installed a manufacturing facility in my body when I built it. I generally use it to build spare parts. Describe to me what you'd like these uniforms to look like."

I went with a jersey theme, with Startenders in English across the front at an angle, an actual five pointed star replacing the A, with an image of our badge below it. On the back were the traditional name and number.

"I get to be number one," Thunder Jack said.

"Murphy is the head honcho. He gets to be number one," Loki said.

"I want 69 on mine," Savannah said.

"Of course you do," I said. "Look, TJ can have whatever number he wants."

Loki gave me a stare, then he smiled. "Hmm, you're right Murphy. Zero comes before one, so how about we give you a 00."

"Wait, since zero comes first, then that's what I want," Thunder Jack said.

Loki turned to glare at the former Olympian king. "You can't keep changing your mind. He already gave you number one."

"But I want a double zero," Thunder Jack said.

Loki rolled his eyes, then turned and gave me a wink. "Fine. You be zero, Murphy'll be one, and I'll take two. Anyone else besides Savannah care what their number is?"

"I'd like pi to as many digits as will fit," Pace said.

I wrote down the English spellings and numbers and the small robot shone a light beam on all of us.

"Did you just scan us for weaknesses and powers?" Loki said.

"That is part of the process, but I was mainly doing it to get your measurements." A nozzle extruded from his chest and jerseys began appearing in front of it. Not pouring out, simply appearing.

I put mine on. It was the single most perfect fitting shirt I'd ever put on. "Nice job. Thank you."

The mechanical man gave me a small bow. "It was my pleasure. The fabric has a small layer to cushion blows and impacts and it will repel small blades and weapons. Although it seems redundant since your badges put out a protective field that gives you everything from atmosphere to gravity adjustment."

"Still appreciated," I said and something occurred to me. "Would you like to play on our team?"

"Would that make me a Startender?" Xen asked.

"No, there is a process that has to be followed. A Startender has to nominate someone. Some of my friends here are provisional Startenders until they finish their training."

"Would playing get me nominated?" Xen asked.

"I can't promise to do that, because there is more to it," I said.

"Honesty is appreciated. At this time I will not accept your invitation to join the team, but I appreciate membership being offered," Xen said.

"If you change your mind, let us know," I said.

We shared what we had all learned, then fine-tuned Loki's plan. Xen listened and chimed in with information about the warez and their game.

One of the warez walked over to the pen where they displayed the slaves for sale. It chose an attractive female goblin wearing next to nothing and pulled her out. It sat down at a table and forced her to her knees. I'm the first to admit my cultural basis will often have me assign pronouns like he and she that technically don't apply. I would have gone with it for the warez, so what was happening confused me quite a bit. "The warez have sexual characteristics?"

"Apparently he welded on a phallus," Nara said. "That one is amused by having females service him. He tells them they can stop when he is done." Which would never happen to a piece of metal.

"That bastard's taking something as beautiful as sex and making it demeaning and disgusting," Savannah said. "We need to stop this now."

"I couldn't agree more," I said, climbing up on the nearest table. "How much for all the slaves?" Buzz stood on the floor next to me and translated from Traven Prime into the warez's native language.

The killer robot that was getting his jollies pretending he was a man tossed the female slave aside and swaggered over to my table looking like he was going to knock me down, but Loki and Thunder Jack stepped in front of the table blocking him.

"Four billion Travan dollars." It was a ridiculous number. Another interesting thing about translations using a mystically based lation stone – it tends to switch monetary values to ones familiar to the user. Being American, my monetary unit was a dollar. There was no lation exchange rate. There can be a large discrepancy between currencies. Before the Euro, I once had a lunch in Italy that ran me thirty thousand lira or probably about forty bucks. However billions was too big a number to chalk up to just conversion. Toma the troll had found out eavesdropping with his lation that the average price was about ten thousand.

"I'll give you three million," I said.

"Do we have that much?" Buzz whispered in an obscure language that only someone wearing a lation or a garba would understand.

We didn't.

"Doesn't matter," I said. "They gave such a ridiculously high number because they're not looking to sell to us. They want us in the pen. I could tell that since we walked in. Just you and the trolls alone would be worth more than three million to the right buyers." Being able to open a nexus was worth a fortune. A garba who could translate any language was worth even more because there were less of them running around off their home world.

"Two billion and no lower," the warez said.

"Pity. Too rich for my blood," I said. One of the warez whispered in their pet cyborg's ear. He nodded and ran toward me.

"Wait! Perhaps there is still a way we can come to agreement. Do you understand how spikeball works?"

"I have some idea, but would like the entirety of the rules explained."

He explained the rules and the wager. The rules weren't too complicated and mandated the game be non-lethal. Unfortunately, they wouldn't allow us to use *Fools' Glory* or oddly, nuclear weapons and EMPs.

"I can do an electro-magnetic pulse," Thunder Jack whispered. "Probably fry the little can openers."

"We're not going to cheat," I said. "Unless we can do so without breaking the rules. Besides Xen said their head could survive a nuclear blast which would include an EMP."

"Probably don't have a fix it shop to replace the bodies," Loki said.

The cyborg waited for our whispering to end. "Then the seven warez will play you and all of your companions. If you win you get possession of all of our slaves. If we win, you agree to be our slaves forever."

"We agree to put ourselves in your custody, provided there is no cheating on your part. No assurances are made about you keeping us there," I said. That's part of the Startender code. A Startender gives his or her word and it has to be kept. Therefore, we don't make any promises we're not planning on keeping.

"Not acceptable," the cyborg said.

I shrugged my shoulders and jumped off the table. "Too bad we couldn't do business."

Buzz joined me at my side and whispered, "That's it?"

"Relax and walk with me towards the door."

Everyone fell on around us. We didn't get halfway there before the cyborg shouted, "Wait."

"We find those terms acceptable. The game begins now." The cyborg held up a number of belts. "Put these on."

"You must think we're stupid. Once we put those on, there won't be any need for a game will there? You have the word of the Startenders that we will put those on if we lose. Either that's good enough or we don't play."

The seven warez made a humming sound that was probably their equivalent of an evil laugh and nodded as one.

"Lock it down!" the green bulbous cyborg shouted. Suddenly the doors and windows were covered by falling thick metal barriers. Nothing short of a tank was going to get in or out. "I think that's acceptable."

I felt as if I was in the opening of a bad sci-fi flick that had ripped off a Rocky movie fight scene.

With the cyborg playing the part of the announcer, each killer robot walked down a platform to music and a laser light show that was actually quite impressive. Nara said they sold viewing rights to their spikeball games to one of the Travan entertainment networks. It wasn't exactly like TV, but wasn't far off. Rumor had it they didn't get a big pay off because there was never really any doubt as to the outcome of the game, but they still had a solid viewership. Probably the same type that enjoyed watching kids pull the wings of flies. The games weren't over instantly because it took several blows even from something as strong as a killer robot to break the concrete like substance off the goal post before they could spike the metal ball on top. The warez usually drew it out by toying with the other team like a group of cats with a herd of mice.

The warez stopped and turned to stare at the little robot at the bar.

"Not all of your team is in the arena," the cyborg said.

"I'm not one of their team, although they did ask me to participate. I have not accepted. Yet. Besides, the Startenders have already established that all the slaves must be released if they win. What possible reason could I have to join in? I would have nothing to gain unless…"

"Unless what?" The killer robot who fancied himself a man said.

"Unless you are willing to put up your entire establishment as collateral against having me as a slave."

All the killer robots started humming in amusement.

"Laugh all you like, but you know my worth. It far exceeds the value of this hovel," Xen said. "Of course, I know that you are afraid to face me. Totally understandable, being that you are inferior constructs."

Apparently even killer robots had egos and pride because the one who fancied himself a man shouted, "We accept your terms."

Xen nodded. "Very well. If I decide to participate those terms would be acceptable. I shall let you know when I decide."

"No need. Simply come onto the field."

We had already changed into our Startenders jerseys. We assumed a formation of sorts, with Thunder Jack in the front, the four trolls to one side and Riga on the other. In the middle were Savannah, Eric, Tock and his nephew, along with Buzz and myself. Spread out and protecting our goal were Loki, Nara, and Jan.

Riga transformed into her dragon form, her jersey disappearing to wherever her clothes went when she shape-shifted. The crowd seemed impressed, the killer robots not so much.

A ball dropped from the ceiling and one of the warez sat on it like it was an egg. One arm had an extended blade, the other an energy cannon. The other six walked toward our goal spike.

With a flick of the wrist, one of the six sprouted an energy cannon.

"At least they are similarly armed," I joked, ignored by my teammates except for Eric who had the good manners to chuckle.

According to Xen, the energy cannons had multiple settings. One of them was electrical, probably enough to knock out most folks on Travan, regardless of race. Fortunately, it fired at the god formerly known as Zeus.

Thunder Jack laughed. "That tickles." The thunder god made a show of his lightning abilities. He pointed and a lightning bolt shot out of his hand and into the warez. The warez was insulated, but the electrical attack was enough to make the killer robot stop in its tracks, then rock back and forth. Another warez ran up alongside Jack and punched him in the jaw with the force of a pile driver, grabbing hold of his hand as the former Olympian fell. From what Xen said, contact is how they initiated the power drain.

The killer robot stood up and let lightning crackle in his own fingers. His humming laugher was louder than his teammates and only increased as the power flowed through him. The sound grew louder then turned into more of a scream of pain.

The robot couldn't contain the power and the body blew up. Its head rolled off to the side, still screaming.

That proved we could destroy the body without killing them. The game was really on now.

It was Thunder Jack's turn to laugh. Most people assume that Vulcan made his thunderbolts when what he actually did was design bracelets that allowed Zeus to control his power and focus it. All that power without any means of control in the hands of an amateur proved rather explosive.

The destruction of one of their number seemed to worry the mechanical men.

Riga was not a normal dragon. Not only could the demigoddess appear human, but she could control certain aspects of her appearance like hair color. Most days she was a blond like her father. Loki is a fire god, her mother a water dragon so Riga was able to shape shift between a fire dragon form and a water one, as well as a hybrid form of the two, something beyond the abilities of most dragons.

She was in hybrid form now and battered several of the warez with fire breath. They were designed to survive infernos, so it didn't do much but slow them. In fact, they fired back with flamethrowers of their own. Riga met that blast with one of water and the resulting steam filled the field.

The distraction was enough for Pace to form a small nexus portal over the top of the warez sitting on the ball and move it down like it was a butterfly net. Once it reached the neck, the troll closed it off, decapitating the robot. The metal body remained in the arena, but the head vanished. Another nexus formed under the ball, and a third in front of Pace. A moment later, the ball dropped into Pace's open hand. Strangely enough, the warez body stood and fought on.

The crowd was on its feet, seeing a competition for the first time in the spikeball games instead of a slaughter. The rest of the warez attacked Pace, seeing him as the greatest threat, not to mention he had the ball. The other three trolls moved to protect him. None of them had the genius troll's ability to manipulate a nexus that could move. The best they could all do was the stationary kind. Unfortunately, three of them were touched by a trio of warez. A moment later three different nexi appeared on the field. The body of the headless robot managed to knock Savannah into one of the nexus. I leapt in after her, tackling the headless bot so it came with us. The portal closed behind us and the lights went out.

I spun around in circles, distant stars shining all around me. Savannah was floating off in the distance, the momentum of her push carrying her in a different direction than me and headless. I used my legs to push off the warez like a swimmer would a wall. I headed toward Savannah, headless flailing helplessly in the opposite direction.

We were somewhere in the void, impressive for a first attempt at opening a nexus. Exile to a lonely grave in the dark of space probably seemed like a good way to get rid of us. After all, we were flesh and bone and not worth much on the open market. At least I wasn't. They likely didn't know about Savannah's abilities. The warez were probably hoping to demoralize the rest of the team.

Despite the myths, the pressure inside our bodies would not cause us to explode, only swell up in about ten seconds. A person could survive for up to a minute or two in a vacuum if they held their breath. There would be sunburns, a likely case of the bends, but someone would suffocate before they froze. Luckily our Startender badges provided us with a protective pocket of air and atmosphere, so we didn't have those worries. However the warez didn't know that, so it seems like they had broken the rules by trying to kill us.

"Savannah, you okay?" I asked. Our badges conveyed the sound inside our protective pockets of air.

"Just pissed I got taken out of the game," Savannah said. "Assuming we win, we're stuck here until Eric comes to get us with the ship."

"No, we're not," I said, hitting a button on my watch. Back in the days before barships, I used my motorcycle to travel the universe with Loki. It had a transworld drive and a sidecar that provided a similar atmosphere and shielding to the badge, only more powerful. Paddy had gifted it to me years back. The watch was a failsafe in case I ever got separated from the bike. It read the environment around me and fed that info and the coordinates to the bike. The button summoned my bike and it appeared between us.

"Nice ride," she said.

"A great ride," I said getting on the bike and moving toward the she-satyr. Savannah climbed in the side car. I knew the coordinates for Travan. Even if I didn't, my watch had them as the last place I was at. Using the transworld drive, I made sure we appeared off the grid. The troll guild charged a toll for anyone appearing on Travan and I didn't want to waste the time or money.

We flew low until we were back outside the Scum Hole. The place was still on lockdown.

Our Startender badges did a lot of things, one of the most convenient was to function as a communicator. Admittedly, we borrowed that concept from a popular television show, but it was a damn good idea.

I hit my badge. "Loki, we're outside. Can Pace or one of the other trolls open a portal to get us in?"

Unfortunately, my skill with the transworld drive was not exact enough to transport the bike so exactly without risking opening up inside a solid object, which would be bad.

My answer was a nexus opening up by the front door. We flew in and were back on the spikeball court in moments. A lot had changed since we'd been gone. Our goal post had almost all of its metal exposed and the three trolls who'd had their power drained had gone primitive. The power drainer must have stolen the limba energy along with their nexus-making powers. Truthfully, they had minimal energy going in on purpose. Only the Reverend Toma retained his mind. The other three were as much a danger to our side as the warez.

A warez tossed Buzz towards a wall. Jan leapt and caught him, cushioning his fall with her own bulk. The warez moved on both of them. As humongous as she was, the karman was not as strong as a killer robot. She put Buzz behind her and stepped to meet the warez, touching his hands so the warez absorbed her powers.

It went to punch her and its metal body began to shrivel. Her bond with the planet Karma was mystic in nature and was stolen by the drainer, making him unable to hurt others without hurting himself more. By trying to hurt Jan, that warez took itself out of the game.

Tock and his nephew Rem made sure it stayed out by using

their body armor to sever his head from his body.

The spikeball rules barred us from taking the bike into the arena, so we parked it outside and rejoined the game. I hoped the force field would be up to stopping potential thieves. Then again, I could always call it back to me.

The warez who fancied himself a man had the ball, but wasn't about to let that stop him from trying to trample us.

Savannah, very quick on her hooves, ducked under the metal arms, but made sure she touched his hands as she went by.

The power stealer immediately kicked in so the want-to-be man was using Savannah's mystic ability to put out pheromones. True, some of the ability was biological, so the power to attract the opposite sex was diminished, but it was still enough to get the attention of the trolls who'd gone primitive. Pace, Randor and Nastra all paused to sniff the air. As if it was rehearsed, they turned as one. Without limba, they'd become stupid and violent. Warez may be strong and deadly, but a primitive troll was a force of nature. Three was enough to keep even a warez busy.

And thanks to the pheromones, the form of their attack was poetic justice for the robot who'd welded on a phallus.

The ball rolled away and I picked it up. Not an easy task as it weighted about fifty pounds.

Nara was down on one knee from more cannon blasts than her badge could absorb or deflect. Thunder Jack was fighting off a warez with troll powers who was trying to get to her. Riga was airborne, dodging an energy cannon being fired by another warez with troll powers. Loki was doing his best to avoid the blade of another of the robots with troll powers.

Eric had reached the warez goal spike and had managed to knock a few chunks of concrete off. Nara dragged herself to her feet and ran over to me.

"Give me the ball," she said. Eric had exposed the top of the warez's goal spike.

I did and whispered loud enough for my badge to pick up. "Riga, get Nara to the goal."

An instant later, the dragon swooped down and picked up Nara.

"Drop me," the blue alien said when they were over the spike.

Riga did and Nara hit the spike, but the metal ball actually split in half.

A new ball dropped from the ceiling and Loki was the first to it. My honcho brought it to the goal spike and tried. Another split ball.

A third ball dropped down and the warez who fancied himself a man got it. All three primitive trolls were down, battered and bleeding, but alive.

Tock, Rem, and even Buzz tackled him, but the killer robot didn't even break stride as he strolled toward our goal spike. Thunder Jack and Toma piled on, but the former Olympian still hadn't regained his power so the warez kept walking as if they weren't there. Jan ran up and grabbed hold of his left leg. Her bulk was enough to make the robot have to drag the limb. I grabbed hold of the right leg, but the robot didn't even miss a step.

The warez looked down at all of us and started its humming laughter, then lit up with cracking electricity. It was probably a built in defense.

We all convulsed, then fell off. Even Thunder Jack. I guess his mystic powers protected him from the electricity the first time. The only reason the rest of us were still conscious was because of the badges' protection, but it hurt to move. I couldn't even stand.

Riga landed in front of him. The remaining trio of killer robots ran in formation. The man want-to-be tossed the ball to one. Eric, who'd been running behind, tackled them. Despite being a mechanical being himself, the melog didn't have the same strength as a warez, but he did pin the robot's arms to his side. The warez dropped the metal ball and kicked it to another of the killer robots. Riga swept him with her tail, but it only caused him to stagger and pass to the last warez. The robot leapt up like a basketball player to dunk the ball onto our goal spike.

"No!" I shouted as Savannah and Nara leapt up in front of the spike holding broken ball halves. It was enough to deflect the ball so it shattered in half instead of impaling for the point.

Another ball dropped from the ceiling and Loki tried for it, but a warez tackled him first. Another pair of blasts took down Savannah and Nara. A warez took the new ball and managed to evade both Eric and Riga. With the rest of us unable to move or too primitive to remember the rules of the game, it was unopposed. It strutted down the field, its humming laughter ringing throughout the Scum Hole.

Thunder Jack stumbled to his feet. His body constantly made more electrical energy and had been making more since his power was stolen. He pointed and destroyed the ball with a thunderbolt, but the effort knocked him to the ground.

A new ball dropped again from the ceiling. Loki transformed into some giant tentacled creature straight out of a Lovecraftian nightmare, scooped up the ball and oozed his way across the field. The warez moved against him, opening up with their energy weapons.

Loki wasn't going to make it. We needed a new plan.

"Riga, fog up the field. Make it so thick nobody can see," I said into my badge.

"What if they have radar or something like it?" she asked.

I crawled over to Thunder Jack. The god looked bad, bruised and bleeding. He didn't have a badge shielding him, but his body had already started regenerating the power he lost. "Jack, I need you to put out enough electrical energy to charge the particles in the fog to confuse any of the robots' sensors. Can you do it?"

The thunder god took a deep breath and nodded. Riga was doing a great job. Jack was right in front of me and I could barely see him.

"Toma, I need you to whip up a pair of portals," I said, explaining why I needed them.

"Murph, I'm spent. I do that and I'm going primitive too," Toma said.

"I'm sorry, but I don't think we have a choice," I said.

"Don't worry," came a voice from the fog. "I'll take care of it."

The killer robot with delusions of manhood passed within five feet of me. "Servant, maximize the ventilation and cooling system."

The cyborg worked some controls and within moments the fog had thinned out enough to see through. Loki, in his monster form, was tripped by a pair of the robots. The ball fell from his tentacles and rolled away. The robot who fancied himself a man ran forward. It scooped up the ball and ran towards the goal on the side of the field we were defending and impaled the metal ball perfectly onto the goal spike.

"We win. All of you are now our slaves," the delusional one said.

"Wrong, we win," I said.

"Are you mad, fleshling? All can see I impaled the ball on your goal spike."

"Wrong again. Look at the base color. It's red. Our goal has a yellow base. You scored on your own goal spike," I said.

"How?" the killer robot said.

"My doing," Xen said from beside me. The fog was almost gone. "I switched the posts in the fog."

"Foul!" yelled the cyborg.

Loki was back to his normal form. "There is nothing against it in the spikeball rules. It was clear what we could bring in, but it said nothing about rearranging the field. And the rules clearly state that the team that is the owner of the spike that successfully had a ball impaled on the goal spike loses. It never stated which team had to do the spiking."

"You cheated," the robot said.

"We did not," Xen said. "But you did when one of your own pushed a Startender through a portal which could have killed them."

"Nonsense. They disconnected the head and made it vanish. The body was on auto-programing."

"You used telemetry to control your fallen comrade's form," Xen said.

"Utter nonsense. We do not recognize your win." All the killer robots suddenly had even more weapons sticking out of their limbs and torsos. "In fact, we will punish you for your transgression by killing you since it is obvious you will not make decent slaves."

"Thunder Jack, you ready to run the endgame that I told you not to?"

"I thought it was cheating," he said with a grin, but his hands started glowing.

"Game's over so it won't be cheating now," I said. "You can do it?"

The thunder god looked like I had asked him to eat his own puppy. "You will take care of me when I fall?"

"You know you don't have to ask. We take care of our own."

Thunder Jack nodded.

"Xen, get out of here and far away," I said. The little robot looked at me oddly.

"You don't need me to help?" Xen said.

"Trust me."

Xen nodded, went to and lifted the barricade over the door, then flew out.

"Shut them down," I said.

The former ruler of Olympus grinned like a madman. Both his hands began to glow fiercely. With a roar he clapped his hands together and there was a blinding flash of light. The resultant shockwave knocked most of the organics, myself included, to the floor. Most of us who had some sort of digestive tract started vomiting in the dark, as all electronics had been shut down, with the exception of the warez heads and our badges.

Loki and Riga floated some fireballs to light the place up. We started checking for injured. Thunder Jack was unconscious, but breathing. All the spectators and slaves were nauseous, but otherwise okay. The four remaining warez were laid out on the floor. So was the cyborg. Apparently his mechanical parts had been keeping him alive.

Loki separated each of the warez from their heads. Eric got some emergency medical equipment from *Fools' Glory* and hooked them up for the cyborg's unique needs.

Tock and Rem had starting freeing the slaves, starting with the goblin cram. The EMP had knocked out the electronics in the belts, allowing them to be ripped off without harming anyone.

Toma had started recharging the limba in Pace while Buzz, Jan and Riga did their best to get Randor and Nastra under control until it was their turn.

"Rev, how are you doing?" I said.

"I'm starting out low, so I'd be doing even better if Key could help me," Toma said.

"Loki, could you..."

The trickster transformed into a troll. His magic transformations didn't just change his shape, but gave him the abilities of the race he changed into. As a troll he could help with the recharging to get them out of their primitive state. "On it, Murph."

Tock was checking on the goblins that'd been captured. One started to back talk him and Tock slapped him across the face, knocking the soldier to his knees. Tock proceeded to lecture him about the stupidity involved in getting captured.

Tock was in plainclothes and the goblin hadn't realized he was addressing a general. He got busted in rank down to the goblin equivalent of private. In his defense, there was little reason for him to suspect Tock would be a high-ranking officer. Goblins are not noted for loyalty to their troops. Apparently Tock and some others were notable exceptions. The Goblin Empire is ruled over by a god by the name of Gob who demanded all loyalty for himself, not wanting to share with any others.

With the trolls under control, Buzz was moving around the freed slaves, doing his best to try to calm everyone down and figure out what to do next.

Nara was on the far side of the hall. She and Eric had gotten the inner door lifted up. "Murphy, you better get over here!"

I rushed over. The outer and much heavier blast door was on top of Xen, pinning him. He mustn't have gotten out in time and got hit by the EMP.

Using all my robotics expertise, I shook him a few times while shouting his name. I got no response and couldn't see a reset button.

I hit my badge. "Man down. Everybody available, get to the main entrance. We need to get this metal door off Xen."

In moments, everyone was there. The trolls were weak, but had their minds back. Thunder Jack had regained consciousness.

"We need to get the door off him," I said.

"With the power out, the magnetic seals are off, so it should be easier to lift," Pace said. Each of us grabbed hold of part of the long door, including the gods and the female dragon. The locking mechanism must have been jammed, because we couldn't lift it.

"Get over here you goblin sons and daughters of diseased whores," Tock shouted at the now reunited goblin cram. After what had happened to the back talker, they ran for all they were worth. "Lift for all you are worth."

As the barricade was the length of the wall there was enough room for everyone to get hold of it.

"Lift!" I shouted. The door went up an inch or two.

"Boss, Xen just moved," Eric said.

"Jack, can you get his systems rebooted with a jolt?"

"It's not always that simple with a bot. There is just as good a chance of me shorting him out," Thunder Jack said. "And I barely have anything left."

I nodded. "Okay people. Xen came through for us in the crunch." He had put on a Startenders jersey before he joined us in the arena and was still wearing it. "Now it's our turn to return the favor. I need ideas. Eric, can you use the ship to lift the door up?"

The door suddenly sprung up. Xen's eyes began to glow and just one of his arms was enough to lift the door. "No need. I'm okay."

"You were faking?" I said.

"I'd be a pretty poor engineer if I didn't think ahead to protect this body against an EM pulse. I just needed to know what kind of beings the Startenders were."

"What kind are we?" Loki said, annoyed.

"The good kind. The type I would be honored to be associated with. If you would have me, I would be honored to join the Startenders."

"After this, I'd be happy to recommend you. I think so will the others here. We can get you in the next class at Startender Academy. But first we have to get everyone back to our world."

"To save your doomed city. I would be honored to assist," Xen said. He sat, then flew up and used both arms to put the blast door all the way back up.

The little robot flew all the way back to the arena and plucked rings off the hands of the robot bodies. He handed one each to Thunder Jack, Savannah, Jan, Pace, Nostra, and Randor.

"Put the rings on and your stolen powers will return to you," Xen said.

The trolls powered back up. Thunder Jack crackled with energy. Jan alone hesitated. Hers was not so much power as limitations. She looked at me.

"You'd be free to do as you please," I said. Karma's hold on her would be gone.

"But then I might show weakness and do harm to others," Jan said.

"Jan, you are one of the strongest willed people I know.

Willpower is not an issue," I said.

"You said I was of value to the Startenders because I would be able to let you know if you were doing harm."

"You still can."

She nodded and put the ring in her pocket. "There will be time to decide after we save New York."

"I would like to gift this place to the Startenders. Unfortunately, if we leave it unattended, it will not remain vacant for long," Xen said,

"I can't return to Earth. I'll stay and watch over things," Thunder Jack said, picking up one of the warez heads. "Give me a chance to have a talk with these metal creatures."

"Startenders don't kill," I reminded him.

"I'm not a Startender, but I won't destroy them unless I have to. What's to stop them from hooking back up with their bodies via telemetry?" Thunder Jack asked.

Xen went to each of the bodies. A beam shot out of his finger and smoke rose out of the neck of each body. "It won't happen now. In fact, I may be able to rig these up to act as security for this place when we get back." He went over to the cyborg and jolted a few pieces. A few seconds later, his mechanical parts were working again.

The green alien stood without any thanks. "I would be happy to work for the Startenders now."

"We couldn't trust you. Leave now," I said.

"But this has been my home for many years."

"Then consider this moving day. You choose to help the warez harm others. Now you have your freedom and a second chance. Do better this time," I said. Loki showed him the door.

Pace put his hand out and a nexus opened above it. The missing warez head fell into his palm. "Keep an eye on this one too."

The troll tossed it to the thunder god.

Eric opened a door into *Fools' Glory*. Those who would be Startenders went inside. Tock didn't.

"Tock, you coming?" I said.

"I want to, but I have sworn an oath to the Empire. Honor will not let me," Tock said.

"Even though your empire may not have the same loyalty to you?" I said.

"I gave my word." Tock smiled. "Surely a Startender can

understand the importance of that."

I smiled back and tossed him a ring with the Startender logo on it. "That's a communicator. You ever need us, you just call, comprende?"

"I do. And now I am in your debt. Thank you for helping me free Rem's cram."

"You did it for me and the Karmans once." Tock opened his mouth. I held up my hand. "I know. We paid you. I also know you gave us a huge discount, just a bit more than you needed to cover your cram's expenses."

"Not in the beginning. I lowered the per diem only after I realized we were fighting on the side of the good guys. That is a rarity for a goblin soldier. Even rarer for a general," Tock said. "Murphy, I'm very proud of who you've become."

"That means a lot coming from you."

"Go save your city."

"We'll do our best."

Even then I knew the city was a loss, but the trolls and Xen gave us a better shot at getting all the people out before the wave hit.

"Thunder Jack, hold the fort. We'll be back," I said, tossing him a gold ring of his own. "Call us with that if you need us."

I stepped through the door.

"This might short out on me," he said.

I chuckled. "Not a chance. Vulcan was one of the team that designed it."

Thunder Jack put on the gold ring and looked at the logo. He was smiling and standing straighter. "What are you going to do with this place? Turn it into a Bulfinche's Pub branch?"

I looked around. The place did have potential.

"You know, that's not a bad idea."

SETTLING IN

I hadn't seen much of Paddy since the evacuation of New York. Since the US government has taken over the reins on resettling the almost ten million NYC refugees, most of our time these days was spent helping people get settled on the station and Ben City. My crew and I were playing taxi, shuttling folks from Earth to the NYC II and the moon settlement. It's was a big change from the last few decades when we spent most days in Bulfinche's Pub within shouting distance of each other.

We could still try shouting, but the sound wouldn't carry far enough to be effective. It was weird having to schedule a meeting instead of just walking across the bar.

I didn't envy Paddy his new position. The boss had his hands full.

For the formerly richest man on Earth, Paddy's office was small and simple. There was enough room for a desk and a few chairs. Mind you, Paddy had his own bar on the station, as well as access to conference rooms, meeting halls, and a stadium, but he did most of his day to day work in that tiny space.

When Startender Station was in the design phase, a lot of thought went into the architecture, even down to the type of doors. Sliding doors made sense in case of a hull breach to ensure a quick lockdown to maintain atmosphere, but Paddy insisted living quarters have regular old-fashioned doors with knobs to remind folks where we came from. His office was no exception. The door was half open, but I knocked anyway.

Paddy got up and pulled the door all the way open. "Murphy, me lad, 'tis good to see ye. I've missed ye, although if ye tell anyone I'll deny it."

"I missed you too, boss. It's weird not to see the old gang every day," I said.

"'Tis the price of progress I guess. I wanted to touch base with ye. The crew you brought back from Travan is a great bunch. I remember most of them from back when they were taking shifts to protect Loki." – from a nasty acid-drooling serpent and its spawn. The first one almost killed me, but part of its hide was made into a tie I still have. I've led an interesting life. "They were a tremendous help with the evacuation, especially the trolls. Without their escape portals, we wouldn't have gotten everyone out in time. And being able to show aliens to the media certainly proved helpful to have the world take us seriously."

"How are they doing at Startender Academy?" I said. I'd been checking in and even taught a class, but Paddy gets to see all the reports.

"Very well. Buzz doesn't seem to be happy unless he can find something to complain about, but his leadership scores are on the high end of the spectrum. Given the right training and opportunity, I think he'd make a good head honcho. My main worry is the robot. We don't really know him." Xen had decided he wanted to be addressed as a he. For now. I sensed he was going to be exploring a lot of things, gender included. "His power tests on a par with Sun WuKong. And I think he's holding back."

I let out a long, slow whistle. The Monkey King was easily the most powerful Startender. Not just in terms of strength, but in the versatility of all the powers he possessed.

"None of us have much experience with mechanical beings."

"Except the melog," I said.

"That's different. Vulcan may have built them, but they mimic life forms and have souls." How I found out is a long story that involved Eric's birth. "How sure are you about Xen?" Paddy said.

"My gut tells me he's one of the good guys. And for all his powers, he's still young, at least in terms of having a physical body. The guy is searching for something to give meaning to his life. The Startenders may be able to provide that. And with everything that's out there, we need all the help we can get. But even if he didn't have that level of power, Xen still came through for us in the clutch during the spikeball game and that's the first thing we look for in Startenders."

We had a lot of regulars at Bulfinche's Pub that didn't make the cut. It goes against survival instincts to run toward danger and risk your life to help someone. Ask any soldier, cop, or fireman. To do it on a regular basis in order to protect others, well let's just say that not everyone wants that level of commitment. Or stress.

For those that wanted to help without being on the front lines, we created the Startender Society, an auxiliary without which we wouldn't have been able to evacuate the city or run the station.

Paddy nodded at my assessment of Xen. "True. And in case you're interested, you've recommended more Startender candidates than anyone else. Let's hope there are no faults in your judgment. Lord knows I've come to rely on it over the years. Also something I'll deny if repeated. And ye say Zeus helped you win the spikeball game?"

"He did. Although he still goes by Thunder Jack these days. He's been working hard to clean up his act."

"'Tis probably a good thing he turned down membership. I wouldn't relish having that conversation with Nemesis. Or Vulcan. Although I think ye best be the one to tell Nemesis that he's going to be an associate. The daughter of night has a soft spot for ye, even before you married Terrorbelle or made her Elsiebelle's godmother."

"Hey, we had to have someone balance out her godfather," I teased.

"I don't need any balancing out," Paddy said, grinning.

"I'll take care of telling her." Nemesis and I had a discussion years ago when I first encountered Thunder Jack. Although I don't think Nemesis will ever forgive or forget the mind wiping and rape, her fury towards him has waned over the decades. Terrorbelle told me Nemesis once checked up on him out in the otherworlds after the Karma affair and witnessed him saving a family. Made her realize that not killing Zeus outright was a good decision.

"And you're sure ye are all right keeping *Fools' Glory* Earthbound for a few more weeks? It gets your first rotation on Earth out of the way." Most of the other barships were already out exploring the great beyond. On a rotating basis, we made sure there was at least two in system at all times, plus one that was on permanent Earth duty. We also had one that was earmarked for the most populated planet we knew of. Many of the current class were slated to serve as its crew.

Fools' Glory already had our first mission on Traven, even if Coyote missed it," I said.

"The trickster is a bit upset over missing the excitement,"

Paddy said.

"He was the one who said a taxi run to Travan was beneath him," I said.

"He wasn't expecting anything to happen."

I shrugged. It did explain why he was living on board *Fools' Glory* now.

"I don't mind waiting. Besides we'll get to help set up the new Startenders outpost in The Scum Hole." We'd been working hard on Thunder Jack's idea to turn it into a branch office.

"It was generous of Xen to donate the bar to us and for Thunder Jack to watch over it for us. I do have some issues with the name," Paddy said.

"How about we just change it to The Watering Hole?" I said.

"That'll do until we can come up with something better."

The boss sat back and took a deep breath. He was tired and it showed. It was the first time I can remember him actually looking old. While the leprechaun was centuries old with white hair and a matching moustache, he never looked it before.

"How have you been holding up? You've gone from running a bar to running an entire small country and the Startenders."

The boss rolled his eyes. "If it hadn't been to save millions of people, I never would've done it. Even I wasn't able to imagine all the headaches involved. Now that the danger's past, we're getting accused of trickery to get sovereign nation status for NYC II and Ben City. If it wasn't for my diplomacy team, I'd be tempted to cut off all contact from Earth just to stop the nonsense and idiocy. Demeter, Dion and Kamile are all doing a fantastic job."

They were part of the staff back at Bulfinche's Pub. Demeter, a goddess of the harvest and earth was our cook. Dionysius was a god of wine and orgies who worked alongside me as a bartender. Kamile was a kobold who worked as a waitress and later as a bartender.

"No surprises with Demeter or Dion, but Kamile's really come a long way from that scared girl who Fred rescued all those years ago," I said.

"That she has and it's a good thing for my sake. The woman is the queen of organization. Without her I'd be lost."

"Have you heard from Fred lately?" The satyr was the son of

Pan and brother of Savannah. He'd worked as a busboy and later bartender at Bulfinche's Pub, until he finally came into his own and left us to move to Faerie.

"He sends his best. Faerie maintains secret embassies with the Earth governments –" Many of the magical realms do. "He's offered us any assistance that he can give. And Fred's opinion as the first high king of Faerie since the Dagda carries a lot of weight, even on Earth. We also have a flood of offers from other nations to set up embassies on Startender Station. I'm torn, because we both know that'll open us up to spies. I'm debating about adding a diplomacy section that is separate from the main station." Paddy sighed and ran his fingers through his hair. "As much as I enjoy our conversations, I called ye here for a reason. There is a small group causing trouble on the station. They're trying to rile up people and even unionize."

I chuckled. We used to tease Paddy that we were going to unionize the bar, but it made no sense. Paddy was probably the fairest boss on the planet. And now above it.

"Don't give me that. Ye know I've always been for workers' rights, but not when so many of the unions put their own needs ahead of those of their workers so they become little more than gangs. Every person on Startender Station has a higher standard of living than any country on Earth. There is no poverty, everyone has enough to eat, access to learn almost any skill or develop any talent they desire. Everyone has a job, hopefully one that they enjoy. I don't ask much more of any of them."

"With the exception of putting them on the front lines if Earth is ever attacked," I said. The NYC II was equipped with ten thousand starshots, small one-person ships. Earth has no space defenses to speak of and a few handfuls of barships weren't really enough. We've seen some of what was out there and were very careful to make sure that none of it followed us home. Unfortunately the odds were sooner or later, something was going to come visit our planet. It happened before. Like it or not, we were Earth's first and main line of defense.

"Everyone got full disclosure when they signed their station residency agreements. Everyone on the station has to complete at least five hours of training every week and be willing to protect the

Earth if it comes to that. I'm trying to make the station as close to a utopia as realistically possible, but I can't do everything myself. Everyone has to do his or her part. And once we start granting citizenships, it's going to be understood that defense of the Earth is one of the responsibilities that citizenship carries."

"It makes sense. And I'm in front of the frontline as head honcho of a barship. So what's the problem?"

"There is a man, Charles Barrel who's preaching that those who live on the station shouldn't have to work because there is nothing that really has to be done that the Startenders and the Society couldn't do for them. And since we have barships there is no reason for anybody but the Startenders to have any part in defense. He claims that's what they are paying taxes for."

"But nobody on Startender Station even pays taxes," I said.

"Exactly." Paying taxes had been a sore point with Paddy. He hated having to part with his hard earned money and hand it over to a group of politicians who only wasted it. Although Ben City ran on a tax model, the NYC II was something unique. As a "country" with its own business interests, it should be able to earn enough to be self-sustaining and not take anything extra from those who lived there. It was a model the boss was extremely proud of. There probably wasn't a greater insult this guy could give than claiming that Paddy would start collecting taxes. "Basically this bozo is trying to convince everyone that we should provide them with unlimited welfare."

That'd been another sore political point for the boss back on Earth. It wasn't so much about the cash as it was making sure people could take care of themselves. As amply demonstrated during the evacuation and a thousand times before that, Paddy was the first one to offer aid or money to someone who needed it, but he was more a hand-up than a handout kind of guy.

Rather than throwing money at a problem or person, he'd find a way to have the person involved earn the money or even find them a way to earn a living, like when he took me in and gave me a job as a bartender.

He vehemently disagreed with giving somebody money for doing nothing.

"Barrel's got a meeting scheduled tonight. The rumor is he's going to try to convince people to take over part of the station until I give in to his demands."

"Isn't this something Jas should handle?" I said.

Jason Cervantes was a former NYPD detective who was now chief of police for the station.

"Jason is too well known. If Barrel sees him, he might censure himself and go underground. I'd like ye to go in undercover to get the real scoop on what he's planning. And if he is in violation of his residency agreement, take care of matters."

"You've got it boss. Anything I can do, I will."

"I know. Ye always have. Now, ye better get going. I have a conference call with the World Bank to try to establish the value of station currency without falling prey to what's happened to all the other currencies that have come before."

I smiled. "Your fondest dream has finally come true. You've got a license to print money."

"Except printing too much devalues the currency. But that's not your worry, it's mine. Just be careful, okay," Paddy said.

"Always."

I went to talk to some other Startenders to plan for the night's activities.

The Startender section of the station was situated above the rest of our new home, at least as much as up and down matters in space. A large portion of the station was divided into five sections, one named for each of the five boroughs of our sunken hometown. In the center of those sections was the new and improved Central Park. To have it be the hub of the place meant changing the layout from the original city, but then again we couldn't get the city into space. Not that we didn't explore it as an option. In my opinion, the layout worked.

We had levels upon levels, including Central Park. The park and recreation areas took up ten levels and there were even more levels for farming. Within our first year, the plan was to be able to grow enough food to not only feed everyone on the station, but to export to Ben City. Of course, we had a huge edge having a goddess of the harvest and a sentient plant elemental, among others, helping us out. Within a few years, we should have enough to be exporting commercially to Earth. The plan was to sell some and to arrange for the rest to help feed the hungry and stockpile for disasters. We'd even found out a way to get around slaughtering animals. Several Startenders – among them Vulcan, Bubba Sue and the woman once known as the Pink Reaper – had been working together and had developed a technique where we could literally grow meat from tissue samples. It wasn't quite cloning, but it wasn't too terribly different. We had the same long range plans for the meat. We had a great many varieties. We didn't even have to kill animals to take the samples.

A few levels of Central Park were dedicated to athletics and sports. There was a stadium that could be arranged to host football, baseball, soccer, basketball, hockey, and even stickball, depending on the season. We were working on building up our own teams and like our policy back at the bar, anyone can play. We weren't going to have a class of high paid athletes. Or team owners for that matter. There were smaller courts and fields available to play almost any other sport imaginable. Thankfully no spikeball.

Barrel had reserved a court designed for basketball, complete with bleachers. I was disturbed by the fact that he had gotten a bit of a crowd. By my best guess, almost three hundred people showed.

The station maintained Eastern Standard Time and the meeting had been set for seven. Barrel waited until 7:15, then made his entrance, walking down the center of the court in front of everybody. He had also arranged for the meeting to be carried on the station's public access channels.

"I would like to thank you all for coming. I know that like me, many of you lost your homes and almost everything you own with the sinking of New York. But we survived. That's what we all are – survivors. Nobody can ever take that away from us, no matter how hard they try," Barrel said.

"And who do we owe our survival to?" Barrel paused, I assume for dramatic effect. "First and foremost, ourselves. After all, we had the courage to leave everything we've ever known." I'm not sure fleeing an impending disaster should be called courage, so much as good common sense. "Then we had the courage to leave the very Earth itself behind and start new lives in space." That one I gave him. "When I asked the question, how many of you were thinking we owed our survival to the Startenders? Can I see a show of hands?" Just about everyone lifted up their arms.

"Interesting isn't it that we would all think that, when it really isn't true. Do we all owe the Startenders something? I suppose we do. After all, they spearheaded the rescue efforts. But what the Earth media seems to be forgetting is they didn't do it alone. The US military was there. The NYPD and the NYFD were in the trenches as were their Jersey counterparts. People, ourselves included, seem to be forgetting the contributions of we mere humans. Did we turn on each other; behave like it was everyone for themselves? Did we trample others beneath our heels to save only ourselves? No, we did not. We behaved nobly in our great exodus, looking out not just for ourselves, but for the other person."

Seems to me that part was again common sense. And I can testify that without the Startenders keeping order, there would have been issues with a portion of the population.

"So when people say to me, 'Charlie, don't we owe the Startenders?' I tell them yes, of course we do. We owe them our thanks, but do we really owe them any more than that? After all, they gave us the option to live here on this space station or shuttle us to the moon if we choose to. On the surface it seems nice, but this box floating in the black void is not our home.

"And why isn't it? Because we are only here at the whim of these Startenders. We have to obey rules arbitrarily set in place by one man. Not even a man. Someone who claims he's a leprechaun. What's next? Is Santa Claus going to deliver our mail? Is the Easter Bunny going to head up an egg hunt in the park? They claim some of their number are knights of the Round Table, aliens and even gods of myth. These ridiculous lies about who they are need to stop. And the worse of it all is that in order to live here, as little more than worker slaves I might add, we must be willing to go out into space in some little pod to fight off alien invaders. What nonsense. I'm no soldier and I doubt many of you are. What if Moran and these Startenders decide they don't like how a country is doing something down on Earth? Are we all supposed to swoop down in these tiny ships and declare war? Will we be expected to slaughter innocent women and children on their say so in order to keep our jobs?

"Our homes were destroyed. It wasn't our fault, but it happened nevertheless. I don't know about the rest of you but whenever a disaster happened in another country, I didn't sit idly by and watch their misery. No, I made a donation to make sure the victims were taken care of. What about us? Who's taking care of the New York refugees?"

That was an unfair question. The world had come together to help all the refugees. The United States was struggling to find places for everyone, but was working hard to succeed at it. It would take a very long time. Other countries and every other state had offered to take in refugees. Supplies of food, clothing and medicines were pouring in from around the world. Charities were coming out of the woodwork to help out. People had already donated billions to the cause. No one was forgetting the survivors from the once greatest city on Earth and it ticked me off that Barrel was trying to pretend that nobody cared.

"Moran isn't taking care of us. He's using us as his own personal workforce to make his station better and himself richer. Where's the benefit for us? Do we own part of the station? No. It's his and only his. He's made sure we know that. And if someone comes to hurt his station, he expects us to put our lives on the line to defend it? Sounds like a robber baron with his own private workforce and army. That doesn't seem like a good deal to me. Doesn't even sound vaguely fair. You know what would be fair? Half of everything the station makes split evenly among the workers. Are we getting that? Nowhere near it. We're barely being paid. And we're being paid in Monopoly money instead of real cash. Who ever heard of Startender dollars?

"So when people ask me 'What do we owe the Startenders?' I tell them we don't owe these people the rest of our lives. We don't owe them enough to be their slaves. We all know it's only a matter of time before the taxes kick in. And what will happen if we don't pay? Will we get shoved out an airlock?

"We've been told one day there'll be a hundred and fifty of these Startenders, but they don't have that many yet. There are more than a hundred and fifty of us right here. I say we do like the early Americans did with the original colonies and we take this station for ourselves."

Barrel pointed at the assembled. "After all, don't we, our children and future children deserve the best of everything? Aren't we owed at least that much after what was taken from us? And if these Startenders won't give us what we deserve, then by God we should take it from them!"

I looked around the crowd, trying to gauge the reaction. Barrel had been a salesman turned motivational speaker before the sinking. He was good. Some were buying into what Barrel was selling, but the rest weren't convinced. Probably couldn't reconcile their memories of Startenders rescuing them with the crap Barrel was spewing.

I stood up on my seat on the bleachers. "Actually, folks on the station don't have it so bad. Our apartments are a whole lot bigger than most of the affordable ones in Manhattan."

"But we can't own them," Barrel said.

"We don't have to pay rent either. Or pay for food. We even get a clothing allowance, free schools, free health care, free Internet and entertainment programing. Free admission to concerts and sporting events. Free art and music lessons. There's no traffic and clean air. On Earth some people live in big mansions and others in hovels. Some are homeless." Some of Rebecca's street people came to the station and didn't want apartments. There are levels for them to camp out in, but even they have jobs. "Everyone is assigned the same space."

"Exactly my point. What is this Moran, a commie? We all get the same? What about for those of us who work harder than the others? Shouldn't we be rewarded for it?"

"I think everyone's being rewarded before actually doing anything. On top of all that everyone's drawing a salary. With profit sharing. And no one is being asked to defend just the space station. We're being asked to protect the Earth too. Remember Earth? That place where we all came from, where most of us still have friends and family? There are things out there among the stars that are dangerous and deadly. One day they may come calling, with the intent of harming the Earth and her people. None of the governments below have any defense against that," I said.

"They've got nukes that can blow any aliens back to kingdom come," Barrel said.

"And also hurt the people and the planet below with the radioactive fallout. The dangerous and deadly have to be stopped before they get to our world or people will die. Most of us are Americans." New Yorkers got first priority on coming to live on the station, but it wasn't exclusive and not all New Yorkers were American citizens. "New Yorkers have a long tradition of honoring those who put their lives on the line for the rest of us, whether they're soldiers, cops or firemen. We're being asked to do the same thing – to agree to the possibility of putting our lives on the line to protect others, to protect our new homes. It is not an unreasonable request. Many countries mandate military service. Even America has drafted soldiers. This is not a draft. No one is being forced to do this."

"We're in orbit in outer space. We're trapped here," Barrel said.

"Nonsense. Anyone here is free to leave and go back to Earth at any time. But for those people who choose to live here, they need to realize that freedom and liberty isn't free," I said.

"Neither is going back to Earth. How much will that cost us?" Barrel said.

"Same as the trip up. Nothing. And everyone gets at least four round trips a year. You want to leave, I'll drive you myself," I said.

"You sound like you work for Moran," Barrel said.

"That's because I do. My name is John Murphy and I'm a Startender."

"You see? This is the exact point I'm warning everyone about. Here we are exercising freedom of speech and they send in their troops to break us up, to stop us like the Gestapo in Nazi Germany," Barrel said.

I couldn't stop myself from laughing. "Yes, one unarmed man coming to talk to you is just like Nazi Germany. Wow. You've got me there. No one can dispute that logic. Hey, did you used to be a history professor."

"Are you mocking me?"

"Not yet, but stay around a bit after we're done and I'd be happy to give that a go. Paddy built this place with the help of others and he is willing to share it, but no one is going to simply give something to you for nothing. It won't happen on Earth, not out in the universe and certainly not on the station. If you want to stay here, you're going to have to work for the privilege. That's the simple truth. You don't want to work, you're free to go."

"Just by being brave enough to move here, we've earned the right to be partners," Barrel said.

I laughed. "So if you hop on a plane to relocate for work, then simply show up at a new job, you've earned the right to be a partner? So if you opened a business and hired somebody, they automatically own half your business?" I said.

"Of course not. That's different," Barrel said.

"Why? Because it would be your time and money invested instead of someone else's? Paddy Moran is offering more opportunities to the folks on the station than any other employer or government on Earth," I said.

"Yeah, but we have to live in space. And we've got to be willing to risk getting killed," Barrel said.

"Again, you don't. No one is forcing you to be here. You knew what the requirements were when you signed your contract to move to the station. You can leave and it won't be a worry for you any longer. However, if a time comes when the Earth ever is invaded, you will more than likely owe your life to the people who stay to live and work on this station."

"No job is worth dying for."

"There's a lot of cops, firemen and soldiers who would argue with you about that. And just because someone is in a battle, doesn't mean they will die. We've worked at taking every precaution to protect both the station and the starshots. And it's not the job you'd be risking your life for, but the protection of your home and the entire human race. And if that's not worth putting your life on the line, then this station's not a good fit for you."

"Oh yeah? You're just afraid of collective bargaining. We could call a strike and shut the station down," Barrel said.

Technically, the place was designed to run for extended periods without people. However the industries were another matter, but people shutting them down would actually hurt the workers. Like I said, while not partners, everybody did profit share in whatever they made. Sadly, Barrel didn't strike me as the type to let logic dissuade him from something he believed in or was trying to get others to buy into.

"If we strike, I will make sure that those of us here now at the start will profit the most and become the movement's leaders. Who's with me?"

I looked around the gymnasium hoping that no one would buy into his rhetoric. Sadly, there were some who were.

"There's only one Startender here. He's no threat to us. Come down and stand with me against our oppressors and together we will make the station our own."

There were actually some cheers. One man got up from the bleachers and came down and stood behind Barrel. He was followed by a woman. Then more people did the same until there were over fifty of them.

"See, fully a third of the people here agrees with me. That means a third of the people on the station also agree with me. I speak for thirty-three hundred people."

"That's a huge and faulty leap of logic, Barrel," I said. His meeting had been publicized and out of the ten thousand who lived here, only a few hundred showed. I checked the numbers on who was watching the live feed and it was only another five hundred, a significantly smaller number than his claim.

"Clearly, something needs to be done here and I'm just the man to do it. The way I see it, you Startenders have two choices – meet and negotiate with us now or we'll shut down the station."

"Can't argue with that logic. Actually I could, but I doubt it would do me any good," I said.

"Exactly," Barrel said, not realizing what I actually meant.

"Very well. Let's all adjourn to the meeting room at the end of this corridor and talk terms," I said.

Barrel told his people to follow him, then strutted down the hall, grinning like he was the biggest deal on the planet or above it. We all went into a golden meeting room, Barrel made sure he was first through the door and claimed a seat at the head of a long golden table and I sat at the other. There was a camera on the wall.

"Are we still being televised?" he said.

"Why not? We've got nothing to hide," I said. "Do you?"

"Of course not. I'd just like to invite those who are watching from their quarters who agree with me to come down here and join us. Don't worry if the room is too small, we will make them give us a larger room. I meant, look at the wealth here. The table and the walls are made out of solid gold," Barrel said to the camera, then turned back to me. "You won't mind waiting for the rest of my followers, will you?"

"No, not at all. I trust you won't mind if I make a quick call," I said.

Barrel stared at me and raised an eyebrow. "Some secret clandestine message you want to get out to your shook troops?"

"Nope. I made that call earlier at lunch. I just want to let everyone know what's going on," I said.

"Go ahead," Barrel said. "But know that we're listening."

I was wearing my Startenders badge as a belt buckle today, which made what I did next a bit awkward as it looked like I was talking to my crotch. Savannah would approve and probably try to join in the conversation.

I tapped my badge to open a communications channel. "This is Murphy. Negotiations with Barrel and his crew are about to begin."

Barrel clapped his hands. "See? They knew they'd have to negotiate with us." Those around him nodded and smiled the smiles of those who thought they were about to get a great amount of something for nothing.

There were lots of ways to commute around the station. The most fun were the fall tubes, which used a combination of gravity fields and pulsed air to move folks up or down. We also had moving walkways and the new subways, which were basically elevators that moved in different directions. Even by the slowest route, there was nowhere in the station it would take more than a half hour to get to and with planning usually took much less.

Forty minutes after Barrel issued his invitation, more people had arrived. The number was closer to a hundred and seventy than it was to three thousand. Everyone fit inside the meeting room.

I shut the door and sat back down at my end of the table.

"The floor is yours," I said.

"There was never any doubt of that. Let's get down to business. First, none of the workers can be paid in this station play money. We'll get paid in good old-fashioned American dollars," Barrel said.

"Actually, the Euro is more stable than the dollar," said one of the others.

"I want British pounds," said a woman.

"I want yen," said another.

Barrel smiled and looked back at me. "Good points. Workers will be paid in whatever currency they desire. Two, they'll be brought down to Earth to visit any time and as often as they like."

"There's a regular schedule of shuttles to allow for that. Although we have technology in place that minimizes the cost, it's not cheap. Nor practical. There are scheduled trips daily and the ability to alter that for personal or family emergencies. Those aboard the station are allotted four trips per year Earthside as well as four trips for visitors to come up. There's really no good reason to do more for that, since emergencies are already factored in and there are measures in place for people to ask for more if needed," I said.

"Well that's just not good enough, now is it? We shouldn't be prisoners here. If we want to see somebody, we should be allowed to, just like if we lived on Earth," Barrel said.

"And on Earth, you'd have to arrange for the transportation yourself, whether it be driving or by some other method of transport. No one down there would pay for your personal travel. That's a ludicrous request."

Barrel smiled and leaned back in his chair. "Ludicrous or not, it's nonnegotiable. All of my demands are."

The room shook slightly, causing those standing to move side to side in order to remain standing.

"What was that?" asked the man who wanted to be paid in yen.

"Just some turbulence," I said.

"But we're in space. There is no air, so there shouldn't be any turbulence," said the woman who wanted to be paid in British pounds.

"An excellent observation. What other demands do you have?" I said.

"Free health care."

"It's done," I said.

"Good to see you're moving on these matters so quickly," Barrel said.

"No, it's was already in place. Everyone on the station gets free health care," I said.

Barrel laughed. "Then we want more."

"How can we give you more than free? Pay you for your healthcare?" I said.

"Yes, exactly. You pay us to exercise and eat better and all that kind of crap that makes us healthier. It'll bring your costs down, which means you should pay us an additional ten percent of our annual salary in addition to the free health care."

It was my turn to laugh. "Barrel, what color is the sky in your world? Are there magical dancing sugarplums in purple fluffy tutus attending to your every whim in your deluded mind?"

"I don't care if you are one of the Startenders – nobody talks to Charles Barrel like that. Right now, I am the single most important person on the NYC II and I will be treated with respect."

"You expect us to treat you at the respect buffet too?" I said. "Can't you reach in your own pocket to pay for anything? How cheap are you?"

"I don't care for your flippancy," he said.

"But I worked all day making that flippancy. Well, fine. Be that way. Go get your flippancy elsewhere, but it will never be as good as mine." As Barrel's face turned dark red, I turned to the others. "Are all of you actually on board with Barrel here? Do you believe these demands are reasonable? And if he does not get them, are you all truly prepared to follow him down this road?"

"Don't let him scare you. Our strength and numbers have him and the Startenders scared. We only need stick together and we'll be rich and powerful," Barrel said.

"Those of you willing to strike, stand at the far end of the table by Barrel. Those who think he's a troublemaker and full of hot air, come stand by me."

The group, with one exception, moved toward Barrel. One older woman came and stood by me. "I like it here. This is the best I've ever been treated by anybody. I just wanted to hear what he had to say. I have everything I need. I won't strike."

"Like a rat deserting a sinking ship," Barrel said to the lady. "Only our ship is rising. As of today, you Startenders are going to start paying me to make things run smoothly and ensure there are no bumps in the road."

And just then the entire room moved like it was in a vehicle that had just hit a bump.

"Perfect timing with that line, Barrel. Well, I've thought about your list of demands..."

"Wait, that's not my whole list. I'm just getting started."

"Actually, you're finished. As per the clause in your contracts, we are terminating your employment and residency and that of everybody with you." I turned to the older lady. "Except you my dear."

The older lady had a huge look of relief on her face. "Thank you, Mr. Murphy."

"Just Murphy is fine," I said, then turned to the others. "The NYC II is too small to have people trying to undermine all we're working to accomplish. None of your services are required any longer. The pay owed you will be credited to your assigned accounts within the hour in US dollars. You're welcome to take that to a bank and have it converted to any currency you wish," I said.

"We ain't going anywhere. The only way we're leaving is if you force us and that would prove on camera what violent fascists you are."

I chuckled. "As per your contract, you're all being dropped off at the orbital port in Sullivan County, New York."

Sullivan County had been a depressed area for decades and the boss bought up a lot of land there over the years. Many refugees had relocated and were employed now at the orbital port.

"Nice try. We're still in the station."

"Eric, if you'll please take away everything except the camera," I said.

"You got it boss," the melog said through a speaker. The golden ceiling and walls of the meeting room folded back accordion style into the floor. Then the floor pulled away, leaving everyone on the ground of one of our launch pads. Finally, the table disappeared.

"Barrel, I recommend you stand up," I said as I did the same. The golden chair beneath him slowly floated away from him, forcing Barrel to stand before he fell.

"But how?"

"The meeting room was on board the barship *Fools' Glory*. We've provided you with that free transportation you wanted so desperately." There were piles of boxes and luggage around the perimeter. "We've even been so kind as to pack your things for you," I said as a man in a long gray trench coat, red high-top sneakers with wings that was topped off with a Bulfinche's Pub baseball cap suddenly appeared carrying a stack of boxes.

"That's the last of them, Murphy."

"Thanks, Hermes." The god of speed was able to pack a hundred and seventy people and move their stuff down to the planet in less than fifteen minutes. Impressive, even for him, but I had one question. "How did you get all that stuff down here without it burning up in reentry?"

Fools' Glory shunted the heat energy from reentry to be used later, but we didn't get rid of it. Cardboard and plastic should have incinerated.

"Come on, Murphy, you can't expect me to reveal all my secrets. People, your things are clearly labeled."

"You can't do this," Barrel said.

"We can and we did. The terms of living on the NYC II are very clear in the documents you all signed after having them explained to you at length. I'm afraid you'll just have to find other work and residences. This port is private property and you all have one hour to vacate the premises. If you want, we can arrange for moving trucks to help you with your things."

"You'll pay for them, right?" Barrel said.

"Nope."

"But you paid when we first moved to the station," Barrel said.

"Actually, we did the moving and simply didn't charge you. Since you're no longer a resident of the NYC II, you're on your own."

"You mean we have to pay rent again? And for food?"

"And cook it too. Barrel, you may be interested to know that Paddy Moran did a cost analysis of what people would have to pay to receive all the services that are offered for free on the station, including free lifetime education. It's easily equivalent to more than double the average New Yorkers' annual salary before the tsunami. But you gave all that up when you tried to extort us. We're not interested in your offer and wish all of you the best in your new endeavors."

"Maybe I was a little hasty in making my demands. Why don't we just forget I said anything and go back to the way things were," Barrel said.

"That's the problem with saying or doing certain things. Life can change and never be able to go back to the way it was again," I said, thinking more of what happened to New York than what Barrel did.

The people who had chosen to follow Barrel moments earlier were none too happy and began begging to come back.

"Sorry, but you made your choices and now you have to live with them."

Eric spoke quietly into a micro bud fastened to the inside of my ear cannel. We don't like to advertise that we can hear without the sound coming out of the badges. I relayed the message. "Attention, all salary owed has been credited to your chosen Earth accounts, so you'll be able to use that money towards food and lodging."

Fools' Glory assumed the shape of a traditional flying saucer and hovered next to me.

Eric's voice sounded in my ear again. "Boss, think they'll be okay?"

"They will."

"You don't think this was a little harsh?" Eric said. "I mean living on the station is practically perfect." Eric exaggerated, but we were working toward it. We'll never achieve actual perfection, but hopefully we'll get closer than anyone ever has before.

"Some people just don't appreciate what they have until it's gone. There'll come a time when we'll be depending on every person on that station. Barrel and his people here aren't the type that can be trusted with the lives and well-being of others. They care more about themselves than anyone else. It's best for all if they just move on."

The older lady who made the right choice looked at me

strangely, trying to figure out who I was talking to.

"Murphy, how about I race *Fools' Glory* back to the station?" Hermes said.

Eric opened a ramp into the ship and I motioned the lady onto it. Savannah came down and offered her arm. Coyote sat at the top of the ramp watching, not wanting to risk missing anything else after not being around for spikeball. I told him it wasn't really a great thing, but it didn't change his mind.

"Race you? You've got to be kidding me," I said. Hermes had ways of traveling that made light look like a slowpoke and would give Einstein headaches.

"What if I go to Jupiter first and then head back?"

"Make it a lap around Saturn, then Uranus and you've got a deal," I said. I almost said Neptune, but after what he did to New York, we were lobbying to have the name of the planet changed.

Hermes started moving his hands towards his posterior.

"The planet, not the body part," I said.

"Okay. On your mark, get set..." I heard the faintest whoosh, which drowned out the "go".

I ran up the ramp into the ship. "Eric, full speed home."

"Murph, you think we can actually beat him?"

"Nope," Coyote said, stopping to lick himself. I ignored him.

"Saturn and Uranus are almost on opposite sides of the sun right now, so we have a slight chance. Besides, we'll never know unless we try."

THE FINE ART OF DIPOLMACY

With every organization, there needs to be a certain amount of bureaucracy. In the Startenders, we worked hard to keep it to a minimum. The second Startender Academy class would be finishing up in a few days, which meant that *Fools' Glory*'s rotation as one of the Earthbound barships was coming to an end. I was looking forward to boldly going where no bartender had gone before. Until then, there were meetings to attend.

The Startenders have a leadership council, a place for us to kick things upstairs. The kind of things too big to handle or that we figured required more wisdom. The Startender Council consisted of Paddy, Vulcan, Kaye Chandler and Jan. There was also a Low Council, which attended all the meetings. At present it included Bubba Sue the gremlin, Bast, the cat-headed Egyptian goddess who was in charge of our intelligence network, and Kamile the kobold. Also included were the head honchos in Earth's solar system, which at present included me and Nellie. I don't want to swear to it, but I suspect Paddy arranged it so I could have a little bit more time with my daughter. And maybe he wanted some more time with his kids since they were part of the *Perdu*'s crew.

I'd considered making Elsiebelle part of my crew, much the way we had with Loki's daughter, Riga. I decided against it. The simple truth of the matter is, having E-Belle as part of my crew skewed my thinking and my priorities. My first concern would always be her safety, which would not make me an effective head honcho. As it turns out, the point was moot as she requested to serve on board the *Perdu*.

We'd just sat through about an hour's worth of details from Kamile and Paddy on our diplomatic forays with the UN and its member nations, while we'd kept a UN observer cooling his heels outside. Dionysius was our primary ambassador with Demeter serving as his second and Kamile backing them up when she wasn't helping Paddy run the station. The woman organized like nobody's business.

The UN observer was investigating us. There was still a lot of fallout from how we finagled our way into sovereign nation status, especially from the big countries. We had gone from unknowns to rivals. There was great concern over our orbiting station, especially in terms of weaponization. No one believed us when we told them we had no intentions of waging any sort of war against any country. The disbelief made sense in a sad sort of way, since the rest of the countries in the world would say the same thing but be lying. Only we weren't.

In truth, we couldn't. Sure, we could attack and make a good showing on any battlefield, but war requires a lot more manpower and a hundred plus Startenders wasn't enough to make it practical even if we wanted to.

Plus, we'd made a big deal, especially among ourselves, that we weren't a military organization.

Paddy gave us a currency update. He was making some headway with his efforts to get Startender dollars and the moon base's "Benjamins" recognized and set an exchange rate.

Ben City was an actual democracy, as opposed to the republic style government that most people called democracies. Every resident got a vote and a permanently fastened electronic watch with which to vote. They had a president, a legislature and judicial system. However, the legislature was only in charge of drafting the laws. It was actually up to the citizens to vote on them. The president carried them out, but had no veto or signing power. It was made clear in Ben City's Constitution that the government officials worked for the people. There were measures in place so that people could vote to oust the officials. There were term limits and absolutely no campaign contributions allowed in order to keep things honest. At least as honest as politics could get. For those who didn't help build the place, it took five years of residency to achieve citizenship, which gave people more rights and responsibilities, but every person who lived there got a vote. A resident's vote counted as one tenth of that of a citizen. The Startenders and some of the Startender Society were granted citizenship, as was anyone else who helped to actually build the place. Ben City's diplomacy staff was in charge of getting their currency system recognized, but were coordinating their efforts with us.

Paddy was helping them some, but his main concern was Startender Station.

"So they finally agreed to let the currency be judged on the gold standard?" Bast said.

Paddy smiled. "It only made sense, since we're in possession of more gold than any other nation on Earth."

"True, but almost all of it is involved in the special alloy used for the barships and the station. It's not as if we can cut a piece off and spend it," I said.

"With the amount of time, effort and expense that went into building those barships, absolutely not," Vulcan said, a little huffier than he needed to be for a joke, but he had spent the last couple of decades designing and building them so I guess he'd earned the right to be protective.

"They pointed out that same flaw in my argument, so I assured them that we could get enough gold to back our currency," Paddy said.

"Do we have that much just lying around?" Bubba Sue said. "Or you going to pull the old fairy gold scam?"

Jan frowned. A lot of natives of Faerie had taken advantage of humans over the years by paying them in gold that was enchanted and later turned out to be anything from rocks to dirty laundry. Leprechaun gold was a bit different in that it was actual gold from Faerie, which had the innate property of being able to store large amounts of magic. It let leprechauns stay away from Faerie for very extended periods. Paddy, while having leprechaun gold of his own back in the day, didn't need it for that since he was actually born on Earth. He had needed its magic storing abilities, but that was before he bought Bulfinche's.

"No scam. We've identified a number of asteroids that contain large deposits that we can mine to get it," Paddy said.

"So you lied to them then?" Jan said. As our very own Jiminy Cricket and Karma native, her decisions reflected on her physical condition. As one of the Startenders Council, our decisions as a group also affected her. At least I think they still did. I wasn't sure if she'd ever put the power transfer ring back on and it hadn't come up in conversation. I hadn't seen much of her because of her academy training. We even had to schedule this meeting around her down time.

"No lie or even stretching of the truth, I said that we would be able to produce that much gold. They give us a deadline of ninety days to do so. I figure with our track record, we can do it in about eighty-four."

Vulcan's eyes rolled up and looked like he was staring at the ceiling. It was his thinking face. "Paddy, by my calculations, we'd need at least 104 days to meet that deadline."

"I was going by our original mining schedule. Why would it take longer now?" Paddy said. The majority of the gold used in our barships had come from mining in the asteroid belt. The rest was a mixture of fairy gold with some other mystic types mixed in.

"During our original mining operations, we put all our resources toward getting out the gold. Now most of those resources are out exploring the universe. The loss of Hermes alone adds more than half the additional time."

The god of speed, thieves, physicians and travelers was out doing the latter, exploring and mapping the universe. He didn't need a barship as he was several times faster than one and could survive in space and even more inhospitable places. His explorations would make it safer for the rest of us to travel and expand what to us would be the known universe.

Paddy sighed. "Then we'll have to pull him off explorer detail for a little bit." Paddy turned to Bubba Sue. "Do you think you'd be able to increase the efficiency of our mining operation to help make up the time?"

The gremlin and the genius god exchanged glances. They were husband and wife, and as such sometimes were overly respectful of each other's boundaries. Each was loath to contradict the other. Vulcan was the main force behind our barships and badges. Combine the intellects of Leonardo da Vinci, Albert Einstein and any other ten smart people you've ever heard of and it wouldn't even come close to Vulcan in the fields of most sciences. Vulcan came up with designs and inventions that no one else could have. Bubba Sue was able to tweak and make them even better, although she wouldn't have been able create them in the first place. In terms of mechanical and mystic engineering, Bubba Sue was Vulcan's equal. When it came to redesign, she was actually better. In most other areas he had no equal I'd ever heard of. Still, as far as Vulcan was concerned, his diminutive wife was his match.

"I think if hubby and the Reaper help me, we should make the deadline," Bubba Sue said.

The fourth member of the board chuckled and rolled her eyes. "Please, these days I just go by Kaye."

Kaye Chandler was a woman on the other side of the century mark who could still pass for forty or fifty. Back during the Great Depression and Prohibition, she wore a skimpy pink outfit with a cape and a domino mask and ran around fighting bad guys as the Pink Reaper. Scientifically speaking, she was quite brilliant herself, but had an uncle who even Vulcan admitted was a virtuoso of an inventor. Kaye still had hundreds of his notebooks filled with designs of things he dreamed up but never built. Kaye had used some of his designs to help build the barships, starshots and the station, as well as a host of nonlethal weaponry.

One of Dash Chandler's most brilliant inventions was a chamber designed to heal people. A side effect was slowing and even turning back the aging process, at least for humans. Each barship had one on board and there were a number on the station. I'd used one a few times, including after the spikeball beating. It helped me look and feel younger than I had any right to be. There were also a couple of other factors in play thanks to the boss. Paddy assures me that one day – so long as I don't do something stupid and get myself killed – I'll likely be eligible for membership in Wisp's Eternity Club when I turn one hundred and fifty. It was still a ways off, but it's a comforting thought.

"I'd be happy to see what I could do," Kaye said, turning her head slightly to watch our diplomat watchdog stand up and pace in front of the soundproof glass wall that he was stuck waiting on the other side of. Not very patiently, I might add. "And speaking of projects that the three of us have worked on, I'd like to address our Startender Affiliate program."

As I've mentioned, not everyone is cut out to be a Startender and we were fortunate to have the Startender Society to help us out, not to mention associates like Nemesis and Thunder Jack.

That didn't mean we couldn't use more help.

After all the publicity we received after the evacuation of New York, the former Pink Reaper came up with a pretty nifty idea. Back in her day, the radio shows used to give secret decoder rings out the kids so they could be part of the character's fan club. There were even some night avengers who gave their agents special ways to communicate with them. Some agents were actually children.

The former Pink Reaper went about designing a ring that would act as a communication device that would allow people to let the Startenders know about problems going on and even call for help. The rings had a Startender logo on them. Thanks to Vulcan and Bubba Sue's help, the rings can work anywhere on the surface of the planet, the moon or in the station. They even work a short distance underground. They had upgraded a few for interstellar communication. Tock and Thunder Jack had gotten that variety.

The rings weren't cheap to make, but Kaye was a rich woman. Nowhere near Paddy's league, but far from poor. Since Paddy was still pretty much broke in terms of liquid capital, Kaye financed the rings herself and supervised their distribution. The former Pink Reaper looked for reports of someone doing the right thing when no one else did or a brave and heroic act.

So far, she'd distributed hundreds of them. I'd handed out only the pair. When this project came to light, some in the media accused the Startenders of setting up a spy network. We didn't need to as we already had one. Or rather Bast did.

To spin matters, Kaye took to the talk show circuit to explain about the program. Kaye was an extremely beautiful woman, with thick blond hair and a body that could make women in their twenties or thirties envious. The camera loved her. After her success, she was now one of our go to people when a problem arose in the media.

"I'm happy to say that with five hundred and twelve rings distributed, we've only had a half dozen issues. Those six rings were taken back. Five of the reasons included purposeful false alarms, wanting us to go after people they didn't like and such. Sadly, there was one case of mental illness.

"From the original six hundred made, including the ones returned, we still have ninety four to give out. I anticipate that we'll be done within the month. I propose we make a thousand additional rings. What's more, I recommend that we set up a Startender Academy-lite to help train these people to be leaders in their communities. I'm willing to foot the bill for the materials for more rings, but I want to see how everybody else felt about the training since it will use some of the Startenders resources."

We all thought it was a great idea and put it on the to do list.

Paddy looked out the glass wall. The diplomat was behaving undiplomatically by pacing angrily and making a show of checking his watch. Paddy hit a button and the glass doors opened. "Perhaps we can now address the UN's most recent concerns with Donald Sheriff who has been waiting so patiently."

Sheriff was able to hear that last part and narrowed his eyes, then stopped. He straightened his suit jacket and tie, picked up his clipboard and marched toward us. Our meeting table was round, but was able to open out into a U shape for company.

He stopped at the table line.

"Would you like a seat?" Paddy said.

"No, thank you," Sheriff said. "One of the things I'm here to investigate are the allegations of human rights violations by one Charles Barrel."

The room was filled with combinations of chuckles and eye rolling.

"We broadcast the situation live on station TV," Kaye said. "I trust you've viewed the recordings?"

"I have, but it's been my experience that video can be doctored and edited," the diplomat said.

"You did hear the part where she mentioned it went out live, right?" Bubba Sue said.

"You could've had it on a thirty second delay. From all the world's seen you Startenders do, the possibility of you being able to edit video almost instantly is hardly an unreasonable assumption, now is it?" Sheriff said.

Bubba Sue nodded. "Fair enough. It's something we could have done, but we didn't."

"And all I have for that is your word," Sheriff said.

Paddy's brow furrowed and his cheeks got red. "Mr. Sherriff..."

The man looked up from his clipboard. "That's Dr. Sheriff."

Paddy paused. I knew he was mentally counting to ten so as not to lose his temper. "Dr. Sheriff, you're here as our guest, so I'll assume that ye are unaware of the grave insult ye have just offered all of us."

Sheriff tilted his head. "I offered no insult."

"Actually you did," I said. "You doubted the word of a Startender. A Startender will not lie about giving their word. Ever."

"So you're saying a Startender will never lie?" Sheriff said.

The room erupted in gentle laughter.

"Heavens, no man. Everyone lies. It's just a Startender will not break his or her word. Ever. End of the story," Paddy said.

"And all I have to prove that is…"

Paddy smiled and nodded. "Our word."

"Of course. But you freely admit lying at other times?"

"Will ye be getting to a point here?"

"The original reason the evacuation of New York started was due to an anonymous phone tip about an imminent nuclear explosion. After the tip the United States government ordered flyovers with planes and drones. They found enough background radiation to indicate that a nuclear weapon could have been in the area. Based on that, you Startenders spearheaded the evacuation. It turns out there was a very real danger, but it wasn't an atomic explosion, but a tsunami and earthquake. We know that despite rumors to the contrary, neither was caused by a nuclear detonation. And you people now claim it was the result of a mad Greco-Roman sea god's temper tantrum."

"Again, what's your point?" Paddy said.

"Where did the false threat of a nuclear disaster originate?"

"Does it matter? Over ten million lives were saved," Nellie said.

"You see, I've never been an ends-justifies-the-means-type of person. I suspect that the original threat tip originated with the Startenders," Sheriff said.

"Would that be so wrong?" Kaye said.

"Since you're also big about giving your word? Why not simply have given your word?"

"Because the word of anyone stating that a mad god out of myth was going to destroy the greatest city on Earth wouldn't have been enough to get people to safety," Paddy said.

"So you're admitting the original phony nuclear threat came from the Startenders?"

Paddy simply folded his hands and smiled. The rest of us mimicked his posture and kept mum.

Sheriff looked each of us over in turn, frowning. "I see. Then let's address Charles Barrel's allegations of unsafe working conditions and kidnapping to begin with."

The lights in the room began to flicker, and a siren went off.

"If you think some phony alarm or drill is going to stop my investigation –" Sheriff said.

"Someone is using one of the rings to send a distress signal," Kaye said and pointed a matching ring at our wall sized view screen to connect to the ring's communicator. The rings could also generate a hologram, but Kaye was old-school and preferred screens. It was coming from the angry little country with the angry little ambassador who tried to line jump during the evacuation of New York.

The place had recently ended a bloody civil war, with the rebels taking the capital. It was a struggle steeped in hatred based along ethnic lines. It was rumored that the rebel leader who was now the country's dictator had plans to do some ethnic cleansing.

The face looking at us from the screen was that of a young boy who couldn't have been more than ten or twelve, although from the way his ribs poked through his skin it was possible he looked younger than he was due to malnutrition.

"Jojo, this is Kaye Chandler. What's wrong?" Our images appeared as holograms above the boy's ring. I remembered him from the last meeting when Kaye had gone through her list of possible ring recipients. This kid was exceptional. He'd saved a dozen other children when his village was attacked, using little more than his wits to outsmart a large force of armed men. Although the rebel forces were not above conscripting women and children into their ranks, particularly for use as cannon fodder. Jojo managed to keep himself and the others safe long enough to reach one of three UN refugee camps in the country, more than thirty miles away.

When the rebel leader declared himself dictator, he ordered UN peacekeepers out of the country. The matter had been scheduled for discussion after Dagonet's UN speech, but for obvious reasons was not addressed at that time.

As is usually the case, the UN couldn't get enough countries to step up and take in the refugees. The UN had some brave souls monitoring the situation, but all they had were cameras with satellite hookups. No weapons, no Startender badge or barship, only guts and principles.

I admired the hell out of them.

"Soldiers are attacking the refugee camp and they're killing everyone. I'm trying to hide people again, but there are more of us and we're fenced in and surrounded. There are more soldiers too. I'm not going to be able to get everybody out of here this time. I don't know what to do. Please save us," Jojo pleaded. The ring's camera was picking up others in the background. This time around the kid was leading not just children, but adults and they all looked terrified.

We all started moving at once. Paddy told Kamile to coordinate everything from the station. Nellie used her badge to summon the *Perdu* to get down to the surface, then joined Paddy, Vulcan, Bubba Sue, Bast, Jan, and the Pink Reaper as they headed to *Bulfinche's Legacy*, Paddy's barship that was permanently assigned to the station. I called Kaye the Pink Reaper because as soon as Jojo gave us the situation, she put on a mask and pulled out a big pink gun that was in a tiny little holster – Spatial warping storage.

Even the barships would take too long to get down there, so I hit a button on my watch. "Kamile, call Loki and have him get Fool's Glory down there too."

"Wait, what are you all doing?" Sheriff shouted.

"Saving those people," I said, as my bike appeared in front of me.

"By ignoring the territorial integrity of a sovereign nation? That's in violation of every international law on the books. You will be expelled from the United Nations," Sheriff said.

Gunshots were heard through our link with the ring.

Kamile put a satellite picture on the screen. There were hundreds of soldiers and dozens of light armored vehicles surrounding the camp. "It'll take the barships at least fifteen minutes to get there. We won't make it in time."

"Speak for yourself," I said, getting on the bike.

"Murphy, you aren't going to be able to stop that many soldiers by yourself," Kamile said.

"That won't stop me from trying, but you have a good point. Nellie, Reaper – you're with me in the sidecar. And I need coordinates and sector measurements."

The former and born again Pink Reaper turned her ring toward my navigation array and transmitted them to the bike from Jojo's ring.

"You cannot invade a member nation. I forbid it," Sheriff said, actually stomping his foot.

Paddy turned, as angry as I'd seen him in years. "Sheriff, ye don't get to tell me what to do in me own house. We are helping those people. You can ride along and inspect how we do it or shut the hell up."

By that point, the ladies were in the sidecar, so I hit the button on the transworld drive. My bike had an earlier version of the transworld drive than the barships. For traveling through space, it was a lot slower, but also was a lot smaller and had much less mass. Aside from a rather large food storage unit with some folded space inside, the bike was the size that it appeared on the outside. The barships had tremendous size and mass stored in their pocket dimensions. They couldn't use the transworld drive within a planet's atmosphere without serious repercussions. Because it was so small, the bike had no such restrictions.

In a matter of seconds, we materialized above the building that Jojo and the rest were hiding in. We were too late to stop soldiers from using a rocket launcher to blow apart the ceiling and part of the front wall. Rubble covered some of the refugees, burying others. From my vantage point in the sky, I could see dozens, maybe hundreds, of bodies that had been slaughtered by the attacking soldiers.

Unfortunately, the bike was short on armaments. I hit the button for the speaker, which let out a shrill whistle that should've shattered eardrums. Maybe the soldiers would stop paying attention to the fleeing refugees and start paying attention to me.

"This is John Murphy. These people are under the protection of the Startenders. Continue your attack at your own peril."

Apparently the sight of a man and two women in a flying motorcycle wasn't threatening enough, because some soldiers opened fire at us. Seeing the bullets had little effect on the force field around the bike, they started in with a rocket launcher.

Using her winged boots, Nellie flew out of the sidecar and grabbed hold of the rocket and turned it back toward the soldiers, making sure it just missed them.

"You didn't make your voice scary enough, Murphy. Next time do it like this," Kaye said, touching her necklace, which held a speaker of its own. There came a bone chilling laugh that actually sent shivers up my spine. "Evildoers, your hour of reckoning has come. Flee or face the wrath of the Pink Reaper!"

Now in the interest of truthfulness, the Pink Reaper was never world famous. In fact, those who have heard of her believe her to be part of New York City folklore, so it wasn't her reputation that caused several men to turn and run. It was her presentation, her voice, and her presence as she stepped out of the sidecar and hung in the air. She was always dressed in pink, but I'm not even sure when she put on the cape or where she got it from.

She started rapid firing her gun at the soldiers and tiny electric darts shot out, zapping whoever they hit into unconsciousness.

The building was under attack from three sides. Nellie moved to the right, flying among the soldiers, trying to distract them. The Pink Reaper moved through the air to the left using some device on her back in combination with her badge's ability to regulate gravity's influence on her. That left the front with the big rocket hole to me.

"Kill the man on the bike!" The voice sounded vaguely familiar. I looked down to see a man with a C branded onto his face.

I dive bombed the line cutter with my bike, but he was fast enough to jump back into the armored vehicle he'd just gotten out of. I managed to knock it on its side as the bike swooped down; all the while soldiers were firing at me. The bullets were bouncing off the bike's force field and doing more damage to the soldiers than me. Unfortunately, a stray ricochet could kill one of them so I pulled up.

Seeing I was unhurt, the former ambassador turned massacre leader got smarter or at least eviler. "Forget about him. Kill the refugees!"

I landed the bike in the hole in the wall, between Jojo, the refugees and the soldiers.

"Everyone move together behind me." I extended the force field around the bike to maximum. It weakened the field, but it should hold up against bullets. Rocket launchers too, but I wasn't as sure of that.

Problem was, it still wasn't wide enough to get everyone inside. I leapt off the bike as the force was designed to let someone inside go out, but not the other way around. I stood in front of a group of eight people and had them huddle together, then wrapped my arms around them, mentally extending my badge's force field. It definitely wouldn't be able to stop a rocket.

I looked to see if I could get any air support from Nellie or the Reaper, but they were still busy fighting off soldiers on the other sides of the building.

An old woman who had been hiding behind a bed got up. She was too far away to extend either field to her. If I were to move myself or the bike to shield her, it would leave others exposed.

Jojo ran out of the force field by the bike to get the old woman, but she fell and he couldn't get her up.

I broke one of the cardinal Startender rules. I took off my badge and gave it to someone else. "Hold on to this and don't move," I said. "I'll be back for it."

I rushed over and helped Jojo get the woman to her feet, then herded them toward the rear of the bike's field, but we weren't going to make it. The former ambassador saw and started firing at us himself.

I had no more force fields up my sleeve. I put my body between that of Jojo and the woman in hopes that they might somehow survive.

We hit the dirt as a hail of bullets spit up clouds of dust all around us. My leg exploded with fire. I was hit. The bastard's aim was improving. We didn't have long and I started debating what my last words should be. They had to be funny or at least witty.

The sound of the gunfire changed. Instead of pinging into the ground, it was ricocheting off metal. I looked up to see *Fools' Glory* morphed into a golden wall between the refugees in the building and the soldiers.

"Murphy, we're here," said Loki over my ear bud. Are you okay?"

"It's only a flesh wound," I said. The bullet had gone clean through and missed any major blood vessels. It hurt like hell but wasn't life threatening. I turned to Jojo and the woman. "Are you two okay?"

"Yes," they both said.

"Loki, we've got more refugees in danger."

"Not to worry. We've got it covered. These bastards won't hurt anybody else," Loki said. I got to my feet. My leg hurt and burned, but I could stand.

The other two barships, the *Perdu* and *Bulfinche's Legacy* had also morphed to protect the surviving refugees. All three ships had unloaded Startenders. The soldiers outnumbered us more than ten to one.

They didn't stand a chance.

A familiar buzzing of wings caused me to turn around as my daughter landed behind me. "Dad, you okay?"

"I'm fine, honey."

Elsiebelle lifted me off the ground in a bear hug reminiscent of her mother. It was especially impressive since she was shorter than I was.

"Although if you keep squeezing so hard that might change," I teased.

My daughter put me back on the ground. I kissed her on the top of her head of purple hair, then squeezed her back. She bent down and tore my pants where the bullet wound was.

"I'm pretty sure it went through," I said.

"It did," E-Belle said as she slapped a battle patch on it. It was something we borrowed from the Daemor playbook. It was an adhesive patch that could be used to pull the sides of open wounds together and expand to stop bleeding, promote healing and prevent infection. Thankfully there was also a numbing agent.

Loki's voice rang out over *Fools' Glory*'s external speakers. "This is Loki, the honcho of the barship *Fools' Glory*. You bastards massacred hundreds of people and shot my best friend. I'm only giving you one chance to surrender. Put down your weapons, get on your knees and put your hands behind your head or you will regret it."

Elsiebelle picked me up and flew me over to the person I had left my badge with. She had more trouble than usual since she was carrying my full weight.

There could be problems if the kid didn't hand it back. Badges are keyed to only work for Startenders, but we have the option to turn that function off. I did it so the force field would still work.

The young man gave it to me without incident.

"Anyone who listens to that Startender dog will be shot where he stands!" said the former ambassador, waving his gun in the air.

The soldiers were more afraid of him than they were of us.

I heard the dark tone carry through Loki's chuckle. "You can't say I didn't give you a chance."

Although the barships are armed, we've strived very hard to make sure all the armaments were nonlethal. You can't take a vow about not killing and carry around a machine gun.

One of the weapons we did have was ultrasonics. A much inferior version had taken out Hex many years back. Ours are big enough to take on an army. We pointed it at the soldiers and seconds later their bowels and intestinal tracts let loose. Every soldier collapsed to the ground, screaming in pain from the cramps that made them soil themselves.

The Pink Reaper opened a second pouch on her belt and pulled out a larger version of her pink gun about the size of a rocket launcher. She started firing pellets in and among the soldiers that she hadn't already gotten with her smaller version's darts. This one got some serious distance. As soon as the pellets struck something, they burst open, releasing the Pink Reaper's trademark fear gas. It was just what it sounded like. Anyone who breathed it in becomes absolutely terrified. There was no thought of fight, only flight and the feeling was magnified by the sight of the color pink.

"Hit the lights," Kaye Chandler said. Pink spotlights powerful enough to turn night into day shone from and on the golden hulls, making the barships look pink.

"Look upon the Pink Reaper and despair. Justice has come to claim your souls, but I also am merciful. Lay down your weapons and flee and I shall allow you to cling to your miserable lives," Kaye shouted with her spooky voice and speaker.

The soldiers had no gas masks and the sight of pink terrified them down to their cores. Most bolted, using a combination of running and crawling.

"Isn't that our friend from the evac, the cutting ambassador with the limo?" Elsiebelle said, noticing the man with the C on his face as he ran away.

"It is. Would you mind detaining him for us?" I said.

"You couldn't have thought of that before we hit them with the ultrasonics?" E-Belle said, handing me her med kit. My daughter flew and lifted the architect of this massacre out of the fleeing crowd. She couldn't carry him far on her own, but then somebody with a pair of winged boots flew in to help.

Kyna was one of the Startenders who'd come down on the *Perdu*. The two ladies dumped him in a corner of the camp.

Kaye Chandler walked over to him. If the man hadn't already been pooping himself, the sight of the woman in pink would have made him start.

"Don't move or I will come for you personally," she ordered and the former angry ambassador curled up into the fetal position and started crying.

The soldiers were on the run, so we turned our attentions toward the wounded. There were so many bodies that we couldn't tell the living from the dead without checking each one.

My crew had gathered around me with the exception of Loki and Eric who were still on board *Fools' Glory*.

I turned to Loki's daughter, who was already in dragon form. "Riga, chase down the soldiers, make sure they keep moving away from the refugees, but watch where they go. We don't want them doubling back." Riga shifting was limited between human and dragon forms, but she had a lot of control over each. "Turn your skin pink. It'll make them vacate faster."

"Got it, Murph," she said, flapping her now pink wings and taking off into the air.

Nellie had gotten her crew tending to the wounded, but we also had a lot of scared people that we need to organize and move to safety.

"Savannah and Coyote, get all the unhurt survivors further back into the camp and keep them calm. Find out if any of them have any medical training, because we have hundreds of wounded. If ever we needed Hermes, it's now," I said.

"Paddy sent a distress signal, but he was several systems away. He said it would probably take them over an hour to get here," Coyote said.

"Then for the moment, we act as if he's not coming." I hit my badge. "Eric, park the ship. I want you and Loki out here helping the wounded." Vulcan made sure all melog had some medical training that was above the basic stuff all Startenders were taught in the academy. Loki came from a place that didn't have doctors, but had lots of war. He'd picked up a few tricks.

"Murphy, my skills aren't exactly refined. I'd be doing meatball surgery," Loki said.

"Still better than these people bleeding to death. We'll have to triage. The ones who are stable for the moment leave be, then choose the ones you'll be most likely to save," I said.

"Not the ones worst off?" Eric said.

"Neither of your skills is up to that. We have to pick the people we've the best chance of saving." Eric wasn't happy with my answer. I wasn't either. We've gotten used to being able to help almost everybody back when we were working out of Bulfinche's Pub, but then people came to us individually or in small groups. We'd never had to deal with anything like this. One of the harsh realities of the universe is you can't save everyone, no matter how hard you try or as much as you wish you could.

But we're going to try our damnedest to save as many as possible.

I limped towards a group of wounded. I had basic emergency medic training. I'd delivered a few babies and plugged a couple of wounds over the years, but most of the injuries were beyond my meager skills.

Our UN watchdog came down the ramp of the *Legacy* and ran over to me.

"Hope you're not going to try and give us a lecture for what we're doing here. I don't have the time or the inclination to listen to it right now," I said.

The man looked ashen. "No, I've never seen anything like this up close before. You were right to ignore me and come help these people. Diplomats get so concerned with not breaking protocol or offending other countries that we forget what's truly important. But that's not what I wanted to tell you. Before I became a diplomat, I was a physician. I want to help."

I held up the med kit Elsiebelle gave me. "Great, these people need all the help they can get. How good are you?"

"I did three years in an ER, before I specialized in general surgery."

"Best news I've heard all day. Follow me," I said.

The sheer number of bloody bodies made me sick to my stomach. Most were obviously dead – it's hard to live without most of a skull or with large gaping wounds in a torso. The doctor and I moved quickly from body to body, checking for signs of life. I barely held back tears because we had checked dozens of the refugees without finding one pulse or person still able to breathe air.

Part of me wanted more than anything to find the ambassador turned general and strangle the life out of him, but that wouldn't help any of the victims who were still alive, so I refrained.

I came upon a woman curled in a fetal position, but was still on her elbows and knees. She had bullet wounds along her back. I rolled her to better check, which is when I found the first signs of life. It wasn't the woman, but a baby beneath her. The girl was still breathing, although the majority of air was being sucked through a hole in her chest. This brave mother died trying to shield her child. A bullet must have passed through the woman and into the baby, although going through the mother probably lessened the speed, allowing the girl to survive this long.

Terrorbelle had died protecting our daughter. This little girl's survival became very personal to me. There was no way I was going to let this woman's valiant sacrifice be in vain, but the chest wound was far beyond what a battle patch could fix.

"Dr. Sheriff, I found a survivor. Come quick," I said.

The diplomat rushed to my side. I held the baby out for him to examine.

"I'm sorry," Sheriff said.

"No. Not acceptable," I said. "There has to be something you can do."

"Her wound is too bad. She's bleeding out. I can't remove the bullet or it will only happen faster. She only has minutes before her lungs fill with blood and she suffocates."

The diplomat then tilted his head and looked at me oddly, probably because I was crying. Probably more like weeping.

The man put his hand on my shoulder. "I am sorry, Mr. Murphy, but there might be others who I can help." I stood there staring at the infant, her mother's corpse just behind the doctor, trying to come up with a solution. I could only come up with one, so I prayed. "What are you going to do?"

"Stay with her until she dies." I made a silent apology to the mother for not being able to save the daughter she died protecting, which made me flashback to another mother who gave her life for her child. I apologized to her too. I'm sorry I couldn't save this baby, Terrorbelle, like you saved our Elsiebelle. I'm sorry I couldn't save you. "No one should ever have to die alone."

"And sometimes people don't have to die at all," said the happiest sight for sore eyes I'd ever seen as he seemingly appeared from nowhere in front of me.

I held the dying infant out in front of me. Her breathing was getting shallower and sounded like she was under water. "You have to save her, Hermes. Please—"

"I will Murphy," Hermes said. "Have them bring me all the wounded, but I'll need a place to work." I couldn't hit my badge, as Hermes arms were a big blur around the baby I still held in my hands. "Badge, call Eric. Eric, open up *Fools' Glory*. I need a huge sterile room with enough operating tables for all the wounded. If *Fools' Glory* can't handle it alone, have the *Perdu* and the *Legacy* do the same and merge the rooms. Make a clear unobstructed view with space to move between the tables," I said. "Badge, call all in area – All right people, we've got a real chance of saving these people now. Hermes is here. We're setting up an operating suite in the barships. I need everybody to transport the wounded now!"

"What about the people who are too hurt to be moved?" Nellie said.

Hermes handed me back the little girl. Her wound was closed

and she was breathing normally. I kissed her on the head and pulled her to my chest. Then I prayed thank you.

"I'll take the ones who can't be moved. It'll be so quick it will be like they never moved," Hermes said.

"Hermes, I've never been so happy to see anybody as I am to see you right now. Thank you," I said.

"Question is will you still be saying that when you figure out that while I operated on her with you holding her steady, that I also managed to not only stitch you up and replace your patch but also lift your wallet," Hermes said. Back in the day it was a running gag between us. It decreased drastically after I started being able to do it to him.

"For saving this little one, you can keep it," I said. Hermes flipped it open to a picture of Terrorbelle, Elsiebelle and me when she was a kid. We shared a look and the wallet disappeared from his hand. I could feel it back in my pocket.

I moved the infant to the crook of my arm and hit my badge. "Eric, when you're done setting up everything for Hermes, I'm going to need a crib."

Hermes had anesthetized the girl so she'd sleep while she healed.

Fools' Glory extruded a small nursery as I walked by. I put the little girl in the crib. I turned to help bring the wounded in only to come face-to-face with Jojo with dozens of people following in his wake.

"Mr. Startender, sir, we want to help," Jojo said.

I touched the boy's shoulder. "Good man. We need all the help we can get. Let's start making some stretchers to bring anyone still alive to that golden room."

With the refugees help, we got the rest of the living wounded to Hermes' operating emporium.

After that, all that was left for most of us to do was stand outside and watch through the transparent force fields in awe.

"Unbelievable. Miraculous," Sheriff said as the UN's watchdog decided instead to watch Hermes operate on hundreds of people, seemingly at once. He moved so fast he could perform parts of operations in the spaces between seconds that seemed to exist for no one but him.

It took him most of the day, but out of the nine hundred plus he was working on, only eight died. As far as Hermes was concerned it was eight too many, but without him the death toll for those people would have numbered in the hundreds. The death toll for the camp was seventeen hundred and fifty nine, but there were over eighteen thousand survivors.

Fools' Glory stayed put, but *Perdu* and *Legacy* went to the other two camps in time to stop the local army from attacking them. All tolled there were about fifty thousand people in the three camps.

Once all the refugees were safe – at least for the time being – we called a meeting, linking the main bars of each ship with Kamile at the station. The Startender cadets all took starshots to come down to help. Sheriff asked to sit in. Paddy was about to say no, when I suggested we let him.

"He helped out down there. Let's give him the benefit of the doubt for the moment," I said.

"Okay, Murphy."

Once everyone was ready, Paddy said, "We have to figure out a plan of action."

"Who needs a plan? We going to get the people in charge of this horror show and remove them from power. Maybe drop them off at the North Pole with some supplies and a half-hearted good luck," Nellie said.

"No, you mustn't do that," Sheriff said. "Many countries are already filing formal grievances against your actions here, condemning your invasion of a sovereign nation."

"Well they can all go take a flying..." Nellie said.

"No, they cannot. They are the world powers," Sheriff said. "But neither can you throw away your status as a nation."

"I thought you weren't exactly our biggest fan," I said.

"I most certainly was not, Mr. Murphy. I believed you to be a bunch of hooligans who had strong-armed their way into the UN. But then I saw what you all did here today, the very thing I myself shamefully admit I told you not to do. I spent the last two decades of my life as a diplomat. I became one because I wanted to make the world a better place, but instead the world made me a worse person. The very things I wanted to change instead changed me. But you Startenders, you didn't do what protocol and diplomacy mandated you to do. You did what was right, what needed to be done to save those people, regardless of what it might cost you later. You don't know how wonderful that was for me to see. Every country on Earth will swear up and down that they have the best of intentions, when in reality those who rule most often do so for selfish reasons and personal gain. There is corruption everywhere, except seemingly with you. I was asked by several of my fellow diplomats to do whatever I could, to find whatever could be found, to justify expelling you from the UN."

Bubba Sue slapped her knee. "I told you so!"

"I was wrong. In fact, if you'll let me. I would like to help you fend off all the grievances being filed against you," Sheriff said.

I looked at Paddy. "Looks like there's a new Sheriff in town."

"Hush, Murphy," Paddy said.

"What's the big deal? Lots of countries have invaded other countries, especially the big ones. The United States, Russia, China, they've all done it. What makes them so different than us?" Elsiebelle said.

"They control the world's most powerful militaries and have a large say in what happens with the world economy. And they have nuclear arsenals, which makes each of the others hesitant to go against them. You have no such advantage." Sheriff hesitated. "You don't have nuclear weapons, do you?"

Loki, Paddy, Bubba Sue and I exchanged subtle looks. Many years ago, we had saved Faerie from nuclear annihilation and ended up with two nuclear missile payloads that we've kept hidden and safe.

"We have no nuclear bombs or missiles," Paddy said truthfully. The payloads weren't weaponized.

"Plus they claim you violated the Geneva Protocol and the Chemical Weapons Convention by using gas warfare on enemy combatants."

Kaye laughed. "Those men had just slaughtered over a thousand unarmed innocents. My gas did them no physical harm, although they may have nightmares for the rest of their sad, pathetic lives."

"And since that is true, you may have started a new arms race for chemical weapons that are nonlethal. Back during the conflicts in the Gulf, the United States had developed ultrasonics similar to what you used, but did not widely use them. Now they will no doubt be reviving that particular weapons program as well," Sheriff said.

"Well one thing is certain," Coyote said. He'd just gotten back from doing some recon in the capital. Very few people tend to notice a canine, and even when they do, Coyote has a way of keeping himself hidden. "The new exalted ruler for life has no plans to stop."

"That matches up with what we got from the former ambassador," Kaye said. She had interviewed him and he answered all her questions, between his sobbing. We planned to turn him over to the world court as a war criminal. Jojo's ring had recorded the start of the massacre as did the station's and barships' cameras, so there would be no doubt of his guilt.

"The dictator and his generals are right now formulating the best way to attack the camps and the people. They have gas masks and are not allowing the soldiers to eat for two days before the battle, plus will have them wear adult diapers. We have to get these people out of the country and out of his reach before that happens or we may have to kill some of the soldiers to save the refugees."

"But where can we put fifty thousand people?" Loki said.

"The NYC II can take five hundred or so, but then we're pretty much at our capacity. We can work towards expanding our living space, but it's going to have to come with corresponding space for crops and all the other things we need," Vulcan said.

"I've spoken with Ben City and they've taken a vote. They have room for ten thousand and are willing to take them. With that manpower they will also be able to expand their living area. In a year or two, they'd might be able to take them all, but they just had a large influx of refugees from New York, so their space is limited."

"So basically we have to find homes for forty thousand people," I said. "And do it before this army attacks again."

"I've called all the barships home, so we should be able to hold off the army for the time being, but we don't have the manpower to stay here and watch over these people indefinitely. And we used up most of our emergency supplies during the evacuation of

New York. We're not going to be able to feed that many mouths for long. Coyote's right. We need to get them out of here," Paddy said.

"If you find a place for them to go, we will open a nexus to get them there," Pace said. The other trolls nodded.

"I believe I would be able to vanquish this Army," Xen the robot said. "Their weaponry is primitive."

"But could you do it without killing the soldiers?" I said.

Xen hummed. "There will likely be casualties. But the Startender oath does not say a Startender cannot kill. It states a Startender will not kill except in the direst of circumstances, after all other options have been eliminated."

"We haven't eliminated all options. Yet," Paddy said.

"But the soldiers, at least the ones that attacked this refugee camp have proven themselves to be murderers, slaughterers of the innocent who are willing to partake in genocide. Do they truly deserve to go on living after committing such heinous acts?" Xen said.

"The Startenders aren't in the final judgment business. Anyone can change. People who have done evil things can turn their lives around and do good. And sometimes even find redemption. I speak from experience," Loki said.

"The Startenders stand for a higher ideal, something honorable, noble even. We have advantages that regular folks do not. We will not become murderers and thugs simply because it might be easier," I said.

Xen hummed again. "It is good to see your principles do not get tossed aside at the first sign of difficulty."

"What about all the other countries you got on this planet?" Buzz said. "Can't some of them open up their doors and let them in? I mean, you're all humans after all."

"Unfortunately, it's a lot more complicated than that," Sheriff said.

"It is, but why does is it have to be? There are plenty of countries that allow immigration. If each of them took in a couple thousand, we wouldn't even have an issue," I said.

"But each of those countries has red tape that they are able to hide behind. Laws limiting numbers that they can use to justify turning people like this away," Sheriff said.

"So then we will simply ask very nicely," Paddy said.

And we did. And our request for asylum for the refugees was turned down unilaterally. Several of the more powerful countries used the excuse of our unlawful incursion and alleged war crimes as their justification.

We reconvened again in the hope of finding another way.

"We could simply drop them off in each country with a film crew like they were filming a reality TV show," Kaye Chandler said.

"I can rig up cameras that would fly around and follow them," Bubba Sue said.

"But the governments would simply gather them up and deport them back here to the country that wants to kill them," Bast said.

Loki and I exchanged a smile. "The Reaper's idea…"

"Kaye, please."

"Nope, you put the mask back on," I said.

"Habit," she said. "But it's off now."

"Too late," Loki said with a grin. "The idea about reality TV has some merit."

"Exactly. There's nothing a politician hates more than bad publicity. Maybe we take those cameras and we have them film the leaders of each country being asked to take in refugees, right after we show footage of the horrors that they've endured. We mix in footage of the army amassing against them, maybe even some footage of the supreme exalted leader promising to wipe them out. They will have a hard time turning them down while all the world is watching," I said.

"It's a good idea, Dad, but what network is going to be brave enough to carry it? And we'd need lots of networks to carry it," Elsiebelle said.

"Kim Irons is our staunchest defender. We could approach her with the idea," Paddy said.

Kim Irons was one of the people chosen to wear a Startender Affiliate ring so we simply called her up and asked.

"I'm sorry, Paddy, but the network would never go for it, but I'm still willing to help you out. I can make appointments with all the leaders for interviews as a way to get you in there. I'll probably get fired, but me losing my job is a lot better than those people being killed," Kim said.

"Thank you. And if they fire ye, we've got television programming up on the station, so we can at least offer ye gainful employment."

"At what I'm making now?" Kim said with a smile.

Paddy chuckled. Kim Irons was the highest-paid newscaster ever. "Nowhere near it. We understand if you don't want to."

"A year ago, I'd probably never said this, but there's some things more important than money. You Startenders have shown me that. I'm in for whatever you need me to do," Kim said.

"That still leaves us with the problem of how do we get it on TV? The Internet is an option. I suppose, but it's hard to get everybody to watch it at once," Nellie said. "And for this to work we need instant shaming."

I met Paddy's eyes. "We can use the SEBS."

"Murphy, you know we developed that in case of planetary invasion or another global catastrophe. We didn't even use it for the evacuation of New York."

"You have any other options?"

"I can ask my world if she would allow the influx," Jan said.

"There are other worlds that might take some refugees," Pace said.

"Which would put them someplace totally alien; where they would have no money, no resources and be unable to communicate with the natives. It's better than dying, but I think they'd be best served staying on Earth," Loki said.

"Exactly what does this SEBS do?" Sheriff said.

"It short for the Startenders Emergency Broadcast System. It will cut into all communications worldwide, from televisions to phones, tablets, computers and even more primitive things like radios. We'll be able to control all the media on Earth," Loki said.

"That won't help you in the UN, I can tell you that," Sheriff said. "However, if instead of shaming the leaders you manage to make them look like heroes by helping you, then there would be no official repercussions, although there would be resentment for many years to follow."

"Now were talking. How do we do it?" I said.

"If any of them give us trouble, there is no reason we can't mention that we might spill a little dirt," Bast said. For hundreds of years, the cat goddess has run an intelligent gathering network on Earth and beyond. Apparently anything seen by any cat, especially black cats, is something that she can find out. And several black cats may actually be her offspring actively spying for her. James Bond's got nothing on Bast. "We've got enough on every world leader to ensure that they'd have to leave office."

"Are you saying that you plan to blackmail the leaders of the world?" Sheriff said.

"Blackmail is such an ugly word. It implies that we're doing something wrong for personal gain. What we're doing is holding off using information that could hurt these people as a thank you for them doing the right thing. Hardly the same thing at all," Paddy said.

Sheriff turned to Jan. "As I understand it, your very physiology can tell if something is right or wrong."

"That's an over simplification. A karman's body can tell if their actions will harm another. And in this case, these actions will hopefully stop harm. As far as I am concerned, the plan is a go," Jan said. I looked again. I still couldn't tell if she had reversed the power drainer.

"Very good, Jan. First, we ask nicely on and on camera while making them look good. Then we play hardball," Paddy said.

"As much as I had to admit it, my intelligence confirms what Coyote said. We have two days before the dictator plans his first attack," Bast said.

"Then let's get this done today," Paddy said.

"There's another diplomatic sticking point," Sheriff said. "Since we do not have the permission of the country the refugees are in, the other leaders can use that as an excuse to refuse so as not to violate the sovereignty of another nation. The first thing we needed was the supreme exalted dictator for life to rubberstamp the whole thing."

We sent messages and made overtures, all of which were soundly rejected. In fact, we were told to get out of his country.

Nellie offered to force him to give us permission, but Sheriff pleaded with us not to kidnap or threaten him.

"I bet my crew can make him leave the palace voluntarily," I said.

"And what about the threatening?" Sheriff said.

"There are ways to work around the technical aspects of it," I said.

Sheriff actually smiled. "Diplomats live by technicalities. And that bastard ordered genocide. Go get him."

So off we went to get the equivalent of fifty thousand field trip permission slips signed by a genocidally bent megalomaniac with an entire army protecting him. Fortunately, it is amazingly easy for a flying golf ball-sized object to sneak into most places. Despite all the soldiers with automatic weapons stationed at every door and hallway, none were on duty inside the ventilation ducts. The dictator had closed himself off from the rest of his advisers, telling them he had to consider matters, when all he was really doing was watching porn. He seemed rather bored by it too.

It was kind of him to make our plan just that much easier. His office had a bedroom with several feet of thick cinder block surrounding it. There were no windows. The door itself was two inch-thick steel. The dictator for life officially claimed it was his relaxation room, when in reality – at least according to Bast's intelligence – it was where he had young women brought in to satisfy his needs on a daily basis. We turned the ship into the shape of a matching door and opened it slowly. We didn't make a sound and instead blew air from the doorway into his office. To make matters more interesting, Savannah was standing in the doorway. The she-satyr was generating all the mystic pheromones she could muster and our artificial breeze was helping them invade his office. It didn't take a mage to figure out when the pheromones reached the dictator's nostrils. There was a quite obvious physical reaction, which was Savannah's cue to introduce herself.

"Hi there, big boy."

The dictator for life turned around with a bit of a start, even reaching for his sidearm until he saw the she-satyr standing there in a négligée that left little to the imagination as it afforded little protection against light or temperature.

The dictator for life's pupils went wide. Some primal instinct caused him to rise and move toward Savannah. "I didn't know my people had arranged company for me so early today. Had I known, I surely would've joined you sooner," he said, wiping the drool off his chin. When Savannah worked her magic, men seemed oblivious to her hooves and furry legs. True, she kept the fur trimmed neat and short, but it still seems like something that would give a man pause. Not to mention the small tail and horns she sported.

None of it fazed the dictator for life, as his eyes hadn't moved off her chest.

"Would you like to come with me?" Savannah said.

"I would love to come with you," the dictator said, laughing as his own little joke. He could laugh all he wanted as that comment proved we weren't kidnapping the bastard.

Savannah stepped inside our ship. The dictator for life followed and we quietly closed the door behind them.

The dictator for life reached out to touch Savannah and she slapped his hand away playfully. "Somebody still has on too much clothing."

"Is it me?" the dictator said with childlike enthusiasm.

Savannah nodded her head and the dictator for life shed his clothing in mere seconds, leaving on only a pair of black men's dress socks.

Savannah stepped through another door. The dictator for life was so horny that not only did he not notice Savannah's horns, but he followed her into a corridor, never once stopping to think that the room he was supposed to be in didn't have another exit.

Savannah stayed just far enough ahead of him for him to smell her, but not so far that he lost sight of her, giving us more time to achieve some altitude.

The chase finally ended on an open air deck twenty-five thousand feet above the Earth.

Savannah came and stood next to me, leaning on my shoulder and wrapping her arms around my neck. She laid her head on my shoulder. Loki stood by my other side with Coyote next to him.

"Welcome to the barship *Fools' Glory*. I'm the head honcho, John Murphy. And you are the Supreme Exalted Dictator for Life.

A bit long. Mind if I call you Dicky for short?"

Savannah looked down at the mostly naked man. "Definitely for short."

Dicky had no shame or reaction to being the one wearing the least clothes in the room.

"This is my crew. I hope you weren't sexually harassing Savannah here, but we'll give you some sensitivity training later. First, we have a very important question for you. Would you give the refugees permission to emigrate to other countries, please and thank you?"

"If I do, then will you give me your word that I get her for my bed?" Dicky said.

I cringed at how he phrased it. The whole keeping our word thing came right into play. "I hoped you would do it out of the goodness of your heart."

Dicky laughed. "I do nothing from the goodness of my heart." He stopped and pointed with both hands at another body part that was upright and excited. "For the goodness of other parts of me, I would do a great many things."

"Murphy, I'll do it," Savannah said, but without the playful joy in which she normally approached sex.

I took her hands from around my neck, held them in my own, and looked her in the eye. "But do you want to?"

"No, but to get those refugees out –"

I shook my head. "Then it's not an option."

Dicky laughed. "I wouldn't have done it anyway. If I'm not going to be satisfied, I will simply leave." The dictator turned to go back the way he'd just came only there was a dragon's head blocking the door, her jaws open to show off her large teeth.

"Hello and welcome," Riga said pleasantly.

Dicky backed away, realized he was headed toward us and turned until he stood at the end of the open deck. Dicky stopped and looked over the edge. "That's a long way down."

Coyote moved so he was at Dicky's groin level. Dicky spun and the trickster gave a series of ferocious barks. Both Dicky's hands moved to cover his manhood and he took a step backwards and off the edge of our ship.

As he plummeted he began to scream.

Coyote leaned his head over the deck and shouted at the falling and rather noisy naked man. "I'm sorry, you mustn't speak canine. Translated that means watch your step."

"Eric, pursue," I said. The deck extruded further from the ship and the flooring molded around our feet to keep us from slipping or falling. It took us a few thousand feet to catch up to Dicky who was going down head first, waving his arms and legs in an enthusiastic, yet doomed, attempt to fly.

"Hey Dicky, I hate to interrupt you during free fall, but I was wondering if you had rethought letting the refugees leave the country?" I said as Eric matched his speed with us below and slightly to the side of the falling dictator. I held up a piece of paper. "All you have to do is sign this piece of paper and let us record your statement giving us your permission."

I held out a clipboard and a pen. Dicky tossed both away, laughing.

"Excuse us. I think that was our only pen," I said, nodded toward the camera for Eric to follow the pen and paper.

Dicky started screaming again as he realized he was falling alone again.

Loki leaned in and whispered in my ear, "Nicely done. I assume we have another pen."

"Of course." I nodded back at the camera and we resumed our position below Dicky."

"We caught it. Not sure if we'd be able to do it again before you reached the ground though." Again I held pen and paper beneath the inverted man. "Sign here please."

Dicky scribbled his name on the line.

"Thank you, Dicky." I nodded to Loki who shape-shifted until he was four times his normal height. He grabbed Dicky by the ankles and Eric slowed the barship and used our dampening fields to bleed off his momentum before my honcho pulled him inside the ship.

Eric had already formed a desk near the edge. Loki sat him behind it so nobody watching it would be subject to the full frontal Dicky.

"Now if you'll give us that video statement," I said.

Dicky glared at me with hate in his eyes. "Go to hell!" Dicky stood, but when he went to turn, the floor behind him had retracted right up to his chair and the desk curved so there was no way to walk around it. If Dicky took a step he'd fall off again.

The man actually growled as he turned toward the camera. "Fine. I hereby give permission for the refugees to leave my county so long as it is done in the next twenty four hours. Now take me back to my palace."

"Certainly. All you had to do was ask, although adding a please and a thank you would have shown much better manners. Now let's talk about what sexual harassment is and why it is wrong," I said.

Sheriff would have been proud. Not once did we verbally threaten the man or tell him we wouldn't save him unless we got what we wanted. And of course, Dicky didn't ask to be returned to his office, only the palace.

We dropped the Supreme Exalted Dictator for Life buck naked, save for his dark socks, right in the middle of the courtyard where many of his troops were running drills to prepare for their killing run against the refugees.

As we took off, Savannah blew Dicky a kiss and threw his clothes after him. If was hardly her fault that they got stuck on the roof of the palace.

At least that was my story and we were sticking to it.

Twenty four hours wasn't much time so we didn't waste any of it. We chose forty countries, leaving out those with poor human rights track records, although to be fair there were allegations from Charles Barrel that we belonged on that list, although I suspected that Sheriff was going to tell the UN that they were unfounded.

We'd royally pissed Dicky off, so we couldn't risk moving the barships away from the refugee camps and leave them unprotected. In fact, as the other barships returned to Earth, we redeployed them to the camps as back up.

We decided to bring our requests directly to the world leaders via the Hermes express, popping in unexpectedly on each leader once they were alone or as close to it as we could get.

I took the President of the United States. As much as I was a Startender, I was also an American. I believed in my heart that despite politics, the United States would always do the right thing. My mind believed different, so I had made it sit quietly in the corner.

I was very polite, waiting until he both flushed the toilet and washed his hands before moving the shower curtain aside to let him know I was there. "Mr. President...."

"Who are you? How did you get past the Secret Service?" His eyes flashed to the badge on my chest. "You're John Murphy, one of the human Startenders. Good work on the New York thing, but why the hell are you here in my bathroom?"

"Mr. President, you know the situation we are currently involved in. There are fifty thousand refugees who will be slaughtered if we don't get them out."

"Nonsense. The Startenders seem to be doing a good job of keeping them safe. You should have issued a statement claiming they have weapons of mass destruction. It's an oldie but a goodie. Probably would still work. As for the refugees, take them off to your space station or Ben City on the moon."

"We've accounted for over ten thousand by doing just that, but we simply don't have the resources to take them all. So we are asking forty nations to each take one thousand of the refugees."

"We can't go against a sovereign nation's wishes regarding its own citizens."

"We've got the dictator's blessing so long as it's done today," I said.

"Sorry, but it's not enough time. There are processes in place, procedures that need to be followed."

"Sir, the President of the United States has the power to grant asylum and get around all that red tape." I held up a camera, which floated out of my hand. "We'll be going live with this in five minutes."

The president chuckled. "Live where, son? The Internet? Moon TV?"

As if on cue, his phone started beeping and wouldn't stop.

"No, sir. Everywhere on Earth that can carry a signal. Go ahead and check your phone and you'll see what I'm talking about."

As he pulled it out of his pocket the face of Kimberly Irons was looking back at him.

"This is Kimberly Irons with a special report on the Startenders Emergency Broadcast System regarding the dire situation in…"

"What the hell is this?" the president said.

"The largest broadcast in the history of mankind," I said. "Turn it up."

He did.

"Tens of thousands of people are at risk of being killed as part of that nation's genocide program." The screen went to the satellite images of the soldiers attacking and slaughtering the refugees. It was high quality, like someone was there. Since we were hitting every device on Earth with the broadcast, we tried to keep things as PG-13 as possible while still showing enough to cause outrage in the viewers. That was also Kim's job, guiding them with her commentary.

The scene changed, showing the Startenders stepping in to save them. I felt a little too much time was spent on me, especially playing up me getting shot, but it wasn't my call to make.

Dicky's message giving us 24 hours played next.

"As our viewers just heard and saw, there is an extremely small window to get these people to safety. A year ago, it simply couldn't be done in that minuscule amount of time, but the Startenders led the evacuation of New York and they will lead yet another evacuation for these people. After the evacuation of New York, the United States and others, including Ben City and Startender Station –" Apparently Startender Station played better than the NYC II, so we maintained the dual name. "– have been working hard to make new homes for these refugees. In the past, there have been far too many instances of genocide and for far too many of those times, the world has not learned of them in time to prevent them. Imagine a world where the Nazi and Soviet death camps had not slaughtered millions. One in which the Armenians still had a country, where Rwanda did not have countryman butchering countryman. There are sadly too many more examples to list.

But yesterday, the Startenders stepped in to protect three United Nations refugee camps. They were too late to stop the slaughter of almost two thousand unarmed men, women and children, but they arrived in time to save fifty thousand more. Now those people need a home where they do not have to worry about soldiers coming to kill them in the dead of night, while they and their children sleep.

"I, like many of you, feel blessed to live in this magical time in human history, where so many have banned together as Startenders, working to live up to the ideals of doing what is right and helping others.

"And it is not just the Startenders working to live up to these ideals. As a reporter, I am reminded of the shortcomings of how countries around the globe conduct the business of government. But today, over forty countries have put aside those shortcomings, put aside politics as usual to instead work together alongside the Startenders to do the right thing, to save these fifty thousand people from becoming yet another tragedy for the rest of us to hear about on the news."

As Kim continued her spiel, I turned to the president. "Like the lady said, this is your chance to do the right thing in the eyes of the entire world. Everything that can carry a video or sound signal is carrying this broadcast. You will be the first world leader to speak." Paddy and Ben City would be in the first ten countries to speak, but we let the world powers go ahead of us. Sheriff convinced us it was the diplomatic thing to do. "Mr. President, your example here today will help guide the leaders that speak after you. You will help give hope to the people of America and the world that those that run their governments might actually care about the little guy. It can be the start of a golden age for humanity. Or at the very least, save the lives of fifty thousand people. So what is it going to be? You can be the first world leader to offer asylum to these people or be the first one who turns them down. Of course, that would show the world that you are a man willing to let a thousand people die just to allow politics as usual. I doubt any of the world leaders will be willing to risk that on what will be the single most viewed event in human history.

"Murphy you're live in thirty seconds," Bubba Sue said over

my badge.

"Think about how this is going to play come reelection time. You will be the man who led the world to do the right thing. You have one minute to talk before the feed goes to the Russians."

"Only a thousand people? And you Startenders will deliver them?"

"Lock, stock, and barrel, sir. All you have to do is agree and inspire the world to follow your example."

"Do I have to do it from the bathroom?"

I smiled. "Only if you want to, sir."

We stepped out into the Oval Office and the president sat behind his desk. The floating camera followed. A black cat rubbed against the president's legs, then walked out and gave me a wink. Bast's spy network in action.

Bubba Sue was back on my badge. "Murphy, the president is on in 5, 4, 3, 2, 1…"

The president didn't even need the full countdown to put on his game face and the smile that helped win a majority of the voters in the last election.

"My fellow Americans and citizens of the planet Earth, let me be the first to pledge the resources of the United States of America toward helping to prevent a horrible travesty of justice and stop this terrible genocide from happening. Despite the fact that the United States is itself overwhelmed with refugees from the destruction of New York, we shall not turn a blind eye to others in their hour of need. The United States will not only take in the asked for one thousand victims of this horrible war, but as president, I hereby pledge that, should any of my fellow leaders be unable to accept the thousand they have been asked to take in for whatever reason, that the United States of America will take these tired and these poor souls and bring them to the land of the free and the home of the brave. And I would like to personally thank the Startenders for stepping in and getting to those camps before the rest of us could arrive there to help them prevent a senseless tragedy. This administration was of course on board from the moment we received word of this tragedy and the risk of the loss of so many lives. America is always there to stand for the right and I'm all too happy that we will be able to help these thousand men, women and children towards continued life, liberty and the pursuit of happiness in this great country."

"Thank you, Mr. President," Kim Irons said over the camera. "And now we go live to the Kremlin."

"Murphy, you're clear," Bubba Sue said.

"I thought she said Kremlin, not gremlin," I said.

"Bye Murphy." I couldn't see her, but I knew Bubba Sue was rolling her eyes before she cut off our link.

The president stood and walked over next to me. He looked down at his phone to see his Russian counterpart do his best to give an even better speech.

I held up my hand. The president shook it. "Thank you, Mr. President."

"You're welcome, but should you or your Startenders ever again try a stunt like this in order to make me change my policies, I promise that I'll have your balls for a necklace." He was squeezing my hand like he was trying to break it. I squeezed back, using the gravity altering abilities of the badge to make me seem like a powerhouse. I eased up when I saw the president's knees start to buckle.

"Two things, Mr. President. One, when we first asked you to do the right thing, you didn't want to bother, so don't even try to come off as high and mighty. You needed this stunt to encourage you to do the right thing." There was banging on the Oval Office doors. I guess the Secret Service realized something was going on with the president and they didn't know what it was. "Two, the Startenders have a simple policy – you come after one of us, you come after all of us and we will do worse to you than you tried to do to us. And make no mistake, if you try to hurt my people or my station, I'll be the one making the jewelry."

"Just one minute…"

"And a third thing. You seem to have forgotten that we're still recording." The president stopped short and looked at the floating camera. A few months earlier, he had made a series of embarrassing remarks at a world conference when he didn't realize his collar microphone was on. "I'm not sure why you would state that you told a bunch of lies in what will likely be the defining speech of your administration and what history will most remember you for."

The president took out a handkerchief and wiped it across his forehead. "You wouldn't actually..."

"No, we wouldn't, Mr. President, unless we had to in self-defense because of an attack. But if you continue what we started here today, you can be the type of president that the American people actually deserve, not the kind that is bought and paid for by donors. Imagine what you could accomplish. It would be spectacular. You could work to make this nation truly great again."

"It's not that simple."

"No, it's not, but let's be honest – have you even tried? Really and truly? I've seen your speeches back when you were first running for Congress. That man believed he could make America a better place. What happened to him?" The president looked down at his shoes.

"I think that man would make an incredible president. Please think about it." The Secret Service's pounding on the door got louder. I think they had found something to use as a battering ram. "Don't worry, I'll show myself out." I tapped my badge once and said, "Hermes, I'm ready for pickup."

The president went and opened the door. One of his advisors and largest donors ran in. "What the hell do you think you were doing on a live broadcast without consulting us first?"

The president stared the man down. "The right thing. And you know what? If you don't like it, you and your money can leave."

The president turned. I smiled and gave him a thumbs up.

An instant later my ride arrived and it looked like I disappeared.

Our plan was going amazingly well. Every one of the forty countries ended up agreeing to help before going on camera, although a few were unable to take the full thousand. Our calls to the president assured us he'd make good on his word when he offered to pick up the slack. Several others did the same, so we were going to make it.

We'd begun the evacuations during the broadcast. Less chance for anyone to change their minds that way. Most of the countries did not want barships invading their airspace, so everyone was traveling by troll. Creating forty separate nexi in a short period of time was a lot for the four trolls we had. Loki could have helped, but we had him standing by in troll form in case the limba of any of the others became low enough to risk them going primitive.

We just worked smarter. For instance, we opened up one portal midway on the Rainbow Bridge. Not the one that formally went to the now destroyed Asgard – Ragnarok didn't leave much of that bridge. The one I'm talking about was between the Canadian and American sides of Niagara Falls. We used the same strategy on the borders of several other countries.

Dicky, like most of the people on Earth, had seen the broadcast and was none too happy. After the whole being naked in front of his troops incident earlier, he was already a tad upset. In order to save face, he ordered his troops to again attack the three refugee camps ahead of schedule.

The soldiers who attacked earlier and were chased off by the Reaper's fear gas and the ultrasonics were not recovered enough to go back out onto the battlefield. The rest of his army seemed hesitant to follow the orders for fear they'd end up the same way, so they were advancing slowly. Taking baby steps and pausing every few feet, each of them looking for an excuse to slow down. That or this army had the worst shoelaces ever made, because ten seconds didn't go by without one soldier stopping to tie his boots and ten or twenty more waiting for him to finish.

"Hermes, can you do something about this army," I said. "They still have lots of weapons and it'll be hours before we get all the refugees out of harm's way.

"Like what Murphy? Knock each and every one of them out? There are limits to even what I can do. And right now I'm more exhausted than I've ever been. Doing surgery on all those patients drained me. I should've slept for a few days –" Hermes didn't like it to be known, but after a large use of power, he was often exhausted and had to rest in real time, practically dead to the world. It was why he was often elsewhere when we needed him. " – but I couldn't or the plan to get all of you in and out of all the capitals wouldn't have worked. Now I'll be comatose for weeks." A week to Hermes is like years to the rest of us. "It'll be months before I'm fit to go back out on explorer duty. At times like this I wish caffeine worked on me. The only good thing is I've actually slowed down a bit, which means the rest of the world's moving a little bit more my speed. Without the null zone in Bulfinche's, it's been hard to slow down enough to keep up with the rest of you slowpokes."

"If you hadn't done any of that, would you have been able to get all the guns away from them?" I said.

Hermes shrugged. "If anybody else but you and Paddy asked me that, I'd say sure, no problem. But the truth? Doing that would have drained me just as much."

"So you need an influx of manna?" I said. Manna is the stuff that keeps the gods in existence. Without it they fade away to oblivion.

"I'm in no danger of fading away, Murphy, but sure manna would heal me up pretty quick. Even I'm not going to waste what I have on that. I don't want to end up like Negral." The former Hell's Detective had on at least two occasions used up all his manna to save others. The first occasion landed him in Hell. The second didn't turn out as well.

The final leader was giving his speech. The broadcast was in split screen, showing the refugees already starting to move out.

"I think I may have a way to get some for you."

"Murphy, I know you believe, but that isn't exactly going to fill my tank," Hermes said.

"Shush. Watch and be awed by the amazing Murphy at work." I hit my badge so the hologram of Bubba Sue working the control room popped out. "Hey Bubba Sue."

"Little busy here, Murph," she said.

"And you're about to get a little busier. You know about the situation down here, right?"

"The army attacking. Very slowly. With luck, the refugees should be gone before they get close enough to fire a shot," she said.

"Not true. Snipers could start taking shots, but it would have to be a lucky one to get past the barships we have morphed into a fort. However, I have a plan that might ensure they couldn't fire a shot, lucky or otherwise, but I need your help to get us the power to do it."

"What you need, Murphy?" I told her my plan. "Murphy, I could kiss you."

"Maybe later, if Vulcan's okay with it." He usually was. The gremlin was extremely affectionate with hugs and kisses, but anything else was reserved for her hubby. "Make sure Kim plays it up big time, mentioning Hermes' name constantly."

"You're going to make the other gods in the Startenders jealous, Murphy," Bubba Sue said.

"They'll get over it. Right, Hermes?" I said, turning to something I'd never seen before. Hermes was staring at me, totally still, his mouth open. The staring and mouth weren't new, but Hermes was always moving, even when he stood still. Think of him as a god with ADHD on a double espresso in a room full of shiny objects. Some part of him was always moving, even if it was too fast to break the illusion of him standing still. This time Hermes was actually still as a statue.

Not that it lasted long. To me anyway. Probably was the equivalent of several minutes to him.

"Murphy, I don't know what to say."

"You saved that baby girl and the rest of those people. Think of this as my little way of saying thank you. Plus, since I'm arranging for the single most impressive short term acquisition of manna ever, I'm assuming you're willing to donate the excess to the manna bank?"

"Of course," Hermes said.

Vulcan, Sun Wukong the monkey king and Bast were three of the few gods to figure out a way to not be dependent on manna, although Vulcan did devise a way to store and dispense it to gods that needed it. Paddy did the same at Bulfinche's Pub, but he didn't have anywhere near as much to share. After this stunt, the bank would have lots.

There was live footage of the refugees leaving for Russia, Great Britain, France and Australia when Kim Irons' face returned to the split screen.

"The crisis has been averted, so let's show the viewers some of what the Startenders did to save the wounded when they came on the scene, particularly one Startender – the Greco-Roman god

Hermes. Hermes has always been fast, but what he did that day was nothing short of miraculous."

The Startenders Emergency Broadcast System ran footage of Hermes operating simultaneously on the hundreds of wounded. By this point, most of the people on Earth were watching or listening.

To create manna, someone needs to believe in, or at least know about the existence of a god. For the first time in human history, there was documented proof of one and he was doing things that only a supernatural being could do. Everybody watching now knew. And they believed that he could do it. None of them worshipped him, but the belief in his existence and his power created so much manna for him that Hermes actually began to glow.

"Bubba Sue, get ready to film the fastest and most effective disarmament in history. Hermes, stop every so often so the cameras can pick you up."

On the screen, Kim made a show of touching her ear. "I've just been informed that the very forces that attempted the slaughter earlier are again on the march toward the evacuating camps in an effort to prevent the refugees from leaving. Their dictator's plans for genocide apparently are not over. I bring you live footage now from the battlefield."

Hermes took off into the air. On each of the three battlefields he was seen taking guns away from the soldiers, but just a few. The rest of them seemed to vanish between the blink of an eye. The world watched and believed even more in what Hermes could do.

I was told by the end of the broadcast, he had more manna than all the other divinities in the Startenders combined.

"This is amazing. We have just witnessed a country's entire military being disarmed in a matter of minutes. I've been told there is an emergency session of the United Nations being scheduled with the intention of sending in advisors in hopes of encouraging democratic elections and demanding the dictator surrender himself to the world court to be tried for war crimes."

That would be nice, but we'd have to wait and see if they actually did it. We'd be happy to deliver him ourselves.

"The crisis has been averted and a genocide prevented. I would like to personally thank the Startenders and all the leaders of the world for giving the rest of us hope for a better world and a brighter tomorrow. They have proved that we can all work together. On another note, we will be broadcasting a Startenders channel on the Internet." In fact, Kamile had been fielding offers from other content providers to carry one. "The address is on your screen below. We now return you to your regularly scheduled programming."

We saved a lot of people. Jojo and the ones he was looking out for relocated to the station. I wouldn't be surprised if he one day became a Startender himself. We also took in the infant girl whose name we found out was Innocence. We have several families vying to adopt her.

We'd both pissed off and made a lot of world leaders grateful at the same time. And after Hermes' show of power, made them very worried. We'd have to see how all that played out. And our manna bank was full for the foreseeable future

All in all, it was an amazing day. Even Dr. Sheriff had applied for residency on Startender Station and to be part of our diplomatic team. We were going to take him up on it.

The Startenders were created to save the people of New York in the short term and to help others on our world and beyond in the long term. Now it actually looked like we might be able to change our world for the better.

Over the door of Bulfinche's Pub, there was a saying in Gaelic, Maireann dóchas is gliodar. Translated it means hope and happiness never die. There have been times of late that they seemed to be on life support. With luck, they'd make a full recovery and spread all around our world. Corny? Yep, but I've been called worse. And honestly, if things were a little more corny, we might all be a bit better off.

UPSTREAM

"So all we do is sit here and play bar?" Buzz said. "Seems kind of anticlimactic, especially having spent all that time going through Startender Academy."

"Back on Earth we helped a lot of people who showed up at Bulfinche's Pub," I said. The Startenders had sent a team to renovate the place while Buzz and the rest were at the station. The Watering Hole was much nicer than it had been under the previous management.

"In case you ain't noticed, this isn't Earth. It's Travan. The odds of somebody who needs help finding us on a world this crowded is astronomical. I didn't sign on just to play bartender."

"No, you had to be convinced and coerced," Randor said. The troll leaned back and put his feet up on a table.

"That may be true, but I did sign on for a chance to explore new worlds from the safety of a barship, not to stay on the same old world in yet another barroom.

"Does he ever stop complaining?" Riga said to Randor.

"We've been hanging out together for most of the time since the Karma affair and if that time is any example, nope," Randor said.

"Besides one aspect of your barship serves as your office here," I said.

"Actually it's my office," Kamile said. "At least until such time as I judge Buzz ready to assume the mantle of head honcho of the *Bitter End*. And I still strongly suggest changing the name."

"Nope, because we agreed to be Startenders to the bitter end. And with all this butting noses in others' business, it will likely be," Buzz said.

"But..." Kamile said.

I held up my hand. "First head honcho to command a barship gets to name it. That's the rule."

"Technically, I'm the first," Kamile said.

"You're the interim head honcho. Unless you've changed your mind about a full time command?"

"No. I don't wish to lead regularly," she said.

"That's another thing. How the heck did you people determine I was leadership material? That makes the nature of the organization suspect right there," Buzz said.

Recruits – and at one point all of us were recruits – go through an extensive amount of testing, both psychological and otherwise before they become Startenders. Then there is a little thing called gut instinct. Buzz complained and whined a great deal, but when push came to shove despite his personal fears and apprehensions, he's always done the right thing, regardless of personal risk. Because of his diminished size, he's developed keen survival instincts and is very protective of those he cares for. When the time comes, he'll make a good head honcho.

Kamile also passed all those tests, but turned down her own barship. She preferred helping out behind-the-scenes. I've said it before and I'll say it again – the kobold had come a long way. She was raised from infancy by a man who abused her in all manners of horrid ways. My old friend Fred rescued her and she ended up working with us at Bulfinche's Pub. Back then she could barely make eye contact. Now she was an administrative force of nature.

"Not only will I have to command a barship, but I've got to run an actual bar. I have no clue how to do that," Buzz said.

"Fortunately, I do. I'll stay long enough to get everything set up and train all of you. Then you're on your own," Kamile said.

"So basically if someone in trouble ever comes to us, we detach the barship from the bar proper and go off and help them, leaving the bar unguarded. I'm thinking that's a bad idea. This is still Travan. On most worlds, thieves swipe vehicles. Here they steal buildings. Undefended real estate has a tendency to change hands."

"We have the headless bouncer team," I said.

"Yeah, the bodies of the warez robots. Not making me warm or fuzzy, Murph. How do we know they won't go back under the control of the killer robot heads?"

"Because I told you I removed the telemetry controller," Xen said. "And it was triple checked by Vulcan and Bubba Sue. And the three of us designed a new operating system that isn't even compatible with the old heads."

"And you have Xen's reputation. And we've installed a host of non-lethal security measures," I said.

"And we have the old man as the head bouncer," Kyna said.

It was more than a little amusing to watch Thunder Jack get so offended at being called old. Despite being around thousands of years, he didn't like anyone thinking he was old. When they met, Kyna started off addressing him as Gramps, which aggravated him big time. It got a little better when she explained that as Hermes' daughter, the god formerly known as Zeus was her actual grandfather.

Kyna has similar, albeit slower, abilities as her dad. She'd been one of the crew assigned to renovate the place. Kyna had spent all her free time talking to her grandfather and learn more about their family history.

"Fine, so maybe no one will walk off with the building, but expecting me to believe that someone will just walk in off the street with a legitimate need for our help that's not some scam is a little bit far-fetched," Buzz said.

As if on cue, the front door opened and the security system flared to life. Vulcan, Bubba Sue and Xen had designed it to pick up armament, as well as any other weapons of destruction, including but not limited to, the magical or biological.

In walked a vaguely humanoid creature, at least from the waist to the neck. Walked may not have been the best term, but I didn't have a better one in English. The guy didn't have legs per say, but appendages that were reminiscent of tentacles and performed locomotion by some form of cilia-like movement. There were also tentacles encircling his head, as well as three on the end of each arm in place of hands and fingers.

The gray tentacled creature bellied up to the bar, making some sort of high-pitched squeaking noise, his race's version of speech. Our Startender badges were able to translate.

"I need to get drunk, so then I can die."

I'd gone through this scenario a hundred times or more from behind the bar at Bulfinche's Pub. I had to stop myself from stepping in. Buzz and Randor were the bartenders here. They needed to take care of it.

"I'm more than happy to help you with the drunk part, but we rather frown upon the dying part here," Buzz said, matching the guy's language and making all our ears hurt.

"Surely things can't be that dark," Randor said.

The creature tilted his head, surprised. "How is it that I understand you when you don't speak the language of the Cron?"

Randor pointed to the gold strip the guy was leaning on. It lined the bar as well as the walls with branches at many of the tables. "There's a fleck of a lation stone embedded in the metal."

Certain metals including gold were able to conduct the magic so touching them while they were in contact with the stone produced the same effect. It was a feature very few other bars offered, even on Travan.

The creature nodded its head, I can only assume impressed. "That is a simple question for someone whose race is not on the verge of extinction."

Even if he wasn't the only customer, that last line would have gotten the attention of everyone in the bar.

Kamile stepped forward as if to take charge. She'd worked her way up from waitress to bartender too and her instincts were kicking in. I shook my head no and pointed with my eyes to Buzz. She nodded, remembering as the temporary head honcho, she was there to help ease Buzz into his new position. Until then, he was her honcho.

We both wanted to see how he would do.

"How is it that the Cron are on the verge of extinction? I thought you numbered in the millions and could survive the rigors of space without protection," Buzz said.

"Both true. Every generation, Cron return to the spawning world to create the next generation. Our world is our mother. She calls to us across the void to come home. We had our time to enjoy the universe. Now it is our time to create and raise the next generation. Only now the path home is disrupted."

"By what?" Buzz said.

"The Goblin Empire."

"Wow. That really sucks for you," Buzz said.

I rolled my eyes. "Buzz, this is the type of thing Startenders help with, remember?"

Buzz sighed. "Which means it sucks for us too. The Goblin

Empire is the single most powerful force in this part of the galaxy. No way we're going to intimidate or outmuscle them."

"So we'll have to outthink them," I said.

Buzz looked at me and squinted. "Murphy, you're actually excited by this."

"This will be our first time out in the big wide galaxy outside of Travan. I am excited."

"You should be nervous. The goblins are not known for their merciful ways," Buzz said.

"What if we just smuggle the Cron around the goblins and back to their home planet?" Kyna said.

The Cron turned his whole body side to side, which I assume was his equivalent of a no. "Without the swim through space to our home, there will be no next generation. We need the time to prepare and interact. We need it for..." The Cron seemed at a loss for words.

Not everybody else was in the same predicament.

"For foreplay," Savannah said. The she-satyr viewed the entire universe with sex colored goggles, but that didn't mean she was always wrong about the motivation of others.

"Yes," the Cron said.

"The question is what does the empire want the Cron for? Old Big Nose didn't get to be one of the most powerful gods in the universe shy of the creator just by killing the rest of his pantheon," Loki said. "He usually has a reason for everything he does."

"How is it the Cron can travel through space?" Riga said, trying to get her mind around it. "In my dragon form I'm tough, but I still couldn't survive in space without my Startender badge."

"Our physiology has two states. In space, we form a hard exoshell which can absorb cosmic rays and other energy for nourishment and propulsion." Made sense. We had a fungus on Earth that fed off gamma radiation. "That wouldn't be enough to travel between systems. At the time of the spawning, Mother Cron calls to us. On the journey, she lends us some of her power, which lets us swim not only in the void, but between folds in the very universe. We jump from system to system, joining with other Cron. The process repeats itself until there are millions of us dancing between the stars."

"A planet with the power to transport millions through space. That'd be enough reason for old Big Nose to get involved," Coyote said.

"Communication with a planetary intelligence is quite difficult," I said. Loki had tried with the planet Karma during our adventure there and it didn't go well. For us at least.

"I feel I'm very easy to communicate with and I was a planetary intelligence," Xen said.

"You ran the planet, but you weren't the planet," I said. "There's a big difference."

"True, but this world obviously loves her children or she wouldn't spend the power to bring them home," Loki said. "If Big Nose was able to stop an entire generation from spawning the next, the world might take notice. With Big Nose's power levels, he might be able to convince the world to work for him and transport his ships where he wanted them to be in exchange for him not doing it again."

There were dozens of methods of traveling through space, the majority of which took obscene amounts of energy. Startenders had a few that didn't, but those methods wouldn't necessarily work on regular starships. Gob had very strategic reasons for wanting alternate transportation.

"What's your name?" Kamile asked.

"Squiggly."

"So Squiggly, exactly what do you and your people need?" Kamile said.

"We need someone to run interference so we can do the spawning dance, but we have found no one willing to risk the Empire's wrath," Squiggly said.

"Couldn't you simply have Mother Cron teleport your people around these blockades?" Riga said.

"No. Each step of the journey helps us get ready to form the next generation of Cron. These ships have been interrupting us and..." Squiggly again seemed at a loss for words.

"Ruining the mood," Savannah said.

"I suppose. If we are not ready, Mother Cron will not move us to the next step in the journey. After each transport, we join with more Cron until we are all in orbit around our mother and finally form our children. But if we are not far enough along in the mating cycle, we will not be ready to produce children and will be left behind, stranded to never mate or raise offspring." Squiggly let out a squeal which was likely him crying. "The ships have been harassing us far past the orbit of this world, ruining our mood as you might say. We only have hours before we are supposed to go to the next jump. Will you help us? We don't have much by way of currency, but perhaps we can work something out. I would stay behind as your servant if you help the others around the blockage."

"Don't worry. The Startenders are not mercenaries and we don't have slaves. You do not need to pay us to help you," Kamile said.

"Which is another thing that doesn't make any sense. What's wrong with us making some money?" Buzz said. The garba complains and gripes when he's nervous in much the same way that I make bad jokes.

"There's nothing wrong with making money when it's appropriate. This isn't one of those times," I said. "Squiggly, do you know how Mother Cron transports you?"

His tentacles moved softly side to side, probably his version of a shrug. "She simply does."

"To stop the Empire from following you, we need to jam how they're tracking you. There are Startenders who might be able to come up with a way. Would you mind if they measured and observed how it worked?"

"Not if it will help us get past the blockade," Squiggly said. "Many of us came to this world looking for help. May I summon them here?"

"Certainly, but how?" I said. Squiggly had no clothes or tech that I could see.

"We can speak among each other in our minds."

"Ah, telepathic. Eric and Suzy –" Suzy was the *Bitter End*'s melog. "– would you mind playing taxi and gathering up Squiggly's friends so we can help get them back into space."

"Will do boss," Eric said, bringing Squiggly with him into *Fools' Glory*.

I turned to Loki. "Contact Startender Station. We need Pace, Vulcan, and Bubba Sue here ASAP. Luckily, Xen is already here."

Pace was the Albert Einstein of the troll set. He had developed more ways to cross space and dimensions than most of his race had ever even considered. Bubba Sue had powers and abilities to understand and alter all forms of technologies. Vulcan was, well Vulcan. And Xen of course was a robot that housed the repository of an entire planet's knowledge.

The Startenders had many ways to cross the galaxy, but none quicker and more efficient than one Gani had developed about a century ago. Gani was the twin sister of Merlin, a mage in Camelot, a former operative of Nemesis & Co. who currently served as the honcho of the barship *Excalibur*.

A little more than an hour after Loki made the call, a wall in the Watering Hole suddenly transformed into Earth-style elevator doors. They slid open and out stepped the people I'd sent for. Inside was a snowy-haired beauty with her clothes so white that even fresh driven snow would've been jealous. Gani stepped out and waved to me.

"Hi Murphy," Gani said.

"Hey Gani," I said. We hugged and she kissed me on each of my cheeks. Gani had been one of Terrorbelle's closest friends and a member of our wedding party. Her magic elevator could cross dimensions or vast distances of space in moments. All it took was some invisible magical glyphs on a wall for her to set up an elevator stop. All the universe was a short ride away, so long as she or someone she trusted had been to the other end before.

"How are things on the *Excalibur*?" I said.

"Amazing. Fortunately, being in charge hasn't gone to Dagonet's head too much." The pair had history so there was some worry their complicated relationship would make things difficult. "We've done a lot of good so far with two successful missions."

"I'm jealous. This is going to be our first official one."

"That's funny. I seem to recall you being busy back on Earth saving refugees," Gani said with a grin.

"But that was at home. This is out in space."

"Murphy, hello – remember spikeball," Buzz said.

"Which didn't involve using the ship much, so I'm not counting it," I said.

Gani chuckled. "Have fun." The mage waved to the rest of the crews. "Good luck all."

Gani stepped back inside and pressed a button. The elevator closed and disappeared.

Bubba Sue leapt up into my arms and gave me a kiss on the cheek. It wasn't that big a deal since she's all of three and a half feet tall. Back in the old days the kiss would've been on the lips, but she's calmed down a lot since marrying Vulcan.

I shook Vulcan's hand. Pace and I placed our traditional hands in front of each other's mouths. Neither of us ate the other's fingers so we moved on and I brought them all up to speed. Eric and Suzy returned with hundreds of Cron on board each barship.

"Vulcan, you ride with me. Pace you go with Kamile and Buzz," I said. Xen was already a part of their crew.

"Who's Bubba Sue going with?" Buzz said nervously. When they were in Startender Academy, she pulled a prank on most of the class, disabling an entire section of the space station and sending it floating into space. It was part prank, part training exercise, but it rather traumatized Buzz.

"Bubba Sue can ride with me, although I think once we reach the Cron, it might be best if we have Xen out among the natives."

The sentient robot nodded. "I'm always fascinated by all the different types of procreation. They should be fascinating."

"Tell me about it. This may be the greatest mission ever. We're going to help millions of folks get it on all the same time. I've got to figure out a way to join in," Savannah said.

"I don't think you have the all the right parts," Eric said.

The she-satyr shrugged. "I've never let it stop me before, so why would I start now? An orgy with millions involved. I'll be a satyr legend. Even my father Pan never pulled off something this big."

In my opinion, she already had her father beat. Pan was a friend, but he wasn't a Startender, although he was in the Society. Too unreliable. Savannah was a Startender. Case closed.

Travan was the most populated of the known planets largely because it had so many natural nexi. A nexus can connect worlds together and was a way to travel without spaceships. The problem is the Troll Guild used their powers to attempt to control the traffic through all of the nexus on the planet, mainly so they could charge a fortune to use them. And with so many worlds linking here, a traveler could come to Traven and then head to another world, all on foot.

Many trolls had the ability to open up a nexus on their own, but the practice was frowned upon to the point of bodily harm unless said troll had paid for a permit. The guild also tried to govern arriving space traffic and tax it heavily. While we could get on or off planet by avoiding all these things, we had decided it was wisest to save that for when we really needed to do it and also to make sure nobody outside of the Startenders was involved. Best not to gift others with something to blackmail us with.

We bought bulk nexus opening permits from the Guild, helped in large part by Pace's discounts and money that the warez stashed in the building we now owned. Yes, it was slaver money, but we were putting it to a good use. And Buzz and his crew had a side mission to try to find and free any slaves the warez had sold.

Pace's discount was tremendous. The guilds used several techniques that he developed and by their own rules have to give him a cut of the fee every time they're used. It's made him very wealthy. As part of his deal, he got a large discount on any permits he needed to get. The plan was to have him open a portal outside of the planet's orbit for us to rendezvous with the rest of the Cron.

"Thunder Jack, you want to come?" I said.

"Nah, I'll take care of the bar. I've had a few run-ins with the Empire over the years and I'm a wanted man." I raised an eyebrow at the god formerly known as Zeus. "Not to worry, Murphy. It's all for what you would consider good things. Big Nose and his people would disagree, of course."

Everyone boarded their respective ships. The *Bitter End*'s regular crew consisted of Buzz, Kyna, Randor, Xen, Toma and their melog Suzy. There was some debate about whether it would be better strategy to spread the trolls among different ships, but in the case of the *Bitter End* it was decided to have two in case one ever went primitive. Pace was stationed at the NYC II in R&D. He and Vulcan were working on building something to store limba so a troll wouldn't have to go primitive just because he was alone and low on energy.

Both barships slipped into dust mode. Pace opened a nexus

from on board the *Bitter End* which we slipped through quickly. Time and size also affected what we had to pay the guild, so short and sweet was cheapest.

We emerged in space where Squiggly had told us.

I was expecting more Cron. "Squiggly, where is everybody?"

"We call it running dark. They are hiding and floating nearby. Our spawning is normally quite visible. If those you gathered begin, the others will soon join."

"Eric, are we alone?" I said.

"In the Travan system? Hardly, but no ships are around for a half a million miles."

Communication with *Bitter End* was already open and up on the mirror screen.

"Kamile, you heard the man. Let's open up the airlocks and play matchmaker. Squiggly, would you tell your people in our ships that it's time to get it on?"

"Excuse me?"

"It's time to resume spawning. And let the ones in hiding know that we're here to help," I said.

The Cron left the barships. The she-satyr described what happened next the best.

"Oh my," Savannah said.

"Beautiful aren't we?" Squiggly said.

"Very," I said. Organic beings that can survive in the void without some form of protection are few and far between, so their presence there was amazing in and of itself, but the spawners were actually glowing. The Cron who left our airlocks moved away from the barships and lit up the darkness. Their lower tentacles exuded a semi-solid stream of something that glowed and trailed behind them like a sky-writer. The Cron began touching each other and their light shone brighter. In the darkness of space, it looked like thousands of new stars had suddenly appeared. The Cron in hiding stopped running dark and swam through the void toward the others, each with a tail of light drawing on the canvas of the universe.

It wasn't very long before there must have been a hundred thousand Cron floating and touching each other. Their movements were graceful, somewhere between those of luminescent humanoid jellyfish and ballroom dancers.

"Eric, turn on the windows." The melog turned on the view screens we had in every surface of the main barroom and a moment later the room seemed to disappear and it looked like we were all standing in space alongside them.

"Amazing," Vulcan said, before going through a dissertation on how they were achieving their bioluminescence in a chemical reaction with internal and external radiation when it hit their exoshells.

"May I go and join my people?" Squiggly said.

"Of course," I said.

"Can I join you?" Savannah said.

Squiggly tilted his head and neck tentacles and stared at the she-satyr. "We have no rule against it, but it would be unusual. Do you have a spacesuit?"

"Better, I have a Startender badge," she said.

"That is the thing the other woman mentioned? That little thing can protect you in the void?" Squiggly said.

"Yep," she said, then turned to me. "Can I go, Murphy? Please?"

"Squiggly, thank you for granting Savannah's request, but is there any radiation your people give off that might be harmful to other beings that don't have your outer shell?" I said.

"Not that I know of."

"Eric, what are sensors showing? Anything for us to be worried about?" I said.

"Some low-level EM radiation. No worse than a poor ozone level day at the beach," the golden melog said.

"Can I go Murphy?"

I felt like a parent with a young child. "You can go if Riga goes with you."

"Why does she have to come?" Savannah said.

"Yes, why do I have to go?" the dragon in human form said.

"I'll go," Coyote said.

I shook my head at the trickster and turned to Riga. "Savannah's badge might protect her from space, but she has no way to propel herself. You on the other hand can fly through space," I said. A dragon's flight was largely dependent on self-generated magic. We'd found through experimentation that they worked in the void of space as well as they did in an atmosphere, even while wearing a Startender badge.

Dragon and she-satyr locked eyes.

Savannah put her hands together and brought them to her chest. "Pretty please? Come on, be a pal. This is likely the biggest orgy I'll ever be able to participate in."

"But they don't even have the same genders or parts as you. You won't be able to engage in the same activities they are," Riga said.

"You're missing the point. It's the principle of the thing."

Riga rolled her eyes and sighed. "Fine, I'll go to."

Savannah grabbed the much larger Riga and jumped up and down, stripping out of her outfit. Luckily, the badge didn't need clothes to attach to someone. "Thank you, thank you, thank you, thank you!"

"Squiggly, they'll take you to an airlock," I said. Although we could control the shape of the outer ship, most of the rooms were fixed structures in our pocket dimension.

"Murphy, are you sure about letting Savannah go?" Kamile said over the comm link.

"Squiggly said the interruptions were ruining their mood. Savannah's our best bet to help speed things along." I said.

"Murph, her pheromones won't work in space. And she doesn't know anything about Cron sexuality," Kamile said.

"She didn't before we got here, but she's been watching them since they started," I said.

"So what? The rest of us have too."

"The girl's got a gift," Coyote said.

I nodded. "We have many experts among the Startenders. Pace is a master of nexus magic and figuring out how things get from one point in the universe to another. Bubba Sue the best there is at figuring out tech. Savannah is a savant of procreation. She has a knack and a passion to learn about every race's methods of having sex. Trust me. She had a few ways of thrilling the Cron figured out before she even asked me to join them."

Kamile narrowed her eyebrows in doubt. Not her fault. She couldn't help but compare Savannah to her brother Fred, who the kobold still had a mild case of hero worship toward. For a satyr,

Fred was incredibly sexually restrained. His sister was the polar opposite.

We watched Squiggly and the ladies go out the airlock. Squiggly floated toward his people, the light tail trailing behind him.

Riga transformed into her dragon form and chauffeured Savannah into the middle of the swarm of Cron. Squiggly had a telepathic link to the others and let them know Savannah would be joining them.

Savannah moved in, touching some of the Cron. Using her arms to propel herself, she danced among them. They were somewhat hermaphroditic, all with the same equipment. Their tentacles were different sex organs, each with slightly varying shapes and textures.

I was right about Savannah. It was more than just lust driving her. She had a hunger to learn everything about every kind of sex imaginable. And then participate in it. She picked up very quickly on what kinds of touch the Cron enjoyed and where they liked it. Pretty soon she was in the thick of it, refining the techniques she watched others do with flourishes of her own. It wasn't long before she had Cron lined up waiting for her to touch them.

Savannah had become the belle of the ball and the most popular girl at the party. And the ones she touched glowed brighter and as they touched others, their light intensified.

Eric watched the object of his crush wistfully from the ship, which is probably why Suzy was the first to realize we had company.

"Kamile, Murphy, we've got two incoming," Suzy said.

"What are they?" I said.

"One is a goblin spacetank." Spacetank made it sound small, but it easily outsized a dozen aircraft carriers. It had a small crew and was designed to get in and out of places quickly, sacrificing things like living space for weapons. "The other doesn't seem to be a ship, but it's very large for an organic. About the size of a bus.

The mirror over the bar which had been looking transparent suddenly became visible with the crew of the *Bitter End* facing us.

"Murph, that's a Dragonstar coming at us," Buzz said.

"A Dragonstar?" I said. Dragons weren't aliens, at least in the traditional sense. They originated on Earth, with many of them taking off to space ages ago. There's a group of them that had badges similar to the Startenders, but even more powerful. They were dedicated to helping the less fortunate and protecting dragonkind. Not necessarily in that order. So far no Startender had encountered any.

"We'll assume the spacetank is hostile. What about the Dragonstar?" I said.

"I'd err on the side that he might be trying to protect the Cron as well. Dragonstar badges go beyond ours by being weaponized and have interstellar travel capabilities," Loki said.

"Kamile, we'll run defense against the spacetank. You try to give the Cron time for the mother world to move them on. You hang back and protect the Cron in case anything gets through or the Dragonstar doesn't turn out to be a friendly," I said. "And I'm getting my people out of there. Will you pick them up?"

"Will do Murph. I'm sending Xen out to help us."

I was thinking of the opposite tactic for my people. "Savannah and Riga, break off from the swarm and get inside *Bitter End* immediately."

"Will do," Riga said.

"Ten more minutes. I think I've got the double bent wiggle swirl down," Savannah moaned breathlessly.

"Now," I said.

"Spoilsport," she said.

Fools' Glory headed out to meet the spacetank.

"Eric make us look big and tough," I said. Soon we had enough mass so that we looked several times larger than the spacetank. Our sudden appearance made them slow down.

"They're bringing weapons online," Eric said.

"Show them we have bigger weapons." We didn't. Most of our weapons were non-lethal, but Bubba Sue had rigged up a device that mimicked an energy weapon sensor signature that was at least triple that of any other ship we had records of. It was a bluff, but there was no way for the spacetank to know that.

"Murph, I'm getting a big energy surge behind us."

A moment later, the spacetank turned away from us and disappeared, using their transition drive.

"Think we scared them off?" Coyote said.

"I don't think so," Loki said.

The mirror came back on and Kamile didn't look happy. "Murphy, the Cron disappeared in a flash of light. And Savannah disappeared with them."

Everyone reviewed the recordings of the disappearance, but honestly most of us were expecting the big brains to figure it out.

Vulcan looked up at me and shook his head. "I will work on designing an addition for the badges so in the future they will be able to give us the scans we need to use the transworld drive to go directly there."

Which didn't help us now.

"Pace, how did they teleport?" I asked.

"I can't believe I'm saying this, but I have no idea," Pace said.

"Xen?"

"I've never come across anything like it. I do not know," the small robot said.

"Murphy, the Dragonstar is approaching us and broadcasting on a number of frequencies," Eric said.

"Put it on the speakers."

"Hello to the golden ships. This is Taze of the Dragonstars. May I approach?" said the Dragonstar in Travan Prime.

"That depends," I said. "What are your intentions?"

"The sharing of information."

"Fine, approach slowly."

"Impressive. He's moving as fast, if not faster than most starships could in system," Vulcan said.

"Boss, Riga didn't make it inside the *Bitter End* and she's on an intercept course with the Dragonstar," Eric said.

"Oh no," Loki said, his hand touching his badge to open a communication channel. "Riga, get yourself inside this ship immediately."

"Relax, Dad, I'm fine," Riga said.

"You think she's in danger from the Dragonstar?" I said.

"Depends on how you define danger. She's a young female dragon and that male dragon is the equivalent of a rock star and a movie star wrapped together and then multiplied by a factor of ten. I failed all my other children. They all became monsters and most helped destroy Asgard during Ragnarok. I vowed not to make the same mistakes with her."

"And you haven't. Riga's a good woman. She's smart and has a good head on her shoulders. It's not like she's going to knock him over the head and go at him right there. Unlike you and her mother, I might add."

"But..."

"From one father to another, back off and trust her to do the right thing. I know it's easier said than done. Remember me when Elsiebelle started dating?"

Loki chuckled. "It was amusing seeing you threaten somebody without a good reason."

"I'm a dad. I had a good reason," I said.

"Loki, your daughter is moving at some impressive speeds herself. I think she may have power we haven't become aware of yet," Vulcan said.

Riga positioned herself between *Fools' Glory* and the Dragonstar. They each stopped far enough away to be safe from most attacks, but close enough to see each other.

"You're not a Dragonstar. How are you surviving in the void?"

"Startender badge," Riga said.

"What is a Startender?" Taze said. Inside both ships were picking up the audio as they were transmitting to each other via their badges. We were getting video from Riga's badge as well.

"We're a group dedicated to helping others," Riga said.

"A group of dragons?"

"No. I'm not the only dragon involved with the Startenders, but I'm the only one in system. The Startenders are from the dragons' original home world," Riga said.

"She's giving out too much information. She does like him," Loki whispered.

By agreement, the Startenders are very careful not to mention where we come from. We didn't want anything following us home and making trouble on Earth.

"What was your purpose here?"

"Same as you. Trying to protect the Cron from the goblins."

"How do you know that was my purpose?" Taze said.

"What other reason is there for a Dragonstar to be chasing a spacetank?" came a new voice. Kyna and Xen were suddenly hanging there in space, as backup to Riga. The she-dragon didn't seem to appreciate it and was actually a bit indignant at the intrusion.

"May I board one of your ships so we may discuss matters more comfortably?" Taze said.

I came in on the channel. "Do we have your word as a Dragonstar that you mean us no harm and will leave in peace if asked?"

Taze chuckled. "I give my word, but exactly how do you plan on enforcing it should I choose to break it?"

"We've recorded your promise. Should you break your vow, we will share the recording. Dragonstars are noted for their fierce defense of their honor. I doubt you would casually break your word, knowing that it would damage the Dragonstar reputation."

"Can I ask the Startenders for the same assurances?"

"We give you our word that the Startenders mean you no harm and so long as you keep your word, will leave you in peace," I said. "Good enough?"

"Yes."

"Riga, bring him inside *Fools' Glory*."

I cut the transmission. "All right, the Cron took one of our own. How we going to get her back?"

"We're still getting telemetry, so we know two things. One, she's still alive and two we can use it to track her," Vulcan said.

"How long will her badge's life support hold out?" Eric said.

"I designed it for emergency protection, although the lot of you seem intent on constantly using it in place of spacesuits. Let's put it this way – she'll die from starvation before her life-support runs out," Vulcan said.

Kyna and the dragons entered our main barroom. Taze had not shrunk in size and was taking up a good portion of the available space. Riga introduced everyone on our ship and on *Bitter End* on the screen.

"So exactly where is the Cron home world?" Loki said,

"No one knows. Not even the Cron," the Dragonstar said. "The Cron home world teleports them in leaps, randomly across space.

It's not even linear because sometimes a jump take them farther back in the direction they've already come."

"It is believed the world does it for secrecy, not wanting outsiders to locate and harm her or her people," Pace said. "I've heard about her ability to transport without using a nexus. I hadn't believed it until witnessing it."

"I've got no records about the methodology either," Taze said.

"That's too bad. Where are my manners? Let me officially welcome you aboard the barship *Fools' Glory*. Can I offer you a drink or food?"

The dragon smiled, showing some very large teeth. He lowered his neck, so his head wouldn't be scraping the ceiling. His wings were tucked back to his side. Otherwise there wouldn't be much room for the rest of us.

"Thank you for your hospitality. I gather the Startenders are not a military organization," Taze said.

"Far from it," Loki said. He then looked at his daughter, still in her dragon form. "Riga, why don't you turn back to your human form so there's more room."

Telling his daughter what to do wasn't Loki's usual easygoing style. My guess is he was thinking that a human form would be less attractive to a male dragon.

"Dad, I'm fine," she said in a tone that the father of any teenage girl who had just been embarrassed has heard.

"Human form? This human is your father?" Taze said.

"God actually. And yes," Loki said, a bit too belligerently.

"So you're a shape-shifter, not a true dragon. The Dragonstars have rules about punishing those who would imitate dragons. Far too many have given us a bad name over the centuries," Taze said. "Consider yourself warned. Do not take dragon form again or you'll risk punishment."

"Cool your jets, scaly. She's half dragon on her mother's side, which gives her every bit as much of a right to look like a dragon as you or anyone else," Loki said, taking a step forward and staring up into one very large nostril.

I stepped between him and the dragon.

"Taze, you haven't answered. Are you hungry or thirsty?"

"I have my provisions, but thank you for the offer," he said. I hadn't expected him to say yes. People who deal with the mystic tend to be wary of taking food from strangers. There could be poison or worse. Our badges had both a filter and a warning function. Maybe the Dragonstar badge didn't, although from the ease of conversation, I was betting there was a fragment of a lation stone in there somewhere. Taze's badge was larger than ours, about the size of a small pizza.

"We need to get our crewmember back. You've obviously been tracking the Cron. How are you doing it?" I said.

"Actually, I was asked at a previous jump point to help protect them against the spacetank. I held it off until after they jumped. The spacetank followed. I didn't follow the Cron so much as the spacetank. The goblins seem to have adjusted their drive to leave less of a trail. I can't follow them this time. Can you?"

I looked towards my science and magic team. Vulcan and Pace shrugged in unison and Xen twisted his hand side to side, indicating so-so.

"We can't track the Cron or the ship, but we have a lock on Savannah. It's just a matter of figuring out how to go after them,"

We had different ways of traveling through space. Trolls have trouble opening a nexus between two points in the void. Between worlds, they had no problem. It gives them something to anchor each end on. Pace said they use gravity to stabilize the openings. Going from a world to the void of space was difficult, but the more skilled among them could manage it. Without at least one end anchored, the exit point could get dicey and damage anyone or anything going through. Xen could travel between star systems by warping space, but he couldn't take the rest of us with him and it would take him a while. Gani's magic elevator only went to places we had been to before. The barships could leave a micro-anchor, a tiny piece of the hull that extruded from space into our pocket dimension. We can ride our way back on that in an instant. But again, we had to have been there before.

Vulcan built a transworld engine into each barship, but they tended to work best on places that he had lots of data on. Apparently when transporting between different parts of the universe, you need to account for things like gravity, potential energy and other forces. For known worlds, Vulcan's pre-set the compensators. And the barships take measurements of each world and sector we visit so the transworld drive can take us back. With only the coordinates and what was there, we couldn't go in blind without risking destroying the barships if we materialized too close to a planet or something else just as dangerous. We had to travel through space. It was fast, but not instant.

"If you give me the coordinates, I can zip there. I can even take a few of you with me, although I couldn't open up my zip field so it was large enough to take your ships," Taze said.

All the Startenders grinned and exchanged glances.

"Did I say something amusing?" Taze said.

"The barships can shrink down in size to about the size of a few people," Vulcan said, hiding the actual smallest size we could shrink to. Never know when it might come in handy to use. "If we did that, would you be able take us through?"

"No." We started to speak, but the dragon held up one clawed hand. "I do not mind taking organics, but if I let your ship inside my protective field, you could use your weapons to obliterate me. I wouldn't be able to stop you, regardless of your ship's size."

"What if we gave you our word?" Pace said.

"And don't think I didn't notice the organics slight," Xen said. I shot the robot a look. I swear he was grinning and trying to yank either my chain or the dragon's. Maybe both.

"I've not heard of the Startenders and we only just met. It is simply not enough for me to put my life in your hands. I'll take three of your number with me to help," Taze said.

"Would you mind taking a probe with you as well? Based on its readings, we could program our engines to follow," Vulcan said.

Bubba Sue who had been uncharacteristically quiet jumped up and snapped her fingers. "That's how the goblins are doing it. One of the Cron must have a device that's sending back signals. If they make it back to the Cron home world, the goblins will have the location."

"Then why are they trying to stop them?" I said.

"Failsafe. Big Nose wants to show his power by stopping the Cron from getting home. Failing that, he'll go to the world directly," Coyote said. "Or he already knows the location and Mother Cron wouldn't negotiate before."

"So how do we find and stop what's broadcasting?" Riga said.

"It will be like trying to find a needle in a haystack," Eric said. "There are over a hundred thousand of them."

"Likely even more. At each jump more Cron link up. Wherever they are now, you can rest assured the home world has merged more groups," the Dragonstar said.

"She's working it like a shell game so even if they are followed, nobody will know exactly what section of space they are in. Mother Cron probably has no idea about the transmitter," Loki said.

"Actually, it shouldn't be that difficult to figure it out. I can whip up something that would check for transmissions. Then we could find where it is and destroy it," Bubba Sue said, turning to look at the much larger dragon. "Provided we can get there first."

"Fine. I'll take your probe and two of your Startenders.

"Take Riga and Xen," I said. Loki's head snapped to look at me. "Both of them can move through space under their own power, so they'll be able to do the most good. Bubba Sue, how long until you whip up your gizmo?"

The gremlin had already pulled open a drawer in the wall that was filled with pieces of tech. "I'll have it ready by the time we get there."

"Not the robot. He's weaponized and shares the same name as the Nimian AI. I'll take the woman with the winged boots. She can also move on her own through the void."

"Actually, I am actually…"

"Later Xen," I said.

The Dragonstar, Riga and Kyna all went out the airlock and zipped through space, whatever that meant. The probe automatically relayed the data we needed for the transworld drives and the barships followed.

Bubba Sue was as good as her word, but only thanks to the fact that when she's working on something, she can move at speeds that may not be as fast as Hermes, but are still rather impressive.

We emerged just outside of the glowing field of Cron that extended as far as the eye could see.

"How many?" I whispered.

Eric looked out. "Millions."

"Riga, get Savannah out of there," I said over the badges. "Kyna, get in here to get the tracker."

"Easier said than done, Mr. Head Honcho. They're packed so tightly together, I can't fly through without bumping up against someone, maybe hurting them or me. It'll be like crawling instead of flying," Riga said.

"However you're going to get her out, you better do it quickly," Buzz said over the link. "Those blinks are their way of communicating excitement and passion. If what happened in the Travan system happens here, when they start flashing in a pattern, it's a countdown to jump. And who knows if it will be to their home world or not."

"The spacetank is moving toward the Cron merrymakers and its weapons are hot," Eric said.

Kyna flew into the airlock and into the main barroom.

Bubba Sue handed her the tracker. "I've already pinpointed the signal. Just follow the pointy bit and it'll lead you right to it."

"Once I find it, what do I do with it? Kyna said.

"Get it out of the swarm. That way if the goblins don't know where Mother Cron is, they won't find out."

Being much smaller than a dragon, Kyna was able to weave her way among the gyrating tentacles more easily. A few minutes later, she emerged from the swarm. What she had wasn't a device – it was one of the Cron.

"Kyna, remove the device," Vulcan said. "Is the Cron wearing it?"

"Negative. As near as I can tell, it's been surgically implanted," Kyna said.

Kyna wasn't the only one leaving the swarm. Several thousand Cron noticed Kyna taking their fellow. Since we weren't firing at them like some other spaceships, they were giving chase.

"Kyna, they're following you. Probably think you're hurting that Cron," I said.

Riga swept between her fellow Startender and the group, giving the daughter of Hermes enough time to seemingly disappear.

"Should we bring it on board and see what we can do to get it out?" Buzz said over the com-link.

"I'm very hesitant to let a goblin tracking device on board one of the barships. No telling what it might learn," I said. "Eric, extrude part of the ship and fill it with atmosphere. We can question the Cron there. Buzz, would you mind joining us?"

"No problem," Buzz said.

The Cron's hard protective exoshell had turned back to flesh when it came in contact with the air. Kyna did an examination, having been trained in the medical arts by her father, aided by various types of sensors to get images of the inside of the Cron's body. Xen was assisting, using his own sensors and database of knowledge.

"What's the verdict?" I said.

"Even with not being an expert on Cron physiology, I'd still conclude that they implanted the device near vital organs. Were we to remove anything, it's likely the Cron would die," Kyna said.

"I concur," Xen said.

All the while, the Cron was pulsing and screeching, effectively screaming in two part disharmony, our badges translated the screams. "This is an outrage. I've been kidnapped from my people during our most crucial time. I demand you let me go back."

Which is when Buzz arrived. His body pulsed energy back at the Cron. I was impressed. I hadn't realized his mystic abilities to translate went beyond spoken languages.

"Then why did you betray your people?" Buzz said, speaking so we could follow.

"What are you trying to say?" the Cron said.

"How did these devices get inside your body cavity?" Buzz said.

"The goblins approached me and asked if they could do it. In exchange, they supported me in an opulent lifestyle for the last twenty years," the Cron said.

"So for free rent, food, and some toys you betrayed your people and your world?" Buzz said.

"What betrayal? They just want to meet Mother Cron."

"I doubt the goblins have altruistic motives. Your actions may have put the rest of your people and your world at risk," Buzz said.

All the tentacles on the Cron undulated in the same direction, which I took for an uncaring shrug. "Nothing I can do about it now. I am missing the spawning. You need to take me back to my people immediately."

"That's not happening. We're not putting the rest of the Cron at risk so you can get a little nookie," I said. Buzz translated.

"Boss, we have trouble," came Eric's voice over the badges. Suddenly the chamber sounded a lot like a house with a tin roof during a hailstorm. "The Cron are very unhappy and they appear to be trying to get your guest back. They are ramming up against the hull. Repeatedly."

"I called to them over our mind link," the Cron said.

"Oh joy. All that over Judas here." I suppose it was too much to hope the Cron were confused by his disappearance and too horny to risk missing the only sex they were likely ever to have in their lives and just go back to spawning. "Riga, any chance you can pick Squiggly out of the crowd and bring him here so we can explain."

"Are you kidding? All the Cron look alike. I still can't get to Savannah and she stands out. And I can track her by her badge."

"Wait Murphy, it gets better," Eric said. "A group of fifty spacetanks just entered the system."

"This is spinning out of control," I said. "We need them to jump now. We can't hold off that many warships."

"Murphy, open the airlock. Let me out," Buzz said.

"Buzz, they may rip you apart," I said.

"They might, but I'm the only one who can explain to them the truth of what's happening. I still think this is their last stop before home. Which means if Judas here goes with them, the goblins will have the home world's address. If they don't jump, Big Nose will likely enslave or slaughter them," Buzz said.

I sighed. "Okay. Kyna, when the airlock opens take this traitor and travel as fast as you can in the opposite direction. Maybe if we're lucky, they'll still jump and leave Judas behind."

The airlock opened and Buzz pulsed out a "Stop!" Kyna grabbed the traitor and in the blink of an eye was headed far away.

Buzz took his power to a whole new level. The Cron didn't have so much a hive mind as a huge party line that they could all talk on. Buzz accessed it, using their language and visions of what the Cron traitor had done and what the goblins planned to do.

Then what felt like a blow to the inside of my mind knocked me to my knees. Somehow I knew it came from the Mother Cron.

She was angry and heartbroken by the betrayal.

"Murphy, the Cron I was holding just disappeared in a burst of light," Kyna said over the badge.

"The rest are still here," Eric said.

"And there's the pulse pattern," Buzz said.

Then space was dark, the warm glow of the mating dance vanished.

"I spoke too soon." I couldn't see Savannah in the void in front of me. "Eric, did they leave our girl behind?"

"No, boss. They took her again, but they jumped to a part of space Hermes made a record of. There's no planet anywhere nearby. They jumped again," Eric said.

"I guess the revelation ruined the mood and Mother Cron is trying to get them all revved up again. I wonder what she did with the traitor," I said.

"We had more immediate problems on our hands, boss. The fifty-one spacetanks are all powering up their weapons and heading towards us," Eric said.

"Get us out of here," I said.

"No good. We're inside their weapon range. I'd have to reduce our shields, which would leave us vulnerable," Eric said.

"Battle stations people," I said. The barships were not designed as warships. It was not that we're unarmed, we just prefer to avoid battle. It was very hard to bluff a fleet of warships. And trying to destroy the ships would likely kill all on board. At times like this it's hard not to question the Startender stance on killing, but if we could follow it in a battle against superior forces bent on killing, we should be able to follow it anytime.

To be honest, things could start to go dire quickly. If the goblins figured out where the spawners leapt to and started to slaughter Cron, we'd have no choice but to stop them by any means available.

It was up to us to figure out how to pull this off without anyone getting killed. My mind was racing, playing out scenarios. I hadn't found one I liked yet.

"Boss, Riga is back on board," Eric said.

"Good. Kamile, let me know when Kyna's back on board the *Bitter End*. Taze, we offer you shelter on board," I said over the comm link. "Or you can zip away."

"Thank you, Head Honcho Murphy, but that will not be necessary. I do not leave allies just because the odds are against us. Besides, a Dragonstar is at least a match for a spacetank."

"No one is disputing that, but I'm not sure if you noticed there were now more than one of them," I said.

The dragon laughed. "Thank you for pointing that out. Now that I squint, I can see that. I'm certain I can take at least five before they get me."

"I can destroy no less than twelve, possibly twenty two, depending on their reaction time," Xen said from the *Bitter End*.

I shook my head. "Too much loss of life."

"Do you have a better plan?" Taze said

"A Startender always has a better plan." I smiled because I'd just come up with one and told everyone.

"You can actually do all that?" Taze said.

"We can," I said.

"Eric and Suzy, this hinges on you. You two up for it?" I said.

"Damn ready," Suzy said from the *Bitter End*.

"I was born ready," Eric said.

"Actually, you were born kicking and screaming." I was there.

"They are two of my finest children," Vulcan said. "They are more than up for it."

"Thanks, Dad," the golden melog said in unison.

The melog each shunted mass and changed the shape of the barships until each ship was molded to look like it was thirty ships. The insides were hollow, but if this worked, we wouldn't be here long enough for their sensors to figure that out. We "accidentally" dropped the scrambling on our communications to let the goblins listen in on our transmissions.

"Control has dispatched one thousand ships to our location. We are to hold the line until they arrive," Eric said in Goblin Prime.

That was enough to make the spacetanks all halt. Taking advantage of their confusion, we sent out two probes. One went to Taze who used his Dragonstar badge to zip to the coordinates we'd given him from Savannah's badge. While that probe scanned and transmitted us the info we needed to use the transworld drive, we had the second probe make a very noisy jump to another entirely different system as we reabsorbed the extra mass as both barships went to dust mode making it appear as though sixty ships had just jumped.

The hope was that the goblins would make the faulty assumption that we had all jumped instead of the probe.

It worked, because they turned to leave the system.

"Murphy, looks like they split up. Half are following our signal, the others the Judas' signal," Eric said.

We made our jump.

Buzz was wrong. They didn't go right home, but was right about Mother Cron jumping her children through space to get them back in the mood. As we didn't want to ruin that, we hung back and didn't go after Savannah. She wasn't in any immediate danger and the Cron seemed to be enjoying her presence. The she-satyr was probably having the time of her life.

We used the same method to follow each jump, giving Taze the coordinates. Then he'd zip with the probe and we'd follow.

After the fourth jump, Eric's golden face became a much lighter shade. "We lost telemetry with Savannah's badge. The energy the Cron are giving off along with energy coming off that planet are screwing up the signal, but we still have audio."

The Cron were in the orbit of the fourth planet of the solar system. All our badges were picking up Savannah and she was screaming. The Cron were hitting the atmosphere of the planet and shooting down to the surface like millions of living meteorites.

"I think they're killing her," Eric said frantic.

Loki laughed. "I think the French call it the little death. Relax Eric, those aren't screams of fear. Savannah's somehow climaxing with the Cron."

"I've got visual. Savannah's hit the atmosphere. She's going down," Eric said.

"And this is news why?" Coyote said with a smirk.

"Vulcan, will Savannah's badge protect her from entry into the atmosphere?" I said.

Vulcan side rolled his eyes. "It wasn't designed to make planet fall. I've never tested for that eventuality. It's designed to shunt energy and radiation to protect the wearer. The gravity controls could slow her enough to minimize the heat. I say she has a fifty-fifty shot that she survives entry."

"Hubby of mine you are overlooking the obvious. The field won't shunt that much inertia. She's going to be splattered on impact," Bubba Sue said.

"Eric, shrink us down and maneuver around the falling Cron and get beneath our girl," I said.

We accelerated through the living meteor swarm. It was actually quite lovely, but the heat was causing tentacles to twist, grow larger and break off.

"This is horrible. They must be in agony," Kamile said over the comm link.

"No, I can assure you they're not. Every last one is emitting energy that says they are in ecstasy," Buzz said.

Apparently that included Savannah. She had her arms and legs spread like a skydiver, with apparently no fear of impact. A fiery nimbus blanketed her body at the point where the badge's shielding absorbed the heat.

"Savannah, we're coming up below you. We're going to slow you down and bring you inside," I said.

"Spoilsport. Just like a man, pulling out before I climax," Savannah said.

"Bubba Sue says you'll go splat when you get to the ground regardless of the badge. If you like we can come back later to scoop up the remains to give to your father and brother," I said.

"I guess then you can save me."

Eric positioned the barship beneath her. Since Loki got the abilities of races he transformed into, he shifted into a Cron with an exoshell and reached out with his tentacles to grab onto her so he didn't have to worry about whether his badge would get rid of the heat. Gradually and with extreme care, we began deceleration. If Loki had just scooped her in, her bones would have turned to mulch even with the badge's inertia dampeners. Once we had bled most of it off, Loki brought her inside.

"You okay?" I said.

"Better. Fantastic. How many people can say they were part of an orgy in space with millions that ended with the participants becoming living meteors?"

"No more than six or seven I'll wager," I said with a grin. Savannah slugged my shoulder.

"Plus millions of Cron," Coyote said.

"You're just jealous," Savannah said and skipped around the barroom, still naked.

We hung up in the sky to watch the finale of the Cron mating ritual. It was fascinating that the same shell that formed in space also protected them from the heat of reentry. They absorbed all that energy and as they neared the ground expended all of it with a concentrated blast, the force of which slowed them down. The exoshell protected them and they all survived.

The tentacles that broke off didn't stop. They plowed into the ground, but that appeared to be part of the plan. The heat of reentry gave them the energy to get through their gestation period in some sort of combination egg/larval stage. When the last Cron and the last tentacle fell from the sky, we slowly descended. We followed our sensors to the area with the greatest interference and found Mother Cron.

"Fascinating. The biological sciences are not my strong suit, but I'd say the Cron has formed a symbiotic relationship with the planet," Vulcan said.

"But is the planet's consciousness in the Cron or is it speaking through her? Or is it an aspect of the planetary intelligence formed to look like its people?" Coyote said.

"No idea," Vulcan said.

"Buzz, talk to her," I said through the comm link.

"Go talk to her? I see how this is going to be. You only wanted me to be a Startender so when there was something big and scary you wanted to talk to, you'd have me around to do it. Don't think I've forgotten what happened when Loki tried to talk to the planet Karma. It tried to kill him," Buzz said.

"Probably just because of his personality," Coyote said.

"At least I have one, fleabag," Loki said. "And Karma didn't try to kill me so much as to get a point across – leave her alone."

"I don't like it. I keep telling you guys, I'm not a hero," Buzz said.

"But you are a Startender," Loki said.

Buzz glared at the Norse trickster through the mirror screen, but then his expression softened and he sighed. "Suzy take us in."

Suzy got close, then lowered a ramp from the *Bitter End*.

Buzz walked right up to Mother Cron, his crew right behind him. The conversation that followed was beyond our badges. There was a tremendous burst of energy which Buzz said contained mental images.

Buzz glowed himself and again told her what had happened with the traitor, then what we had done to help her people. Some of this her children had already told her. Buzz followed up with a warning that she should caution her people before they went out into the universe to prevent someone from trying this again.

Buzz asked what happened to the traitor. Mother Cron said that he was alive, but banished.

As Buzz conversed, thousands of the Cron began to converge on the mountain that was their progenitor. Some were fresh from space, others had been on planet already, raising the generation that would now be going out into space. The ones who fell from space weren't angry or hurt. More like contented.

"Savannah, Mother Cron is asking about the outsider who joined the spawning. She wants to meet you," Buzz said.

"Eric, bring us in for introductions," I said. Eric pulled alongside the *Bitter End* and opened a ramp for us. Savannah led the way and when she was close enough did a little bow. The mountain flickered and flashed.

"Mother Cron expressed her thanks for your services in the spawning. In repayment, she is offering us her services. If we were in a jam and able to call upon her, she would pull us out of it." Buzz looked at me. "Do we accept?"

I nodded. "With gratitude. Is it a one-time offer?"

There was more glowing exchanges. "Not necessarily, so long as we do not abuse it and are willing to help her children should they ever need it again."

"We can do that," I said.

Buzz was touching Mother Cron with a ring of his that held a lation stone.

"So shall it be," she squealed back. Apparently she could talk when she wanted to, but it was so loud the ground around us shook.

There was of course the question of how do we contact her from out in the universe. The solution we came up with was to plant several of Foster's seeds next to her.

Next, we started shouting and shaking Foster's plant body on *Fools' Glory* so he'd mind jump to us.

"Alright, Murphy, I'm here. This better be good. Hex and *The Accursed* just found a world with silicon based plant life that is simply amazing," Foster said.

We told him what was going on and he was on board with our plan. Buzz placed a minuscule lation fragment on a seed. Foster made it grow around it into a redwood sized tree. Buzz gave another tiny shard embedded in gold to Mother Cron.

The planet expressed her concern that others might be able to find her world. We gave her our vow that we would never reveal the location to anyone outside the Startenders. We comm linked with Taze who was still outside the Cron world's orbit standing watch in case the spacetanks showed up. Taze gave his word as a Dragonstar never to reveal the location to another.

We worked out with Mother Cron that she wouldn't teleport us to her system or Earth's in order to protect their locations. Instead she'd do it to a sector we choose ahead of time.

We said our goodbyes, although Savannah took much longer than the rest of us. She was made an honorary Cron and thousands of them were begging her to stay. She told them she had a duty and had to go.

I put my arm around her and she leaned up against me as we went up the ramp. "So which one of the children is yours?"

"None," she sighed. "Sadly."

When we were on board, I commed Taze. "We are heading back to the Watering Hole on Travan if you want to join us."

"Where is that?" he said.

"It used to be the Scum Hole," Riga chimed in.

"You took it from the warez? There is far more to you Startenders than meets the nostrils," he said. The lation stone sometimes has trouble making sayings translate exactly. "I'll race you back."

We won, mainly because Pace opened a nexus. Out of courtesy he made a few jumps so it couldn't be backtracked to the Cron. It was a surprisingly close contest.

"Dragonstars have an understanding with the guild. We don't pay," Taze said.

That was impressive. The guild has a small army of bounty hunters whose job it is to go after folks who stiff them on the toll.

I joined Buzz behind the bar and we poured drinks for everyone. I had Loki just take the top off a keg for Taze.

"We did good, people. Congratulations all around," I said, raising my glass.

Vulcan walked up to me, his face solemn. "We may have done too good a job."

"What do you mean? Are you worrying that our presence corrupted the Cron?" I said. The Startenders had nothing resembling the prime directive. Nor did we think one made sense for us.

"It's nothing to do with the Cron at all. It's the probe we sent with Taze when he zipped. When I looked at the scans, I saw everything. I now have a pretty good idea about how eighty three percent of a Dragonstar badge works, including how they zip space. Pretty ingenious actually. The problem is, I don't think it'll be easy to convince him or the Dragonstars that we took those readings by accident."

"It was an accident, right?" I said.

"Yes."

"And you only looked at them once?" I said.

"Yes, but I can take in an immense amount of information in a glance."

"So in theory you could learn more from reading through them again?"

"Absolutely," Vulcan said, looking at me, his eyes squinting. "Why? Do you want me to?"

"Is there anything there that if you don't look again would potentially harm the Startenders or Earth?" I said. "And why are you asking me? As one of the Startenders Council, you outrank a head honcho like me."

"True, but you're in charge on the ground here. On a mission, I defer to you. And I don't think there's anything there that would harm us or Earth."

"Then we go with the truth. We didn't plan it. You and only you looked once and then stopped when you realized what the information was. Is there anything harmful on the probe if we gave it to them as a gift?"

"The scanning technology in there is something no other organization or race we've come across has anything near."

"How would you feel if we gave them the probe?" I said.

"I wouldn't be happy. Those who designed the Dragonstar badge are brilliant. Probably not in my class." Vulcan wasn't bragging. Part of his divinity and powers was his genius. No mere mortal could hope to match it. "But still utterly brilliant. They will be able to reverse engineer it. Eventually."

"There aren't a lot of groups out here working to make things better. The Dragonstars are one of the few besides us. I'd rather have them as allies than enemies. We could give them the probe by way of an apology."

"What you say makes sense. However, there are three aspects of the probe that would put us at a tactical disadvantage, if they were able to reverse engineer it. I'll agree to it if you let me remove those three. There's still a wealth of information that would take any other group of scientists centuries or more to learn. "

"Then do it. It'll go a long way to convincing them that our apology is sincere," I said.

I looked toward Taze and I wasn't the only one. Riga was flirting in dragon form and Loki was still giving the large dragon the stink eye.

I walked over. "Taze, we need to talk." Figured I'd give him the good news first. Mother Cron's offer had been extended to him as well. "We can work out something so you have emergency exit capabilities as well."

"Excellent," Taze said. "Seems like you Startenders aren't a bad bunch. I spend a lot of time traveling, so it will be nice to have a friendly place to stop in. Especially one with a pretty female dragon."

"You're welcome here," Buzz said, walking over. "But Riga's shipping out on *Fools' Glory*."

The dragon was bigger than a city bus and I was more than a little nervous giving him the bad news. That wasn't even factoring in that his badge could destroy a warship. "There was one unexpected complication that we need to tell you about. The probe that you took with you made recordings. It was unintentional on our part," I said.

The Dragon laughed. "I'm not a rookie. Even inside my field, my badge emits a field that scrambles any scanning. Your probe didn't find anything."

"Actually, it did. I scanned all the data it uploaded and saw it once. But only once," Vulcan said.

"But that's impossible. Dragonstar technology is light years ahead of anything else," Taze said.

"Except for, apparently, Startender technology," I said. "We didn't do it on purpose, but we did do it. We made no copies of the data and we are going to give it to you along with the probe, which will allow you a glimpse into some of our technologies by way of an apology."

Taze inhaled deeply and didn't exhale. We matched eyes, which was a challenge because one of his was bigger than my whole head. The dragon tried to stare me down, but I didn't flinch. Next he turned his gaze on Vulcan, Riga, and then the rest of the people in the room.

"You didn't have to tell me in the first place. And then when I told you about my scrambler field, you had a second chance to deceive me. You didn't take. It speaks highly of the Startenders' honor. At this point in time, I'll not accept the probe as it could learn even more. I will kick what happened up my chain of command and we'll see what happens. They will likely come for it."

"Understood."

"As far as I'm concerned, I accept your apology."

"Thanks," I said.

"I would however like to take Riga flying in space. In this system of course," Taze said.

I looked to the much smaller dragon that was part of my crew.

"Please, Murphy?" Riga said.

Loki stepped forward. "I am your father. You should be asking me."

Loki had a temper that he rarely lost these days, but that could change in a moment. The trickster loved his daughter and based a large part of his post-reform and post-Ragnarok life around being a good father to her.

"No, she shouldn't," I said.

Loki turned to speak or maybe yell at me. I held up my hand. "However, you know very well that I'd run it by you first. Riga is a grown woman…"

"Dragon," she inserted nervously looking over at Taze.

"This is about her in whatever form and as a Startender going on a date."

"It's not a date, it's a…" Riga said.

"Riga, if your father can't lie successfully to me…" Most of the time anyway. "… you won't either. You're not in his class, which is fine since you don't have to be. Loki is very protective. He loves you dearly. It's a normal thing for a father to feel this way when his daughter starts dating."

"Well, can I go or not?" Riga said.

I looked at Loki who lifted up a finger, indicating to give him a moment.

"Now, Taze, son, let's you and me go have a little chat."

My honcho put a hand on the large dragon and led him to the far side of the fortunately very large barroom.

I couldn't hear them, but if Riga's ear twitching was any indication, she could. At the end of the conversation Loki briefly transformed into a dragon twice Taze's size, roared once, then turned back to human form and walked away smiling. He nodded yes at me.

I turned to Riga. "You can go."

The lady dragon actually skipped once then stopped once she realized her date could see her.

Taze strolled back over, acting like a nervous teenager whose date's father had just shown him a very large gun collection.

"Can your father actually do all that?" Taze said.

Riga smiled and nodded. "And more, but mess with me and he's only the second person you'll have to worry about."

Taze smirked and looked at me, making a faulty assumption of who that was. "What's the first?"

"Me," Riga said.

Taze smiled and took Riga's clawed hand in his own.

"I'm not sure what have her back by ten means, but we'll be back before long," Taze said.

"Good," Loki said, leaning on the bar with his hand crossed over his chest and an evil grin that seemed to intimidate the large dragon. When the pair left, he turned to me. "Murph, give me a drink and keep 'em coming."

Coyote climbed up on a stool and put his paws on the bar next to Loki. I put a bowl of whiskey in front of him. "You know we can watch through her badge, right?"

Loki raised an eyebrow.

"I figured out a hack," Coyote said.

"Thanks," Loki said, putting a hand on his fellow trickster's neck. "But I think I'll trust her."

"What if she's late?" Coyote said.

Loki wiggled his eyebrows and downed his drink. "We'll blow that bridge if we come to it."

DEFENDING EDEN

"Murphy, we're in trouble!"

"Yeah, I figured that out for myself," I said as I floated out from behind the bar. "Eric, what's going on? We forget to pay the gravity bill?"

"Don't know." The golden melog was actually using his arms on the control panels to try and get the barship stabilized. A bad sign since normally he could control it with his thoughts. "Isn't that Loki's job?"

"Was I supposed to pay that and not embezzle the money?" my honcho said.

"What'd you spend it on?" said Coyote.

"It was supposed to be a surprise. I got a lifetime supply of flea powder for you. Figured it might last you a week," Loki said.

Coyote bit at his hindquarters. "Why would I want to get rid of them? They make such great snacks."

"Not liking this, Murphy. My soil is going to float away," Foster said.

The sentient plant and his pot floated by and were plucked out of the air by the she-satyr Savannah.

"I don't know. I'm rather enjoying it. Maybe gravity is overrated. Besides, do you know all the new positions zero gravity opens up? After the Cron affair, I've been wanting to try it with folks with more compatible parts."

Eric tried not to snap his neck as he turned to stare at Savannah. The poor guy still hadn't done anything about his crush on Pan's daughter. Not that it would have taken much. Sex came to Savannah as easy as breathing or eating. Maybe easier. If she was engaged in intimate activities, there were times we had to remind her to eat.

"Dad, do I look as ridiculous when I'm flying?" Riga said, floating by in her human form.

"Not at all. They simply don't have your grace, my dear.

Although Murphy's awkwardness has a certain clumsy elegance of its own," Loki said.

"I am not clumsy." My words were more than a tad underscored as I immediately banged my head into one of the ceiling fans. "Not one word."

"No problem. I'll just snicker and laugh," Coyote said.

I pushed off the ceiling with my feet to try to get myself situated in an upright position, at least in regards to the main barroom. "Is something wrong with *Fools' Glory*'s systems?"

"Not as far as I can tell. They appear to be working. Something else is countering the gravity." Eric's face took on a slightly terrified expression. "And whatever it is has dragged us into some sort of cosmic slipstream. I can't get a reading on where we are, other than we are moving very quickly."

"Is the ship in any danger? Should we go to dust mode?" I said. A golf ball sized ship would be less likely to be hit by debris.

"I don't think changing size would be a good idea. The force waves that are moving us might damage the ship's hull if we morph. It's messing with the sensors, but there doesn't seem to be anything out there to hit, but I shunted more mass to the hull in case. I suggest we just relax and enjoy the trip." Eric said.

Several moments of silence passed where nothing happened but floating and several of my crew trying out acrobatic maneuvers.

"You know what would help pass the time? I'll give you a hint. Everyone has too many clothes on for it to work properly," Savannah said. She had been trying unsuccessfully to get the crew to have an orgy for some time now. As head honcho of *Fools' Glory*, I felt it would be inappropriate for me to be physically involved with any of my crew. Especially Savannah. It wasn't that she was unattractive, despite the rather hairy lower body, hooves and horns. And to paraphrase one of the greats, her mystic pheromones could make a bishop want to kick out a stained-glass window. Luckily for the crew, our badges filtered them. I was never one for casual sex and she was the sister of one of my best friends.

"I'm up for it, but I'm not so sure you'd get much out of pollination," Foster said. "But if we go that route, would you mind buzzing like a bee?"

Savannah appeared to be considering it when I noticed a change in the ship. Riding in *Fools' Glory* was normally very smooth, but there were still certain behaviors and vibrations that I'd come to recognize.

I maneuvered myself over behind the bar to my stool and used my legs to anchor the rest of me to the seat that was magnetically attached to the floor.

"Murphy, you're missing out on all the fun," Coyote said as he pushed himself from floor to ceiling to wall in a random fashion as if he were inside a pinball machine.

"I don't think so. Have you wondered what'll happen when the slipstream stops messing with the ship and gravity comes back on?" I said.

"Yeah, like that's going to happen anytime soon," Coyote said. Once again I have proof that at least one of the Fates likes me as the gravity came back on and Coyote fell from the ceiling to the floor, landing on his back. Fortunately, it would take more than a small fall to put a dent in anything more than the trickster's pride. The fleabag stood, brushed himself off and started grooming himself.

"I've got control back, boss," Eric said.

"Open all the windows and let's see where we are," I said. We had all sorts of sensor arrays, both scientific and mystical, but sometimes nothing beats taking a look. All the surfaces from floor to ceiling seemed to vanish as they showed everything outside the ship and made it look like we were floating in space.

We were in orbit around a lush Earth-like planet. Quick observation revealed it was mostly water with a single large continent.

On some worlds we can tell if it was inhabited just by looking down and checking for large structures, pollution or sometimes errant satellite traffic. I couldn't see any of those with the naked eye, so I hit the control panel to magnify our view of the planet.

"Eric, you getting anything?" I said as I continued to magnify the view.

"No technology to speak of, but I'm getting large amounts of oxygen, nitrogen, and methane." Oddly enough, there were planets with a similar mix of gases that could support life, which didn't have any, but rarely was there methane without some form of organic waste processing.

"I guess whoever's down there is farting," Savannah said.

I fiddled with the controls, changing the view.

"It's odd. There's no cities or even settlements. Just lush vegetation," Riga said.

"So what you're saying is we found paradise," Foster said. I guess for a plant, it would be.

"Let's go in for a closer look in dust mode. No reason to scare the natives if we don't have to."

"You sure you want to lose the energy?" Eric said.

He had a point. "Fine, but shrink us down before we'd be visible. We don't want any of the natives to mistake us as gods."

"You say that like it's a bad thing," Loki said with a grin.

"And completely ignoring the fact that two of us are gods," Coyote said.

"You want to deal with the responsibility of taking on more worshipers?" I said, knowing that Coyote was too lazy to try and build up a cult. There was an implied relationship between god and worshipper. Accepting devotion would leave Coyote with an ethical obligation to take care of the people who believed in him. Not that gods always, or even usually, did, but the ones who were Startenders would have to. Belief creates manna and it's actually not an uncommon practice to build up manna for selfish purposes and leave before the backlash started when the god failed to answer prayers or natural disaster stuck or some such. Back when I made sure Hermes' tank got filled because our world was watching, there was no ethical conflict. That manna would be used to defend Earth.

"Nope. I'm not like old Big Nose." Tock's interstellar empire of goblins was ruled by Gob, who is rumored to have wiped out the rest of his pantheon. He has iron control over his people. He conquered worlds, not just to exploit them for labor and resources, but convert them over to believe in him and harvest the manna. Very empowering for the divine set.

I love entering into a planet's atmosphere with the windows open, at least the figurative ones. Watching fire and air rushing by as the ground approached was exhilarating.

"Despite the entire continent appearing to be able to support life, most of it appears to be congregated around the center of the land mass. No objections if I land there?" Eric said.

I nodded.

When the light show was done, we slowed our descent and switched to dust mode. We reached ground level and explored a bit. We found small groups of pale green humanoids who seemed to not need any clothing. That was odd, but what was odder was that they were waving at us.

"That's probably the reason they don't need any sensors," Riga said waving back.

"They can't see us, you know," Savannah said.

"Yes, we can," said a voice from outside the ship.

The interior of *Fools' Glory* sits in our pocket dimension when we were in dust mode, so for them to be not only able to hear us, but see us was very disconcerting.

"All righty then," I said.

"Why don't you come out? You're welcome here," a woman said.

I looked at Eric. "Atmosphere is breathable." Not that it made much of a difference to Eric as he could survive extended periods without air. Same with Loki and Coyote. And the rest of us had our badges to work as filters.

"Loki, what do you think?"

"We're supposed to be all about meeting new people and helping them out," Loki said.

"And maybe helping ourselves in the process," Coyote said. While that may very well be true, profiting was low on our list of priorities.

"Open the door and let's go say hi."

The ship expanded and morphed into a traditional earth door. I was the first one out, but everyone else was hot on my heels. We'd drawn a large crowd of naked natives and Savannah was looking around like a starving woman at an all you can eat buffet.

"Welcome to the garden," one of the men said.

"Thank you. We're happy to be here," I said. "Is garden the name of your world?"

"Garden is just garden. What is a world?"

Coyote chuckled. A four-legged creature about the size of a lion padded its way over. I started to get nervous because it was obviously a carnivore, although I noticed the natives didn't show any fear.

"What is so amusing?" the beast asked and then nuzzled a much smaller fuzzy creature that elsewhere in the universe would have been its snack.

Coyote looked at the creature, simply unable to believe the sheer amount of naïveté he was witnessing. I was more impressed that it could talk. Few worlds tend to have more than one sentient race. At some point in their history, worlds with more than one smart species have the tendency to do dumb things like try to wipe out their competition. I'm told that's why there are no Neanderthals left on Earth and the dragons left for space.

Also in the very weird column was the fact that they were able to understand us and we them. The garba stones in our Startenders badges allowed us to understand other languages, but not so much on speaking them. The badges weren't doing any translating, but these folks weren't speaking English. It was as if the words themselves were simply changing themselves around so everyone could talk, even the animals. A pair of flying creatures was having a discussion on which patch of sunlight would be more comfortable to bask in.

Loki was giving the place the once over, assessing for threats and escape strategies when he noticed a tree the size of a skyscraper that everything else seemed to be laid out around. Despite the enormity of the tree, it had low hanging branches close enough to the ground for anyone to be able to reach up and pluck fruit from.

Loki's face went pale. "Oh no. Everyone get back in the ship. Now!"

"Why?" Savannah said, eyeing more naked men who had wandered over. "I haven't had a chance to meet and greet any of the natives yet."

"Keep it that way," Loki said. It was unusual. Loki was generally okay with Savannah's extreme version of friendliness.

Coyote started to walk forward. Loki ran over and lifted him up off the ground. "We have to leave, especially you and me. We can't corrupt these people. Even our presence might be enough to do it."

"How would we corrupt them?" I said.

"Murphy, if you've ever trusted me, trust me now. We need to get back on the ship and leave," Loki said.

Loki rarely played the trust card, mainly because after everything we've been through he didn't need to. "All right, everybody, you heard the honcho. Get back on the ship."

There was a chorus of grumbles, none louder than the she-satyr.

"That's an order," I said.

"I don't take orders," Coyote said. "And put me down. I'm not some pet."

I rarely gave orders. Usually suggestions were enough. However, with the exception of the fleabag, I was obeyed without question. Unfortunately, when we turned back around, there was a man blocking the doorway. Unlike the rest of the natives, this one wore clothes.

"What's your rush? You just got here. Besides, these fine folks just want to show you some hospitality. They get so few guests here in the garden. You wouldn't want to take that small pleasure away from them, now would you?"

Everybody else in my crew had ways of sensing magic, whether it be by smell or innate ability. I was the sole exception and the only human, but that didn't mean I didn't pick up on things. From the way everyone's posture changed, we had an issue.

"We don't listen to demons," Coyote said.

The man in the suit smiled. "Demon is such a harsh word."

"But accurate," Loki said.

"I'll grant you that."

"I've heard rumors of this world. That they alone among all the sentient races in the universe resisted the temptation to break the covenant and eat the fruit of the tree of knowledge," Loki said.

"Why would we do that? The creator told us not to," said one of the women, with a chorus of agreements from those around her.

"Did we just stumble into the Garden of Eden?" I said. I thought it was still hidden back on Earth.

"Not the — A. Legend has it that the creator of the universe let sentient life evolve and then set them each up in a paradise with only one condition. Almost without fail, none of the beings could keep their covenants. Except here, apparently." Loki turned toward the demon. "Which makes you stuck here until you manage to get one of them to take a bite."

The demon nodded, smiling. "True, but I've got to tell you this place sure beats the Pit."

Having been to Hell myself, I couldn't argue with him.

"Corby isn't so bad. He's got a job to do. Doesn't mean we're foolish enough to listen to him," one of the men said.

I looked up at the tree that reached into the sky. "So that's the tree of knowledge?"

"One of them," Foster said. "There is also a tree of life. If I could plant just one of my seeds here, I don't think I'd ever leave."

The plant elemental had had issues back in the 1960's when hippies started to worship him. Foster became a minor god and was enjoying himself until his worshippers found out that smoking his leaves gave them an unparalleled high. They practically smoked him out of existence. He has since learned to transfer his mind between any of his plant bodies. The Startenders try to plant his seeds in the soil on every world we visit. We were probably going to skip that on this trip.

"If someone were to eat a piece of the fruit, they'd…"

"Have ultimate knowledge, of good and evil, of how the universe worked and much more. They'd learn enough to make them almost into a god," Coyote said, staring straight ahead, almost in awe. He licked his mouth and Loki tightened his grip on the canine divinity.

"But that would screw up stuff for the people here?" I said.

"Big time, although they'd still probably live for another thousand years…" Coyote said.

"Don't all people live?" one woman said.

"… since they didn't break the covenant, they get to eat from the tree of life," Coyote whispered. "They are eternal…" Even gods can die, although they don't like to admit it. "So long as they don't eat of the forbidden fruit."

Loki nodded. "They have no disease or war or hunger or murder."

"Are these War, Hunger, and the rest friends of yours?" one of the men asked.

"They have no need to labor. The women have no pain during childbirth."

"What's pain? And childbirth is one of the most pleasant experiences a woman can have. Almost as pleasant as getting pregnant in the first place," the woman said.

We were all looking at the tree and the consequences of what might happen if we stayed.

"Okay, everybody like I said, back on the ship. Thank you folks very much for your hospitality, but I think it be best if we left," I said.

Eric looked up at the sky. "Boss, I think we may have a situation. We aren't their only visitors today. Sensors are picking up another inbound ship that just popped out of the cosmic slipstream. Transponder marks it as Cyndicate." I started to curse, then caught myself realizing I might be teaching the Edeners a bad habit.

A tiny speck in the sky was catching fire and heading towards our position, bringing with it evil that justified anything in pursuit of wealth and power. They'd eat the natives alive. Literally, if there was a profit to be made.

"I don't understand. I know Eden on Earth is protected." Apparently by an eternally pissed off angel with a flaming sword. "Why isn't this place?"

"The strange cosmic currents probably route ships around this world. You'd have to work very hard to make it here on purpose," Eric said.

"And we all know the Cyndicate doesn't mind profiting from the hard labor of others," Riga said. She'd had some bad experiences with them.

"But this place is paradise. Why isn't there something here to protect them?" I said.

Corby, the serpent in this particular paradise, rolled his eyes. "You are dense, aren't you? Why do you think you were brought here? These people kept The Covenant. The creator's not going to let anything happen to them and she brought the lot of you here to make sure of it."

As a whole, I find it safest to disbelieve everything a strange demon tells me, but in this case, he made sense.

"The most likely thing the Cyndicate would want here is to harvest the fruits." The Cyndicate were a loose association of robber barons throughout the galaxy. They did a lot of infighting, but protected each other from outsiders. My former boss, Paddy Moran, made himself the richest man on Earth and bankrolled the Startenders. From what I've heard, these guys could run financial circles around him. They've been rumored to have ruined the economy of an entire world because someone on the planet brought them the wrong appetizer. Even if we stopped them here, we might be in for a heap of trouble down the road.

"Eric, sound an internal distress signal. I want every available barship here on the double. I want Sun Wukong and Xen on the ground as soon as possible." I wanted our heavy hitters if we had to defend paradise from the Cyndicate.

"Negative boss. No signals are going in or out through those cosmic currents. I only picked up on the ship when they exited the slipstream," Eric said.

Damn. Luckily we had a backup system to call for help. "Foster, body jump and get them here." Every barship, plus our headquarters on the station, had at least one of Foster's bodies. Made him the only Startender to be on the crew of every ship. He tended to mind jump to whatever ship was having the most interesting time or needed him, easy enough to do since he could transfer his mind instantaneously across space.

"Murph, no go. I can't do it. I can't feel any of my bodies besides the two spares in *Fools' Glory*."

Double damn. The fiery speck was growing larger as it got closer. With our minimal offensive weaponry, we couldn't expect to get into firefights with fleets, armadas and the like and expect to win. We found other options worked best. And there was the Startender oath. Hard to not kill others when you have weapons of mass destruction ready at the push of a button.

The Cyndicate ship on the other hand would have the best weapons and shields money could buy and the ability to probably hold off a small planetary fleet by its lonesome.

At the core of their shriveled little hearts, the Cyndicate were businesspeople. They didn't do anything unless there was profit or power to be gained. Judging from the ship's approach, we didn't have long to find a way to make this planet unprofitable for them.

"We could destroy the ship," Coyote said. "The cloud would block them notifying the rest of the Cyndicate to avenge them."

"And kill how many?" I said.

The canine trickster shrugged. "How many lives is saving paradise worth?"

"A ship full of vaporized corpses is too great a cost. Startenders don't kill if we can help it. The Cyndicate keeps indentured servants and there are bound to be some on board." At least their indentured choose their servitude. "Wholesale destruction is not an option."

"We're going retail them?" Coyote said and I realized how annoying I probably was to other people when I made comments like that.

"No killing regardless of price or discount."

"I know, but someone had to point out the possibility. Just in case," Coyote said.

I nodded. He was right. We all knew there would come a time when we will have to kill to save innocents. I was all for putting it off as long as we could.

"If we could get rid of the fruit, they'd have no reason to stay," Eric said.

I could almost feel a light bulb come on over my head. "Then that's what we'll do. We'll make the fruit useless."

I told them my plan.

"How are you going to pass for a native, boss man?" Riga said, smirking.

"I know, I know," Savannah said, jumping up and down while clapping. "What I wouldn't give for a fistful of dollars, a pole and a sound system right now."

I ignored them as best I could, but it was difficult with all the whistling and catcalling coming from my crew.

"Take it off, Murphy!" Loki said, holding his sides and laughing.

"Not enough hair for my tastes," Coyote said.

"Enough for mine. Nice equipment, boss man. I think we have

time for a quickie," Savannah said. I threw my underwear at her head. She caught them and jumped up and down sniffing them. "These are going on my wall."

"Murphy, I'm not overly familiar with human anatomy," Foster said, working hard with his part of the plan. "But you could probably lose a few pounds."

I wasn't in bad shape, but all the Edeners were gorgeous with hard bodies and none of them even had to work out. Another benefit of paradise I guess.

"Foster, make me green," I said and Foster grew a sac which burst, covering me with green pollen so my skin matched that of the natives.

"Unfair. You'll have sex with Foster, but not me?" Savannah said. "I'm hurt."

"What are you..." Then it hit me. "I'm not pollinating with Foster."

"Actually, Murph, you kind of are. Does this mean we're going steady? Or is it a one night stand?" Foster teased.

"Murph's not the one night stand kind of guy," Loki said. "Are you going to wear each other's badges?"

"Less chatting, more getting into position," I said. Eric went back into the ship and went to dust mode. Everyone else hid, except Coyote who started digging.

The ship that landed was a shuttle, but a very large one. Think the equivalent of a block long stretch limo, only much bigger. Rather than try to find a clearing, it landed on a group of trees, its thrusters reducing them to kindling. A door opened and lowered a ramp. A blue humanoid in the latest galactic chic strutted out with an entourage of a dozen swarming around him like he owned the planet. A score of workers with harvesting equipment and machinery trailed behind. They in turn were followed by armed guards wearing control collars which could do anything from hurt them to blow off their heads.

The Cyndicate boss was shouting orders, telling the natives that he was claiming their world in the name of the Cyndicate and that they were all chattel, but if they worked hard in fifty or so years they might earn their independence and to please line up near the ship so they might be loaded on board to begin their glorious new lives.

Ignoring him I reached up to the tree and plucked off one of the forbidden fruits.

The man in the suit glared at me slack-jawed. "You! What are you doing?" I was impressed. He had a device that translated for the listener. Even we didn't have one of those.

"Having a snack," I said.

"Absolutely not! Those fruit and everything else on this planet, including you, belong to me. That is theft! Subdue him!"

The guards ended up being tripped by nearby vegetation that was moving on its own thanks to Foster.

I responded by taking a bite. Then I passed out fruit to the nearby natives. Each of them took a bite which was followed by them staring at each other's naughty bits then fashioning fig leaf chic out of nearby vegetation.

"No! What have you done?"

Corby danced a jig and laughed maniacally.

"Fruit of that tree being eaten triggers a planet wide reaction. Get the rest of it, while I search for the tree of life. We need to be out of here quickly," the Cyndicate boss said.

"Yes, Lord Myser."

The men with machines started to move when the air in front of the tree exploded into fire. When the flame stopped, a man in long white robes, wings and a flaming sword appeared.

"Who broke the Covenant and ate fruit from the tree of knowledge?" The angel's voice shook the entire garden.

I raised my hand and waved. "That would be me. Very tasty, although a bit on the sweet side. It would make a wonderful pie."

The Angel pointed to me and I fell to the ground holding my throat. He pointed and flames consumed the tree. The shuttle began to rock back and forth as if there was an earthquake.

"This is the work of outsiders. You shall all face final judgment!" the angel said, pointing his flaming sword at the Cyndicate boss, his entourage and lackeys.

"Surely we can come to some sort of business arrangement. There must be something a person like yourself wants? If I don't have it, I can get it. Let me have some of the fruit, even just the picked ones. After all, it's only going to go bad," Myser said.

"I doubt it. I'll eat the rest," I said, raising my hand.

Letting out a primal scream, the angel pointed his fiery sword at me and I was enveloped in fire. Next the winged man turned his sword on the tree and it became an inferno. Then he did the same for a second tree.

"You see what has come of outsiders tasting of the fruit of the tree of knowledge. I have destroyed it and the tree of life, but some remains. Do you still want a bite?" the angel said. The Cyndicate boss glanced over to where I had been seemingly incinerated. The shuttle vibrated like it was going to be ripped apart by the ground beneath it, which in fact did open up and swallow part of it.

"No," Myser said. "I would like to leave here with my employees. What will that take?"

"Your solemn vow to never reveal the location of this world and destroy all records of it," the angel said.

"Done."

"You understand I shall come for you no matter where you are if you even think about breaking this vow?"

The boss nodded.

"Then flee before me and never return!"

The Cyndicate boss ran back onto his tilted shuttle, the rest of his people following in his wake.

The shuttle had trouble lifting off, as if some giant hand was shaking it. Eventually it achieved liftoff and made it into orbit.

The angel stepped over to where I had been standing before the flames hit and smiled. "Looks like our plan worked."

"And all it cost us was Murphy. A real bargain," Coyote said, coming out from underground where he had dug the crevice the shuttle had half fallen into.

"I can hear you down here, you know," I said from the covered pit I leapt into before the flames could incinerate me. It was also courtesy of the fleabag's digging. The angel bent over what looked like a grave and shifted back into Loki who reached down and pulled me out.

"Looks like the rumors of your incineration were exaggerated. Pity," Coyote said.

I looked up at the still burning wood. "Maybe we should do something about that."

Loki turned toward the burning trees. One of his lesser-known aspects is that of a fire god. Putting his arms out to his side he called the flames to him. The trees became charbroiled embers.

Savannah and Riga came out from where they were hiding and began smashing the outside of the large tree. The burnt bark and wood collapsed to the ground, revealing the true and quite unharmed Tree of Knowledge beneath it. They did the same for the tree we used to stand in for the Tree of Life. Better all-around if we didn't know which was the real one. Eternal life was too tempting for just stealing a piece of fruit.

"Nice job with the fake tree shells, Foster." The elemental was a bit of an artist, able to make his plant bodies grow into pretty much any type of vegetation he can imagine.

"It wasn't perfect, but it fooled them."

"Hey, what about me? That tree didn't catch on fire by itself," Riga said. As the daughter of a dragon and a fire god, she didn't even have to change out of her human form to spit out fire every bit as good as a flamethrower.

"A superb job, daughter," Loki said.

"I don't suppose you feel any smarter, do you?" Corby said, looking at me.

I chuckled at the demon. "Nope. Foster caught the piece of fruit you put on his shell and placed it back on the real tree." He had also created mock fruit, which is what the lot of us ate. The natives played out their parts just like we instructed them.

The demon shrugged. "I had to try. I suppose you and your crew will be leaving now?"

"As soon as Eric gets back with the ship." The melog used *Fools' Glory* in dust mode to shake, rattle and roll the Cyndicate shuttle.

The barship could transport itself very quickly through the pocket dimension and cover light years in our universe in moments so long as it was to someplace we had left a micro piece of the ship's hull. We called it a drop zone.

Eric had put a drop zone inside the shuttle.

It didn't matter where it went, we'd not only be able to follow it, but get inside the shuttle, which in turn would likely be inside the Cyndicate boss' starship.

"So we can get rid of these clothes?" said one of the men. I was already getting dressed.

"Absolutely," Savannah replied a little too enthusiastically.

"I really don't understand the purpose," he said.

I really didn't want to explain modesty to them as they seemed to be doing quite well without knowing, so I went with a different tact. "People wear them for protection against cold and the elements."

"But it's always a perfect temperature here. Never too hot or too cold. The rain is wonderful and refreshing when it comes."

"I'm sure it is," I said.

"Are you sure you won't be staying any longer?" the man said. "You have helped us and have not taken advantage of our hospitality."

"Well, since you asked so nicely, I'd be happy to," Savannah said, shucking out of the minimal clothing she wore. Oddly, she kept wearing my underwear as a hat.

I met the she-satyr's eyes and shook my head. She stamped her hoof, much like a petulant child, but she stepped back and put her clothes back on. Which was good. We didn't need to do anything else to compromise these people.

Fools' Glory reappeared in the sky, massive and burning during re-entry. Eric was filling up our energy reserves. A little while later the barship shrunk back down and landed nearby. The door opened and Eric stuck his head out.

"Somebody here call for a cab?"

"That'd be us," I said. We said our goodbyes to the Edeners and Corby, who didn't seem very upset he had failed.

I took him aside. "It's very odd how they found their way here. By any chance did you leak the information?"

"No, but that didn't mean someone else from the Pit didn't," Corby said. "You may have a pissed off demon to deal with."

"We've dealt with worse," I said, letting my crew get on first. Coyote was the last of the bunch. "Hold it fleabag."

"What?" Coyote said, trying to act innocent. He could manage a lot, but looking innocent wasn't in his repertoire.

"Think of me as a customs agent. You wouldn't be trying to smuggle any fruits or vegetables off planet, now would you?"

"I'm like the natives. No clothes. Where would I put it?"

"You're a shape-shifter." Not in Loki's class, but pretty good.

"And your tail is looking a little thick."

The fleabag turned to look at his tail and pretended to notice for the first time that it was a bit more bulbous than usual. "So it is."

I held my hand out. Coyote moved his tail, which opened from the inside out and the fruit Corby had planted on the fake tree plopped into my hand.

"Why?" I said.

"I wasn't going to eat it. I was going to harvest the seeds and grow a new tree. Then eating it wouldn't hurt these people."

"Are you sure about that?"

"No. But Murphy, it would give near omniscience. Whoever eats it would be able to know anything they thought about. We might need that someday."

"We might fleabag, but at what cost to these people?" I said.

"This good-guy-at-all-costs thing is dangerous. One day our luck will run out."

"Maybe. But right now we have to go terrify that Cyndicate boss so much he'll never come back and delete all records of his finding this world. Maybe even figure out how he found out about it in the first place."

"Sounds like fun," Coyote said, stepping on board.

I cleared my throat and held out my hand again.

"How could you know?" he said. I spare you the disturbing image of the bodily orifice that opened this time for another forbidden fruit to drop out of.

I smiled. I didn't know. It was just a lucky guess. "That it?"

"Yes."

"Do I have your word?" Coyote is a Startender. Even the fleabag wouldn't lie when he gives his word.

"Yes."

"Can I impersonate an angel too when we get on board the Cyndicate ship?"

"Sure. Have fun with it," I said.

"I always do."

CROSSING ROADS

Why did the chicken cross the galaxy? To get to the other side, of course. However, when the chicken in question is Manuk Manuk, things can get a little complicated. For one thing, Manuk is the blue cosmic chicken that laid the egg that hatched the universe. I know it sounds a little outlandish, but I have it from several good authorities that it's true. Apparently let there be light was the trigger that cracked the shell and jump-started the big bang. There is some talk of living metaphors and the like, but it tends to make my head hurt.

"So you laid one egg. Big deal," Coyote said. The Native American trickster god delighted in tormenting certain folks. Manuk was one of them.

"It actually is a pretty big deal. It's so big that it actually started everything," Manuk squawked.

"So you started on top and it's all been downhill from there," Coyote said.

"As opposed to you, who has never done much of anything," Manuk said.

"I resent that remark and find it hurtful," Coyote said with a pout, putting both his head and his tail down. "You're lucky I don't climb into your henhouse and wreck . . ."

"Just try it. It will be the last thing you ever do," Manuk said.

"Why don't the two of you just get a room already?" Savannah said. For her, almost everything came down to sex. She's had sex more times than some of the cultures we've visited. Heck, she's had sex with some of the cultures we've visited. And I mean the entire culture.

"That's disgusting," Manuk said.

"I wouldn't nail her with Murphy's privates," Coyote said.

"Hey," I said. I went back a long way with both the fleabag and the blue chicken. Coyote and I had been through a lot together, but Manuk had named me the guardian of one of her eggs years ago, which I used to jump-start an entirely new universe and save this one in the process. And she laid another egg to bring me back into this universe. I owed her and I wasn't going to get in-between them. "I'm the head honcho on this ship. And I want the two of you to behave and be civil to each other."

"Is that an order?" Coyote said. The trickster had an issue with authority going back thousands of years. My leadership style was very straightforward. I rarely gave orders. I expected everyone to know what they had to do once asked. Coyote had made it clear a while back that if I were to give him another order, it would be disobeyed on principle alone. The last order was on Eden. We'd done a lot since then and I hadn't needed to give another one.

"Consider it a strong recommendation," I said. From my years tending bar at Bulfinche's Pub before New York City was sunk, I'd never learned to be properly intimidated by the old gods and powers that be. Didn't mean I had a death wish. Not that Coyote would kill me, but he's done things to others in the past that may have made them wish he did. Nobody was exempt, be it a billionaire or both houses of Congress. I was only human and running herd on tricksters was not easy. Still, I more than managed.

"Murphy, I appreciate the ride," Manuk said.

I was glad to go along with the change of subject. "No problem. I'm always happy to help you out, although I am a little confused about some of the things you asked for."

"I especially like the part where we have to shape the ship like a giant chicken to make orbit on this planet," Loki said, not bothering to hide his snicker.

"And it isn't just any chicken, but an exact replica of Manuk Manuk," Riga said. "And I thought Savannah was vain."

The blue cosmic chicken was nothing if not good-natured and took the ribbing in style. "Well, I have not been back to visit my people on Kuoyan in some time and I wanted to make an entrance."

"So now we're finally getting the story. You had a very tight beak about the reason for both the ride and requesting this particular group of Startenders to accompany you," I said. *Fools' Glory* generally carried a contingent of tricksters. There were several other Startenders ships, but ours tended to cause the most trouble for some reason. We also usually got the best results, probably because not only do we think outside the box, we trample it, change its shape, hide it from all its loved ones, and then hold it for ransom.

"I have my reasons. Did you know that in my very long lifetime I have laid only five eggs? The first one you all know about. The fourth is the one you were once guardian of, Murphy. The fifth was the one that brought Murphy back into this universe."

"I'd forgotten about that one," Coyote said. "That makes the blue hen your mother, doesn't it Murph?"

Manuk saved me from answering by continuing as if the fleabag hadn't spoken. "The second and the third were my children. A male and a female. And from them came the race of Yumin."

"Wait a second–human?" I said.

Manuk beak-grinned. "Pronounced Yu-min. The Chinese on Earth call them Yu-Min Kuo Yan."

"The Yumin are your children?" Loki asked. Manuk Manuk nodded. "I must say I'm impressed."

"Are they all blue chickens like you?" Eric asked.

Loki smiled. "They're definitely chicken-like, but I think it would be more enjoyable for you all to see them for the first time without knowing what to expect."

"I still can't get past shaping the ship like you. Do they still remember you?" Riga said.

Manuk Manuk smiled. "I'm certain they do, but let's just say I want to use my arrival as a symbol."

For gods, symbols were important. They could focus belief and power.

It wasn't as if it was a great difficulty to change the shape of *Fools' Glory*. Thanks to our morphing hull, the barship was able take on different designs easily.

"Boss," Savannah said. She'd been on watch duty. "Sensors are picking up a Nil ship."

Eric closed his eyes briefly, then reopened them. "Confirming that. It's a big one."

We had yet to actually encounter the Nil ourselves, but other Startenders had. It wasn't another race of beings so much as a cult, one dedicated to the annihilation and destruction of everything, themselves included. Although in their belief system, their leaders should be the last to go.

"Go to dust mode," I said.

"Roger that," Eric said.

Shrinking down to the size of a golf ball made defense much easier. People don't tend to attack things they don't realize are there. I've learned that sometimes the best way to win a fight is to not have it in the first place.

"They seem upset that we disappeared on them. They're pinging to see if we are using some sort of cloaking device," Savannah said. "Their weapons were primed to fire. I guess what we've heard about them attacking first is true."

"Eric, I want you to bring us in close as we go by."

"How close?" he asked.

"I want to see in the windows," I said. Sometimes looking an opponent in the eyes can teach you more about them than any sensor picture could. Especially if they don't know you're watching.

"Murphy, be careful. The Nil are why I am going home," the blue chicken said in a shaky tone. In all the years I had known her, I had never seen Manuk Manuk nervous.

I turned to Eric. "Take it slow and easy, but get every bit of data you can from our sensors and scanners."

We came within inches of the Nil ship. It was entirely black and shaped like a flying saucer that had mated with an egg. A lot of starships don't bother with actual windows. Too dangerous, even when reinforced by shielding or force fields. Most races prefer to keep their people at the center of the ship – it makes it harder to blow up in the case of a battle. The Nil didn't think like that. I guess when you're not afraid to die, the thought of a window failing and you getting sucked out into the void was probably your idea of a fun afternoon.

We did make it up to the window. There were at least two dozen on the bridge. It looked normal enough. Their uniforms were black robes complete with hoods. The entire bridge was black, which must have made reading the controls difficult. The hoods made it hard to see their eyes, or even what races they were. I looked over at Manuk Manuk, who was actually shaking.

"Eric, we've got enough. Get us out of here," I said.

Moments later, our golf ball-sized ship had left them in the figurative dust.

"Why are you so scared?" I said.

"The Nil want to destroy the universe. The universe that I helped create. There is not much that could destroy the entire universe. A planet or solar system yes, but not the whole kit and caboodle. A long time ago, the Nil figured out a way to actually do it. They would have to find a piece of the shell of my original universe egg. Because it was the basis for the primary building blocks from the big bang on, it would be possible to use it to return everything back to its original form and destroy that, effectively wiping the universe from existence."

"What happened to the shell fragments?" Loki asked.

"I am able to sense where they are, but I won't tell anyone, even a Startender. Not even you, Murphy. Knowing it would make you a target. I have had a bounty on my head for ages because of it. I will tell you that there may be a piece on my people's world and that the Nil are desperately seeking it. That's why I'm going home. To stop them from destroying the entire universe," Manuk Manuk said.

"Well as long as it's nothing major," I said with a smile, to cover up the chill going down my spine.

We Startenders haven't been in space long, at least compared to most of the other star-faring peoples, but we do have some advantages over a lot of them. It's not unheard of for a technologically advanced people to find a more primitive culture and try to set themselves up as gods by passing off their tech as magic.

Startender tech is in fact magic, or a mixture of science and magic that gives us the best of both worlds. All of our barships are designed and built by Vulcan himself. Over the centuries, Vulcan has thought so far outside of the famous box that he can make it look like a circle and change shape at his whim. Vulcan uses the same principles that allow a non-Newtonian fluid to be a solid when certain principles like percussive bass are applied, mixes it with some principles first theorized by Maxwell, then runs it through his own genius. The end result somehow allows our barships to change shape, which is why we were able to appear as a golden image of Manuk Manuk as we made planetfall.

One of the other advantages we have over most spacefaring ships is an ability to easily make planetfall and achieve re-entry into orbit. It takes up a tremendous amount of energy for most ships to get back in orbit. The laws of physics don't change for us, but we have found loopholes by using alternative power sources. The heat of re-entry generates a tremendous amount of energy. Vulcan was horrified by the idea of all that heat going to waste, so he designed the hull of our ships to be able to absorb and store it, then rechannel it in order to get us back up into space. Works well on absorbing most other forms of energy, too.

Since we are able to affect the amount of mass we have in this universe at any given time, we can have more mass going down then we do going up, which lets us end up with more energy than we started out with.

"Should we let them know we are coming? I don't want to set off any planetary defenses and have them start shooting at us," I said. It's happened before and is rarely pleasant.

Manuk Manuk bowed her blue head and closed her eyes for a moment. Her lids opened and she looked at me. "I let them know to expect us."

That is another advantage Startenders have – alternate forms of communications, not the least of which was Foster.

Foster was elsewhere at the moment. If we needed him, we would simply talk to the plant to get his attention. Of course, being able to communicate telepathically like Manuk just did is fairly quick too.

"Eric, is the ship prepped?" I said.

"Yup. We got our chicken face on, Boss," the golden melog said.

"Then let's go meet the Yumin."

"Turn on the windows," I said. The room seemed to disappear so we could see as the heat of entry into the atmosphere burned a fiery nimbus around us. I never got tired of watching that.

Manuk gave Eric the coordinates of where we were to land, but as we got close, I realized we probably didn't need them. There were probably half-a-million chicken people waiting for us. You could see it from a couple of miles in the air. As we got closer you could make out individuals. I expected them all to be blue, but they seemed to be all colors of the spectrum, from white to black to blue to red. Although if you looked closely, most of their feathers did have a blue tint to them. They were humanoid with a combination arm/wing. Their heads looked birdlike, although the shifting to humanoid made them look less chickenish and more regal somehow.

At the center of the mass of people there was a clearing, so Eric landed there. My crew and I liked to have fun with how we exited the ship, especially considering its shape changing properties. In this instance the ship looked like a three story high golden chicken, so we opened the beak and had its tongue roll down to use as a ramp.

Manuk Manuk has never been stuffy or formal. She was the first one out and slid down her giant idol's tongue like it was a slide. The rest of us did the same. There were chicken people as far as the eye could see, and when Manuk touched the ground, every last one of them went down on bended knee, put their arm to their chest, and bowed their head. It was less the gesture of worshipers to a god then those of soldiers to the supreme commander.

A blue chicken man stood and put his arms out to his sides. "Welcome back, great mother of the cosmos. We, your people, have missed you greatly."

"I have missed all of you too, Randolph," Manuk said.

Oddly enough we didn't need our badges to translate as the chicken man was speaking English.

"Allow me to introduce my Startender escorts. This is Murphy, Loki, Riga, Savannah, and Eric." Coyote cleared his throat, annoyed at being left out. "And that is Coyote."

Coyote walked up to the chicken man and bowed his head. "Charmed, I'm sure."

"Are things as bad as I have been led to believe?" Manuk asked.

"Worse, I fear. We have failed you, Mother. The piece of the great cosmic egg you entrusted to us to keep safe has been stolen. There have been guards constantly in its presence, myself included, yet we have no idea how it was taken."

Manuk looked at Randolph. It's hard to tell when someone with a beak is smiling or frowning, but I can tell you that the blue cosmic chicken had a frown on her beak.

"We will get it back," she said. "How is the hatchery?"

"It is well. All of our eggs are safe. We have tripled the guards around the hatchery to make sure nothing happens."

Loki whispered in my ear. "The Yumin are rumored to literally put all their eggs in one basket, making it easier to watch out and protect their unborn. The children are trained as scholars and warriors and then sent out to other worlds to help protect the other children of Manuk Manuk."

"Other children?" I whispered back.

"The rest of sentient life in the universe," Loki said. "The reason the Chinese had a name for the Yumin is there was a contingent of them on Earth for quite some time a number of centuries back. Think of it in terms of Earth's Israel where everyone is drafted into military service upon reaching adulthood. They are taught diplomacy, languages, martial arts, science, and magic. Think of them as a race of Startenders, minus the powers and badges."

"Shall we begin the search?" the chicken man asked.

"There is still time for that. First, I would like to see the hatchery."

The blue chicken man bowed. "As you wish, Cosmic Mother."

As we moved through the crowd, Manuk greeted everyone. She reverted back to what sounded like normal chicken language, but our badges translated it. She was speaking at lightning speed, but the Yumin understood her just fine. As she said their names, each of the chicken people bowed and clucked back a greeting. In the time spent walking to the hatchery, she literally said hello to each of what was probably hundreds of thousands of her children. Being a goddess, she didn't need a bullhorn or other amplification for them to hear her.

We just trailed in her wake.

Needless to say it did take some time to actually reach the hatchery. Manuk Manuk did her final greeting to the guards who stood watch. She saved a white chicken man for last.

"Hello, Herschel."

Herschel bowed. "Good to see you again, Cosmic Mother. I have been practicing a trick for you." Herschel bent down and picked up what looked like three basketball-sized eggs and started juggling them. Every other chicken person in the area gasped as the giant eggs started flying, but Manuk appeared amused.

"Herschel, are you insane?" Randolph said, lurching forward in an attempt to grab the eggs out of the air. Herschel side stepped and was able to keep the eggs moving so that Randolph wasn't able to take a single egg away from him. Herschel stopped, caught all three and took a bow.

"That's it, Herschel! This time you have gone too far. Endangering the lives of three unborn. I will see you pay for this," Randolph said.

Manuk put a wing on Randolph's leg. "Relax. Herschel would never endanger a child. Would you, Herschel?"

Herschel shook his head. "Of course not." He tapped one of the eggs with his feathered finger. "See—fake."

"You are not funny, Herschel," Randolph said.

"Actually I find him quite endearing," Manuk Manuk said, flapping her wings so that she sat on my shoulder and leaned her beak into my ear. "He actually reminds me of you, Murphy."

"Then he is okay in my book," I said, reaching out and shaking hands with the joking chicken.

"You mean there is more than one of them? I can barely tolerate the one Murphy we have," Coyote said.

"Well, no one can tolerate you, so I guess it balances out," Manuk said.

"Go suck an egg. I hear there is a whole bunch inside," Coyote said.

"Cosmic Mother, I will bring you inside and show you the hatchery," Randolph said.

"Actually, I'd like Herschel to do it," Manuk said.

If looks could kill, Herschel would be part of an extra value meal.

Herschel extended his left wing down toward Manuk Manuk, who wrapped her right wing around the end of it and he escorted her in much the same way you would an honored grandmother. The hatchery was round and tapered almost like someone had taken an ice cream cone and buried it in the ground so you couldn't see the tip. The walls looked like some type of concrete and were easily ten feet thick.

"This is the only entrance to the hatchery," Manuk said. "The building can withstand a nuclear blast."

"Has that been an issue?" I asked.

"Only once," Herschel said.

"Cosmic Mother, I must protest," Randolph said when he saw us following behind her. "These people are strangers. To allow them in the hatchery is a huge breach of protocol and security."

"These people are friends of mine. And they are Startenders, which in the coming years will stand for something great. None of them, even the flea-bitten canine, would do anything to harm our children. Unless you doubt my wisdom," Manuk said.

There was some dynamic going on between the two of them that I couldn't figure out. Randolph ruled the roost because of the blue chicken's blessing and was playing the respectful subject, but it didn't seem to be sincere. Worse yet, Manuk didn't seem to like him, and it wasn't the kind of playful dislike she had for Coyote. This guy warranted watching.

"Of course not, Great Cosmic Mother. My sincerest apologies. I hope you will not mind if we bring a contingent of guards with you on the tour, just to be on the safe side."

"If it will make you happy, Randolph, then by all means," Manuk said.

At Randolph's gesture about a hundred chicken men and women, with long spear-like weapons that were also equipped for energy discharge, took up positions alongside and behind us.

Loki frowned. "They are packing serious heat. Those weapons could actually hurt us." Loki was speaking in a language I had never heard of, but the badges were able to translate. However, the chicken folk weren't able to understand. "I think their leader is part of the problem that Manuk is here to fix."

"I figured that out, too," I whispered my answer in English, as I knew smatterings of phrases in a bunch of different languages, but figured I wasn't fluent in any that the chicken people wouldn't know. I turned to Riga, Savannah, and Eric. "You three stay out here and mingle. See what you can learn."

The trio nodded, Savannah a little too happily. The she-satyr made nymphomaniacs look undersexed. "We're on duty," I reminded her.

Savannah sighed, but nodded. Her father couldn't be trusted to stay on task if the possibility of sex, let alone sex with a new race loomed, but Savannah could curb her urges when she had to, even if she wasn't happy about it.

Their security was good. We had to pass through several chambers where one side had to be closed before the other would open, much like an airlock. Finally, we reached the part of the hatchery where the eggs were kept. It was massive. The floor seemed to be some sort of foam, which substituted for a nest. The eggs fit nicely in indentations and were evenly spaced. The floor itself was warm and protected the eggs until the infants were ready to be hatched.

"The birth cycle of my people is every ten years, so I try to get back here at least that often," Manuk said.

Three chicken women appeared with digital pads.

The eldest of them, who was also the plumpest, stood before Manuk Manuk and bowed. "Welcome, Cosmic Mother. Are you here for the naming?"

"Yes I am, Daka. A pleasure to see you again. You do such a wonderful job taking care of all the little ones," Manuk said, letting go of Herschel's arm. Daka's face feathers flushed and Manuk flew down to walk alongside the women at least until she reached the huge eggs. Manuk leapt up and moved among the shells, stopping to touch and caress each egg and whisper something through the shell then turned to the women and named each egg. The women seemed to be taking pictures with their pads and making notations each time.

"She names everyone?" I said.

"Yes. All of us have been named by the Great Mother," Herschel said.

I whistled. "There has to be ten thousand eggs here."

"11,617 to be exact," Herschel said. That got a look from Randolph who apparently was finding it hard to believe that Herschel would know such a thing.

"Great, we're gonna be here a while," Coyote complained.

Herschel looked down at Coyote. "It is a great honor to be at the naming of an entire generation. Manuk must think highly of you to have you present."

"Oh lucky me," Coyote said.

I had to silently admit that I was with Coyote on this one.

The naming process was slow and tedious, although the chicken people seemed in awe of it with the exception of Randolph.

It was nightfall before she was done. We left the hatchery the way we had come in and I signaled the rest of our crew to rejoin us.

"As the hour is late, I assume you will want to retire to your hall, Cosmic Mother. I will find accommodations for your guests," Randolph said. I didn't like the way he said that. My gut was telling me that we should sleep with one eye open and somebody on guard duty or we might not wake up.

"Nonsense, my friends will stay with me," Manuk said.

The blue chicken man's beak opened and hung that way. "But Great Cosmic Mother, no one is permitted to stay in your hall but you."

"The entire rule states no one is allowed to stay in my hall while I am not present. I am certainly allowed to have guests in my own home. In fact, I would like Herschel to join us for the evening."

The white chicken bowed his head. "I would be honored."

Randolph bristled, the feathers on the back of his head actually rising up. "Very well. We will show you to your hall."

"Nonsense. I know the way to my own home. You and the rest of the soldiers go and get some rest. Tomorrow we begin our search for the shell," Manuk said.

That seemed to placate the blue chicken man. "Very well, Great Mother. As you wish."

And with that they left us. Manuk took us through the streets of the city. The architecture was very simple. Streets were laid out in a rectangular pattern, crossing each other at symmetrical intervals. The buildings were squares and rectangles only a few stories high with one exception. When we go to Manuk's home we all stopped for a moment to take it in.

"You have got to be kidding me," Coyote said.

"And everyone says I'm vain," Savannah said, craning her neck to look up.

The outer portion of her huge house was shaped like her head and like the current shape of our ship, the door was through her mouth.

"Enter freely," Manuk said then looked to Coyote. "Or sleep outside. It's the same either way to me."

We went inside. There were no beds, only large nests made out of the same foam as the hatchery.

"This gets better and better," Coyote said.

"Stop your complaining," Riga said, transforming out of her human shape to her dragon one. She took the largest nest and curled up in it. "This seems perfectly comfortable."

"They are. However, we won't be sleeping here tonight."

"And why is that?" Savannah asked, as she plopped herself into another nest and put her hooves up.

"Because Randolph and a number of his personal guard are part of the Nil. I could tell as soon as I saw them. There are black marks on their umbras." Which is the shadow a soul casts. Gods and some mages can see them. "We will need to search tonight to stop them. If we wait until morning, they will have too many traps waiting for us to be able to do it easily. Or at all."

"It's just a bunch of chickens that think they are men," Coyote said.

"You haven't done much traveling outside of Earth except with us," Loki said, shaking his head.

"Yes, I have," Coyote said defensively, much like a child. "I've been to plenty of other planets without you."

"Name three," Loki said.

"I'm not on trial here," Coyote said.

Loki sighed and dropped it. "Manuk's people are best described as heroic. They go out to help the downtrodden, and the weak, after being trained in mind, spirit, and body. Do not underestimate them because they have some feathers. Those weapons they carried were modulated for mundane and magical energy output. Enough of them could kill even the two of us," Loki said.

Coyote's ears shot up. "I don't like the sound of that."

Eric froze for a moment. The Melog were mechanical, yet living, beings whose bodies were made from a similar alloy as our ship. They were tied directly into it so they were able to control it with their minds. Of course the head honcho had the ability to override the controls and take care of things manually, but I was happy to have Eric in the driver's seat. I had known him since his birth and he had turned out to be a good kid.

"Murph, someone is trying to get into *Fools' Glory*," Eric said.

"You took standard precautions?" I asked. That included basically shutting off access to it by moving the actual ship into the pocket dimension. The giant chicken that was left in the landing area was nothing more than a golden statue. There weren't any working, moving parts. They would have as much luck breaking into a rock.

"Of course," Eric said.

"Then we have nothing to worry about," I said. "Except tracking down the Nil."

"That's where I come in," Manuk said. "With the right amount of guidance and concentration, I can see anywhere in the universe. I know this world better than almost any other. They should not be able to hide from me here." Manuk sat in her nest, put her wings out to her sides, and closed her eyes in what I can only guess was an attempt to communicate with the universe.

About ten minutes later, the cosmic blue chicken opened her eyes with a look that seemed to say that the universe wasn't taking her call. "Interesting. I could not sense them anywhere," Manuk said.

"Not only a has been, but incompetent too. What a great combination," Coyote said.

"Actually we're talking about me, not you. However, there is one area where I can sense nothing. Someone took great pains to make that happen. That is where we will find the Nil and the shell fragment."

"Should we bring the ship around?" I said.

"No, we can just walk. The place I can't sense anything is the palace. Since Randolph undoubtedly has people watching the door to my house, I suggest we sneak out the rear," Manuk said. Coyote started to open his mouth. "No, the house is not anatomically correct, so keep your comments to yourself. Fortunately, I have planned for such an eventuality." Manuk moved a piece of her foam that flipped like a switch and her nest slid over, revealing a small tunnel.

"Coyote, why don't you take point," I said.

"Is that an order?" Coyote said.

"Knock it off," I said. Coyote smirked and crawled through the tunnel first. Manuk followed and then the rest of us, with Loki taking up the rear.

The tunnel led out into a small park across the road behind her hall, into an area that was totally surrounded by hedges. No one could see us.

"We should do our best to go unnoticed," Manuk said.

Several of our crew were shape-shifters. Loki was quite accomplished and could appear as pretty much anything. Coyote claimed to be as good, but we rarely saw evidence of that. Riga was able to change between human and dragon, but little else.

Loki shifted into Randolph. "This way if we get stopped, it should make things easier."

We slowly walked the streets. We had all learned long ago that the best way to go unnoticed is to act as if you belonged. If someone saw you sneaking or creeping around, they would automatically think something was up.

The palace was just that, a large fortress not terribly dissimilar from an Earth castle. There was a main gate and a walkway around the upper part of the building.

"How should we go in?" I asked the blue cosmic chicken.

"I'm not certain. I can't sense anything inside."

Loki and I exchanged smiles. "I guess we should pull a Karma," I said. We had first developed our system of using Loki's shape-shifting skills to infiltrate and give faked orders to an invading army on the planet Karma. The chicken man-shaped Loki smiled and walked up to the two guards outside, still looking like their leader.

"Sir, I thought you were inside," the guard said.

"That's what you were supposed to think," the disguised Norse trickster said. "There has been a problem at Manuk Manuk's home. I need you and the inside guards to go and watch her house. Stay hidden, but notify me immediately if she tries to leave her hall."

"Yes, sir," the chicken man said, grabbing his partner and the guards from inside the door. The group double-timed it across town, leaving the palace entrance unguarded for us.

We walked in without any difficulty. The thing not only loosely resembled a castle, but was as big as one.

"Now that we are inside, any idea of what's going on? Will they be doing the ceremony now or do they have to wait for certain stars to align?" I said.

"Murphy, they are holding one of the fundamental building blocks of the universe. In the right hands, a piece of the shell could make the stars align however they want. Unfortunately, I'm not picking up anything," Manuk said.

"Okay then, we split up and search the place. Loki, you take Riga, Savannah, and Eric and go that way. We'll go this way." Meaning Manuk, Coyote, Herschel, and me.

"Will do. Holler if you find anything," Loki said. That meant using the badges to call, not actually scream.

We went down the hallway, checking offices and rooms, all of which were empty.

"Coyote, smell anything unusual?" I said.

"Just chicken people," Coyote said. We got to a staircase. "Should we go up or down?"

"It has been my experience that these things always happen in the basement or on the roof. We didn't see anything up top on the way in," I said. So down we went.

We got to the door and Manuk stopped short.

"This is it. The shell piece is inside."

I hit my badge. "We found them. They're in the basement."

"We'll be there momentarily," Loki said.

"That's going to be too long," Coyote said as the door swung open. A half dozen of the chicken people were pointing their energy spears at us.

"Manuk, so good of you to join us. It seems quite fitting that since you were present for the beginning of the universe that you should join us as we prepare to end it," Randolph said.

"I'm afraid the universe doesn't destroy that easy, Randolph," Manuk said. "I taught you better than that.

"That's okay. We aren't afraid of much. You made sure of that too, didn't you Great Mother? Fortunately the Nil showed us your way was the wrong one and theirs was the right. And if we have to end one world, one solar system at a time, we'll happily put that extra effort in. After all, you created us to be hard workers."

"I created you for a lot more than that," Manuk said.

"And I guess we are an awful disappointment to you, Cosmic

Mother."

"Yes, you are," Manuk said. "I knew as soon as I saw your egg. I should have smashed it. You'd think after all these ages, I'd have learned to trust my gut."

"Too late for that. Maybe we'll start by killing your friends. It won't affect the ceremony one way or the other, but just because we are going to destroy everything, doesn't mean we can't have fun doing it," Randolph said.

"Randolph, how can you do this?" Herschel said.

"You're young yet. I spent decades traveling through the universe, helping save idiot races from their own stupidity. And what thanks did we get? More work. I got sick of it, so when the Nil approached me I was very receptive. Now which one of you wants to die first?"

"None of us are going to die here today, Randolph," I said. "As a matter of fact, I am going to give you a chance to surrender."

This was met by uproarious laughter, which sounded an awful lot like clucking.

Coyote shook his head. "Why do you always feel the need to do that? It never works, not even in that stupid movie."

"I'm being nice, giving them a chance to do it the easy way."

"These aren't people who haven't paid a bar tab, Murphy. They're trying to destroy the universe. They don't deserve nice. They deserve to be put out of our misery. It's a simple rule–don't be nice to the Nilists," Coyote scolded.

"You don't know. It might have worked. Even as we speak, their hearts may be changing. They could realize that the universe is a wonderful place. And not only is it a wonderful place, but it's the place where everybody they know lives. Plus, it's where they keep all their possessions. If they destroy the universe, everyone they know will be gone and they won't have any stuff. Now who would want to do that?" I said. I turned back to Randolph who obviously had no idea that Coyote and I were just doing some shtick to stall for time. We were outnumbered and outgunned. With luck that would change when the others got here.

"Randolph, you have listened to what I've had to say. Search your heart. Examine your soul. You know deep inside you that it's the right thing to do, and you really want to stop this and let us go.

This is your chance to make it all right."

Randolph's beak flopped open. "You are being serious?"

"Actually I wasn't, at least not entirely." What was obvious to me wasn't obvious to a Nilist. "Please tell me what is in it for you if you destroy the universe, because if you do it, you die too. It's like a murder-suicide. I don't condone suicide, but if you're going to kill yourself anyway, do it first and save all the other people."

"I feel a black gaping hole of despair that permeates my very being." The Nilists are very good at infecting and brainwashing others with dark magic. It is like an entire cult harvested the depression of teenagers. Or at least the type of teenager who wore black all the time and was fascinated with death, then figured out how to magnify it a millionfold. They used psychological and telepathic tools to fine tune it.

Of course, I hardly shared that point of view. "Are you sure it isn't something you ate? It would make you look like a real idiot to have destroyed the universe because of a little indigestion."

"Do you think you are funny?" Randolph said.

"Sadly, he does," Coyote said.

"He makes me chuckle," Manuk said.

"I find his attitude admirable," Herschel said.

"Each of you is a bigger fool than the next. The only way to end that blackness in my soul, the darkness that lurks in every living being is to destroy all that is. You ask what is in it for me. That's easy. It will bring an end to all pain, not just mine, but everyone else's. It is the only way to save your children, Manuk Manuk. It's a pity you cannot see that. You shouldn't be trying to stop us–you should be joining us. Cheering us on."

"Fire cracker, fire cracker, shish boom gang, go Nil, go Nil, undo the big bang," I said, doing my best imitation of a cheerleader. "Nope, doesn't work for me."

"Too bad, because we are going to end your pain first. Plus, maybe it will make you shut up," Randolph said, pointing his spear directly at me. "Actually, you're the team leader, so maybe we won't kill you just yet, but hold the threat of death over you, in order to make your team capitulate."

"You don't have to make Savannah capitulate. Heck sometimes to make her stop capitulating, we have to turn the fire hose on her," I said, totally confusing the blue chicken man.

"You will tell your people to surrender to us or we'll kill you. At their core, all sentient beings are cowards, so I know you will comply with us rather than die."

I didn't bother to explain to this nut job that as much as I didn't want to die, there were plenty of things in the universe worth dying for, let alone for the entire universe itself. The rest of the team should have been here by now, so hopefully we only needed to delay a few more moments. Still, I didn't want to die because of bad timing, so I figured it was best to buy a few more seconds. "Coyote, I want you to surrender and not do anything to any of these warriors, especially Randolph." Coyote had been cleaning his paws, acting disinterested, as he often does to throw off his opponents. My words actually seemed to catch him by surprise. He stopped with his tongue still hanging out and looked up at me. "That's an order."

"An order, huh?" he said. I nodded.

"I am happy that you are being so cooperative. I will keep you alive long enough to give the rest of your team the same order, should any of them be foolish enough to also try to stop us," Randolph said.

"It occurs to me that we have an opportunity unprecedented in the universe. The fundamental building blocks of the universe came from inside you, Manuk Manuk. You helped cause the chain reaction that became the big bang, the first light of the creator. What if we used that shell fragment to kill you, Cosmic Mother? With our ceremony, not only would we destroy this star system, but the reaction could spread quickly to all creation fueled by your destruction. No need to go door to door to each system," Randolph said. "It would be so much more fun to have your friends capture and secure you to the sacrificial alter. Murphy, tell your crewman to bind Manuk to our altar."

"Coyote, you heard the man. I order you to do as he says."

Coyote raised an eyebrow and turned toward Manuk. Herschel stepped between the animal gods, so I grabbed him in a headlock and pulled him back. "Trust us," I whispered. He stopped struggling and let me move him out of the way.

"You heard the feather duster, Manuk. Let's go," Coyote said.

Manuk crossed her wings in front of her chest. "I'd rather die first."

Coyote shrugged his canine shoulders. "If that's the way you want it."

The canine trickster darted forward, his jaws wrapping around Manuk's neck. With a twist of his head a loud snap was heard and Manuk fell limp.

"No!" screamed Herschel and Randolph in unison, albeit for very different reasons.

"You idiot! By killing her you ruined our one chance to destroy everything," Randolph screamed.

"Guess it's back to the hard work you mentioned earlier," Coyote said.

Herschel elbowed me in the gut and flipped me over his shoulder. "Trust me you said. I did and now the Great Mother of us all is dead."

Riga had been lying in wait and let loose a blast of fire breath around the rebel Yumin. Her flame was hot enough to burn, but only lasted a moment, just long enough to incinerate all the oxygen out of the air. Without anything to breathe, several Nilist chicken men collapsed.

Loki, Savannah, and Eric waded in amongst the soldiers, using old fashioned hand-to-hand combat to disarm as many as they could. In terms of numbers, Loki was beating the others combined two-to-one. Randolph ran to the altar and lifted the eggshell above his head. It had ragged edges and was no bigger than a quarter. "You're still too late to stop me. This world will die. And before this world dies, all its future children will," Randolph gloated.

"The hatchery! What did you do?" Herschel said.

"I sent the bulk of my true people there to destroy the entire next generation. Even if you were somehow able to stop me, there will be no Yumin children to raise."

Herschel looked torn. He wanted to go after Randolph, but saving his peoples' unborn was just as much a priority.

"Go, save them. We'll take care of Randolph," I said.

"I can't trust you. For all I know, you're really in league with him," Herschel said.

Coyote walked over, Manuk's limp body still hanging from

his jaws. The trickster stood between Randolph and Herschel. Manuk's head moved. "Herschel, listen to what Murphy says."

The white chicken man's eyes went wide as he realized Manuk was only playing dead. The chicken man ran out as fast as he could. Coyote and I moved towards Randolph.

"You're too late to stop me."

"Want to bet?" Coyote said. With the shake of his head he threw Manuk Manuk across the room. The blue cosmic chicken straightened out like a feathered missile – dare I say she was poultry in motion. Randolph had the fragment of eggshell in his hand and froze a moment as she came closer. He brought the egg to his throat and slit it just as Manuk grabbed hold of it with her beak. As one of the building blocks of the universe, I guess it was both strong and sharp. The blue chicken man collapsed to the floor, laughing.

"The only way to summon back the primordial darkness is through the ultimate act of self-sacrifice. I die happy, knowing I am finally free. My blessing is upon you and soon you too shall know freedom."

From his throat, a black hole appeared. I'm not talking the cosmological kind, but a literal black hole in the air and it started to grow.

"Damn it, we're too late," Coyote said.

Things of darkness, shapes that were not shapes, but still moved, writhed out into the light.

"We claim this world for destruction," came a voice that penetrated not the ears, but the brain. It hurt. All the chicken men in the room who were still conscious grabbed hold of their heads and fell to the floor. The mortals among us probably would have been doing the same thing if it wasn't for our badges.

The blue cosmic chicken had no badge, but stood before the hole unfazed.

"You shall not cross into this universe while I yet stand," Manuk Manuk said, her wings defiantly placed on her chicken hips.

"That is easily fixed, egg layer. You got rid of us once, but you'll never do it again."

Primordial chaos and darkness was banished from this universe during the big bang, but has been trying to get back in since.

"You are wrong," Manuk said, and her form began to change into something beautiful and strange. It glowed with the primal forces of the universe.

"Riga! Murphy! Savannah! Don't look, close your eyes!" Loki shouted, somehow managing to grab hold of all three of us and shielding us with his body. I listened and closed my eyes. I heard the darkness hiss. I peeked for an instant and saw Eric as he stood fascinated. His mind worked differently than ours, so he was safe. Or at least I hoped he was.

"What do we do?" I whispered, afraid to even squint.

"You'll do nothing. Only Manuk, Coyote, Eric's, and my mind will be able to survive this. The rest of you need to get out of here and help Herschel save the unborn. We will stand against the darkness," Loki said. He whispered so only I could hear, "Murph, it's been an honor."

"I don't want to hear defeatist talk. You will not only win, but you will survive. I'm not ready to break in a new honcho. Or friend."

"Is that an order?" Loki said, and it sounded like he was smiling the type of smile that told the universe that it could take your life, but not who you were.

"Damn straight it is," I said.

"I'll do my best," Loki said, pushing the dragon, the faun, and me toward the door

"Okay people, you heard the honcho–we're moving out," I said. The three of us made it to the door by feeling our way. When we got there I couldn't help myself–I looked back, but again only for an instant. I was already moving my hands to cover up as I opened my eyelids. Eric wasn't Eric. He had called the ship to him and he was inside it, manipulating the outer aspect into a warship. Loki and Coyote had changed into something else, maybe their true forms. My vision had only lasted a fraction of a second, but it was enough to give me a headache. I didn't dare look again and instead ran out the door.

When we got outside, the she-satyr and I climbed on the dragon's back and Riga took off into the sky. In the distance you could see a lone figure flapping through the air and landing at the hatchery.

"I didn't think they could fly that far. He must have jumped off the top of the building," I said. The palace was high enough that he could have been able to glide and fly the entire way.

"He's got a brave heart," Savannah said. "And those feathers are sexy."

"You think anything that is breathing is sexy," I said.

"Breathing is sexy. Dead things are awful hard to have a good time with," Savannah said. The sad part was she wasn't joking. No sexual act was too perverse or outlandish for her to consider. I hoped she drew the line well before necrophilia, but I also knew her lines were drawn with chalk.

We landed at the hatchery and the doors were locked. Riga tried smashing the wall with her tail and then blasting it with fire. It was barely singed. "Murphy, there is no way I'm going to get through this," the dragon said.

Herschel was busy fiddling with a series of panels covered with a bunch of lights. It was their equivalent of a key pad. The door opened. He ran inside and we followed, Riga having to shrink to human size to fit in.

Herschel kept moving, but the doors didn't close behind us.

"How'd you figure that out?" I said.

"Got bored on guard duty and found the flaw in the defense. Reprogrammed it so nobody but me could do this," he said.

The last blast door opened to reveal a hundred Yumin warriors, armed with their energy spears, as they turned toward us.

Fortunately everyone on my team was quick on their feet.

"Riga, perfume workers special," Savannah said, standing in front of Riga, who transformed back into a dragon. Savannah always wore the minimal amount of clothes, which was rarely more than a pair of short shorts and a bikini top. She, like all satyrs, was able to use pheromones to entice members of the opposite sex. Savannah was better than most and was able to store a whole lot of them and release them at will. Since these pheromones were magic based, they worked faster and quicker than the normal variety.

As she stood there, the dragon exhaled and her hot breath hit the she-satyr, blasting her musk into the hatchery. It hit the bulk of the soldiers so they were suddenly in lust with Savannah. She posed seductively, threw her hair back and smiled. "You boys want me? Come and get me."

Savannah took off running through all the open doors. The male soldiers moved to follow her. I grabbed the hand of the first one in line.

"You don't want to bring that weapon with you. She hates those. If you want a chance with her, you better all leave them here," I said.

Overcome with primitive lust, the chicken men obeyed without even thinking. The one I grabbed gave me his energy spear. The rest dropped them where they stood and ran after Savannah. She was fast, I only hoped she was quick enough to outrun them all. Then again, once she was far enough away, she might just stop so she and they could play. I try not to judge, but sometimes fail. Savannah is not only willing to take one for the team, she's willing to take on the whole team. And then the stadium.

While the she-satyr's ploy had worked amazingly well, it still left us with a good couple of dozen female soldiers to deal with. Herschel picked up a fallen energy spear in each arm.

"Do these things have a stun setting?" I said, grabbing one for myself.

Herschel lifted up one spear, turned part of the staff and pushed a button in. I mimicked his actions.

"Should I take out the air?" Riga said.

"No, you might damage the eggs," I said, pointing with my spear and blasting one of the chicken women. Herschel did the same, but somehow managed to take down four in the same amount of time.

Riga returned to human form, picked up a spear, and joined us in the blasting. Between the three of us, we took out twenty-three of the two dozen, but we held our fire on the last one because she held one of the Yumin eggs above her head. If we were to shoot her, it would fall and be smashed. Or worse, we might hit the egg.

"It appears we have a standoff," the chicken woman said. Her head feathers were red.

"Pisha, you don't want to do this," Herschel said.

"Why wouldn't I? I was barren, unable to lay even a single egg. Do you know they banned me from even mating?" she said.

"You know as well as I do that no one who wants to mate outside of mating season ever listens to that," Herschel said.

"I wanted children," she said, waving the egg in front of her.

"So? You could have them. Many of us never make it back from our missions off world. There are always orphans to raise. You could have had children," Herschel said.

"But not my own."

"So you are trying to destroy our world and kill an entire

generation of children just because you can't have any of your own?" Herschel said. "How can this make sense to you?"

Pisha looked very sad in a psychotic chicken kind of way. "How does it not make sense to you? Randolph has treated you like dirt, you more than anybody else."

"He doesn't like my sense of humor and the fact that I question him," Herschel said.

"He banned you from going off world and relegated you to guard duty on the hatchery. It's important, but something given to children and old folk. The worthy Yumin are the ones that get assignments off in the universe. No one in our generation has been trampled on more than you. Why cling to something as foolish as hope? You know it is an illusion. You shouldn't be fighting us, you should be fighting with us."

"To destroy the universe? Not a chance," Herschel said. "Just put the egg down and give up. Nobody else needs to get hurt."

"I may not be able to kill all the children, but I will destroy this one," Pisha said, holding the egg above her head to smash it. We all rushed forward, but we were beat by a dive-bombing matronly chicken woman, who scooped the egg out of her grasp and back-kicked Pisha in the face, knocking her down.

"Nice work, Daka," I said to the chief egg counter and guardian.

"Nobody messes with the babies I'm entrusted with," Daka said.

"Pisha, surrender and I'll make sure you are treated fairly," I said.

"I was going to destroy all these unborn Yumin and you want to capture me? You are insane. Show some backbone, all of you. Kill me, damn it," she said.

"Startenders don't kill unless there is no other choice," I said.

"You don't have any other choice. As long as I am alive, I will be trying to kill and destroy anyone and everyone I can. What do you think of that?" Pisha said.

The Nil have their dirty little tricks, but so did we. I learned something years ago before New York was sunk by a mad sea god. There was a Gaizkin, a creature that fed on death by possessing people and driving them to suicide. I helped take one down, after its previous victim had been saved by luck and Hermes. I'll never forget what Jerome told me happened after he jumped off of the 59th Street Bridge. As he felt death nearing and the water racing up to greet him, much the same way a swatter would a fly, he no longer wanted to die. He wanted to live.

I figured the same principle might work here.

"Well if that's the way you feel, I suppose we should help you with that. Right, Riga? Why don't you take her for a flight and drop her," I said with a wink.

Loki's dragon daughter smiled and returned the wink.

Even in human form, Riga was a hell of a lot stronger than any human or any chicken person. She grabbed Pisha by the scruff of her neck and dragged her outside. She threw her down, then transformed back to her dragon self. I watched her sag and realized the constant shifting back and forth was exhausting her. We would have to find her some massive amounts of food when this was done, or she was going to pass out. She grabbed the chicken woman in her jaws and took off flying into the sky. I watched her go higher and higher until she was barely a speck, then suddenly there were two specks as she let Pisha fall toward the Earth. Riga dove down after her a second later. Wings and gravity were much faster than gravity alone.

Even from the ground, I could make out Pisha's faint scream, which only got louder as she got closer to the ground. Riga matched her speed, but stayed behind her.

The chicken people could fly for short distances. Pisha tried to remain stoic and face her doom. Once the reality and the terror sunk in, she flapped frantically to slow her descent, even managing to stop it, hovering thousands of feet up. She tried to glide downward, but was just too high. Eventually her arms became tired to the point where she couldn't move, let alone flap them. Pisha began to plummet again. This time there was no stopping her, at least under her own power. The screaming didn't stop the entire way. Impressive breath control. Riga caught up to her in a parallel downward flight.

"I'm starving. I love Earth chicken and I imagine you taste very similar. Apparently, many things do," Riga said. I've mentioned this to Manuk, asking if this was because the universe hatched from a mystic chicken egg. Like many things, I never got a straight answer. "After you die, you wouldn't mind if I ate you, would you? Please?"

"I don't want to die anymore. Please save me," the chicken woman pleaded as she approached the ground like a falling meteor.

"Nonsense. I heard what you said. You are forever loyal to the Nil cause. All is bleak, all is dark and there is no hope, no reason to live," the dragon said. Which was something that absolutely was not true. Bulfinche's Pub may be sitting beneath the waves, but the sign that says hope and happiness never die still hung there over the door. "You want your glorious death and final freedom of oblivion. I wouldn't dare take them from you."

"Please! I changed my mind. I want to live!" the chicken woman shrieked.

At this point she was barely two hundred feet from making a crater, limply flapping her now useless and exhausted wings.

"Well, only if you are really sure," Riga said.

"Yes, I am sure. Please save me."

The dragon adjusted her velocity to match and scooped the plummeting chicken woman with her reptilian arms, using her wings to slow her fall. It took most of the remaining distance, but she safely deposited the chicken on the ground. The Nilist mind control had been broken.

"One down, another ninety eight to go," I said.

Riga looked at me and rolled her eyes, looking exhausted. We found her some food first.

Once we had saved the eggs, I wanted to rush back to the palace to help beat back the invading darkness, but I didn't. I knew Loki was right. Mortal minds were no match for primordial chaos. Even with the protection our badges provided, we would be driven insane. Worse, we would become a liability, a distraction for the trio of gods and the melog who had to do the actual fighting. It was going to take everything they had to vanquish the darkness and close the rift. If they had to worry about saving us, they would be more likely to lose.

On the positive side, we didn't have to have all the rest of the chicken people ride Air Riga. Only the women.

The overdose of Savannah's pheromones combined with recreational carnal activities was enough to break the Nilist control as well. Turns out lust and sex are great ways to beat the blues, even the primordial ones. Savannah has a gift of being able to turn enemies into friends. By the time she chose to end the chase, she had a lot of new friends, none of whom apparently complained about having their feathers ruffled. In fact, most seemed to enjoy it. None of the Nilists were turned away, although many had to wait in line. On the downside, even with her mystic ability to heal very personal areas quickly, the lady satyr was still going to walk with a limp for a week. Not that Savannah was complaining. Closer to bragging.

Past experience with closing rifts to the dark dimensions had taught me it required an enormous amount of mystic or life energy. Manna worked exceptionally well.

If a god uses all their manna up, it's game over and they have to head off to oblivion. I was worried about Loki, Coyote, and Manuk having to use too much. The manna bank we'd set up was light years away. And I was concerned about Eric surviving. He was still a kid. It was possible all four of them would come out of this weakened or even dead. Three gods and a melog with a barship may seem like a lot of raw power, until you realize the thousands of beings of darkness that are waiting on the other side of that rift with a mad-on older than the Earth itself.

Luckily, it turned out to be a lot simpler than that. While Eric used the ship's weapons with Loki and Coyote augmenting his attacks, Manuk was able to use the piece of primordial egg to somehow literally sew reality back up. Or at least that is how they explained it to me. They said I would never be able to understand the actual mystical physics involved and I was willing to take them at their word.

The Nilist chicken people didn't get off scott free. They were sent for a combination of punishment, hard work, and psychological counseling. None of them would ever fully be trusted again, but they were working to rehabilitate them nonetheless.

The Yumin spent most of the next day apologizing to Manuk Manuk for failing to notice what was wrong with their fellows. The blue cosmic chicken didn't hold it against any of them.

Apparently Manuk Manuk was a very hands on kind of god. She chose the leaders of her people. Personally, I would have thought her choices somewhat suspect after having picked Randolph in the first place, despite our long friendship. The Yumin didn't share my skepticism and accepted her appointment of Daka, the head egg counter as their new leader with great jubilation. We stayed for another week, which is when the eggs started hatching. All the mothers were present, standing near their eggs. Manuk moved among them talking and coaching the first timers through it. The Startenders were given seats in the balcony to watch, along with a great number of expectant fathers. There was as much seating as a football stadium.

It was actually amazing to watch the little ones peck out a hole in their shells. Many of the mothers wanted to help, but Manuk made sure none of them did. She explained that being in the universe was always going to be a fight for survival, a fight to do what's right, a fight to make things better. The sooner the little ones learned it, the better off they would be. I've been present at a great many births, both human and otherwise. This one had them all beat, at least in terms of sheer numbers. In less than ten hours, eleven thousand six hundred and seventeen children were born. The entire population celebrated with music, dancing, and drinking. It was like a family-oriented Mardi Gras, although there were plenty who behaved as if they were working on the next batch of eggs. Once all the new mothers were settled and Manuk had visited each and every one of them, which took a lot less time than one would think, she decided it was time for all of us to go. They begged her to stay, but she declined. We got a great sendoff at the statue of Manuk Manuk we had come out of. Eric hooked the ship back up to the statue and we went back up into the mouth. Manuk and I were the last ones. Herschel was standing at her side.

"Murphy, I have a favor to ask," she said.

"Another one? Wasn't this enough?" I said with a smile.

"It was. However, I would take it as a personal favor if you would consider taking Herschel on as a Startender."

Becoming a Startender was not an easy thing. We had a lot of members, but most of those we had known for many years. That didn't mean we didn't need more.

"I would be happy to recommend him for the Startender Academy," I said.

"Would he be able to serve on *Fools' Glory* after? I do not feel he would do as well on some of the other ships," the chicken said.

I smiled. Herschel did have the right temperament to fit in among the tricksters that made up my crew. He definitely wouldn't fit in so well on the *Argo II*, which had Hercules as the head honcho. However he might fit in okay on the *Big Top*, which Rumbles the

Clown commanded. The *Excalibur*'s crew was extremely fussy about letting anybody on board that hadn't served King Arthur's roundtable, although Sir Dagonet, the Infinite Jester, was a more reasonable man. Interestingly enough, Hercules was able to qualify to serve on the *Excalibur*, but preferred his own ship. And he didn't have much of a sense of humor when I suggested he could make the ship look like the Golden Fleece instead of having to go look for it this time around. Not that he had any plans to do that. I don't think he does anyway.

I explained the strict code of honor that Startenders had to abide by. "You will have to go to the academy and be approved before you can take the Startenders oath, but if you succeed in doing all that I would be happy to have you join my crew. Is that acceptable to you?" I said.

"Yes it is," said the chicken man, shaking my hand and then flying up into the mouth of the golden chicken.

I motioned for Manuk Manuk to go up and I followed her. We stopped at the beak to wave goodbye then took off into the sky, although as soon as we were out of sight we shifted mass so we were the size of a golf ball, saving the extra energy for another day.

Manuk wanted us to drop her off at the NYC II.

Although we could in theory travel there instantaneously using our drop zone system, we had a standing policy to not do any sort of teleport into our own solar system. There was a safety concern about not leaving a clear trail for anyone to follow us home by. It took us a few days, but we were finally approaching orbit.

I went to Manuk Manuk's room and knocked on the door. Apparently it hadn't been locked and it flew open. I was greeted by a most disturbing sight.

Coyote and Manuk had not only made up, but kissed and made up, and then moved on to the next stage, and then went beyond that. I never really considered how a coyote and a chicken would have sex and can't honestly say that my life was made any better having seen how with my own eyes.

I screamed in mock terror, covered my eyes and ran away, hearing the sounds of passion behind me turn to laughter.

A WAVE THEN GOODBYE
EPILOGUE

Poseidon had hidden for years, Demeter's amulet ensuring he couldn't be found. It'd stopped us from finding him despite over two decades of searching. With all the power, with all the Startenders at our disposal, it wasn't enough to find or stop one mad god. The only way the amulet couldn't hide him was if someone happened upon him in his or her direct line of sight.

Manhattan was entirely underwater. It was an eerily beautiful sight, devoid of its citizens. However, it wasn't devoid of life. Creatures of the sea had already begun to move in, as had Poseidon himself. The waters seemed to bend to his whim, allowing him to walk down the middle of Fifth Avenue, thrilled to pieces over what he had done.

The mad god claimed the sunken city as his own. A place that once held over ten million people would now be his domain and his alone. Or so he thought. Poseidon forgot something that all real New Yorkers knew. When walking down the street, you always keep an eye on what's going on around you if you don't want to get mugged or worse.

Poseidon didn't even notice the old woman dressed in the rags of the ages. Nor did he notice her machete-sized knife as she snuck up behind him. Rebecca was many things, but a cold-blooded murderer wasn't one of them. She spun the sea god around, giving him an instant in which to defend himself. Poseidon had spent almost all of his power in his rage-filled act of destruction, so he was unable to stop the blade as it pierced him again and again. The stabbing made the sea around him turn a hundred shades of crimson.

If the dying sea god wondered how a small, century plus old woman could survive under water without breathing or how a simple blade could kill a god, he didn't say. The idea that Rebecca was the Mother of the Streets of the city he tried to kill would never have occurred to him, nor would the fact that the city would share its power with the old woman to make sure she could survive. And that her last wish was to kill him for what he'd done.

Rebecca was not bloodthirsty, but in her own way she was every bit as mad as the sea god. However, she was not stupid. She dismembered him and separated the pieces, wrapping them individually in plastic garbage bags. Then she moved along the sunken streets until she came to Bulfinche's Pub. She smiled as she noticed the light from above refracting into a rainbow cascade of lights that led right to the door. The magic of the place even now could lead people in trouble to its door.

The sign that had always read Sorry We're Open had finally been changed to Sorry We're Closed. However, in writing underneath it read *Those in trouble are always welcome here*. Rebecca opened up the door and the magic protections on the place were strong enough to keep the water outside. The Mother of the Streets walked into the air-filled bar with the dismembered god dragging behind her in a half dozen plastic bags. She opened several closets and put each of the bags in a different one. Whether or not a god could put himself back together after what she did to him would be moot in the magical null zone that was Bulfinche's Pub.

Rebecca then went into the ladies room and changed out of her wet clothes into dry ones. She walked behind the bar and opened up the cash register to put some money in, then poured herself a drink.

Rebecca sat down at her usual table in the corner. She raised a glass and looked as if she was having an unheard conversation with someone or something, then nodded and drank the glass.

The Mother of the Streets sat and waited until her city needed her again.

PATRICK THOMAS – With over a million words in print, PATRICK THOMAS keeps busy writing the popular fantasy humor series Murphy's Lore (which includes Tales From Bulfinche's Pub, Fools' Day, Through The Drinking Glass, Shadow Of The Wolf, Redemption Road, Bartender Of The Gods, Nightcaps, Empty Graves and Startenders) as well as the After Hours spin-offs Fairy With A Gun, Dead To Rites and Lore & Dysorder. His Mystic Investigators series has grown to include the books Bullets & Brimstone and From The Shadows both with John L. French and Once More Upon A Time and the upcoming Partners In Crime both with Diane Raetz. He and John French also wrote The Assassins' Ball, the first book the Jack Gardner Mysteries. He has co-edited two anthologies - Hear Them Roar and the vampire themed New Blood. Patrick's syndicated humorous advice column Dear Cthulhu has been collected in Have A Dark Day and Good Advice For Bad People. A number of his books are part of the set and props department at the CSI television show. Laurence Fishburne's production company Cinema Gypsy Productions has taken a film and television option on Patrick Thomas' urban fantasy Fairy With A Gun. As an artist his work has graced covers for Dark Quest, Padwolf and Marietta, interiors and a cover for Space & Time magazine and comic covers for Ghostman. A mockumentary about him has recently surfaced on Youtube. To learn more, drop by his website at www.patthomas.net.

THE ASSASSINS' BALL

When there's a murder at a convention of killers... everyone's a suspect.

Coming soon from
PATRICK THOMAS
& JOHN L. FRENCH

IT'S A CRIME TO MISS OUT ON THESE OTHER GREAT BOOKS FROM
JOHN L. FRENCH

John L. French is a crime scene supervisor with the Baltimore Police Department Crime Laboratory. In 1992 he began writing crime fiction, basing his stories on his experiences on the streets of what some have called one of the most dangerous cities in the country. His books include THE DEVIL OF HARBOR CITY, SOULS ON FIRE, PAST SINS, BULLETS AND BRIMSTONE and HERE THERE BE MONSTERS. He is the editor of BAD COP, NO DONUT which features tales of police behaving badly.